High o...

Down in the village the main street was momentarily busy as the last customers tottering out of the public bar of The Sow's Ear mingled with the worshippers hurrying towards St Anthony's. Huddled beneath their umbrellas they made their way along the pavement beside Rose and Gregory's cottage and those who glanced through the badly drawn curtains could not help but see the naked pair sprawled dormantly in front of their fire. It was fortunate that Georgina's route to church did not take her past their window. Puffing heavily, she was the last member of the congregation to enter the damp, candle-lit nave.

The church bell was silent. The great south door boomed as it was closed by the verger. The clock struck midnight and the service began with a resonant chord from the organ.

'God rest you merry, gentlemen,' Slaughterhouse sang in quavering unison. 'Let nothing you dismay . . . O tidings of comfort and joy, comfort and joy.'

It was Christmas Day.

By the same author

THE YELLOW BOOK
THE DARK ANGEL
A FATHER'S DIARY
A WINTER'S TALE
TRIVIAL DISPUTES
STRANGE LAND
THE LIVING LANDSCAPE

HIGH ON THE HOG

A Christmas Story

FRASER HARRISON

Illustrated by Harriet Dell

Mandarin

A Mandarin Paperback
HIGH ON THE HOG

First published in Great Britain 1991
by William Heinemann Ltd
This edition published 1992
by Mandarin Paperbacks
an imprint of Reed Consumer Books Limited
Michelin House, 81 Fulham Road, London SW3 6RB
and Auckland, Melbourne, Singapore and Toronto

Copyright © Fraser Harrison 1991

I would like to thank the Royal Literary Fund
for the generous help it gave me in 1989.

A CIP catalogue record for this title
is available from the British Library
ISBN 0 7493 1364 1

Printed and bound in Great Britain
by Cox & Wyman Ltd, Reading, Berks

To Jane,
my cousin and oldest ally,
with much affection.

Christmas Eve

Britain goes home for Christmas

One

It was Christmas Eve, and despite the numbing cold the nation was convulsing itself in a last, wild spasm of present-buying. December's weather had been the foullest in living memory, yet more people had made the journey to Regent Street to look at the decorations than in any previous year, more Americans had come to stay in London for the festivities and, best of all, the tills had rung up record-breaking sums of money. Christmas was already a success!

That part of the nation which was not shopping or getting drunk at office parties was travelling. 'Britain is going home for a real family Christmas,' announced a reporter on the lunchtime news, while pictures were shown of airports seething with frustrated passengers, docks clogged with cars waiting for ferries delayed by storms at sea and motorways blocked with lines of vehicles, motionless except for the action of their windscreen wipers.

Conditions at railways stations were no better, and when Gregory Burton emerged from the tube onto the concourse of Liverpool Street Station he found it so congested he could not move without a continual struggle. He fought his way to his usual platform where a huge, shapeless queue was gathered angrily round a sign declaring in chalked letters British Rail's regrets for any inconvenience to passengers. The public address system made announcements nobody could hear.

In due course a train pulled in. The information board made no reference to it, but before it had reached the buffers a small war broke out as those disembarking met the charge of those rushing to climb aboard. Gregory himself was dragged forward bodily and deposited in the carriage just beyond the buffet car. Every seat was taken and he stood in the passageway pressed from both sides by the force of people cramming through the doors. A gang of young men, still hot-headed from the pub, shook their lager cans and sprayed the crowd.

The platform staff, quite unable to control the torrent of people rushing past the barriers, panicked. They blew their whistles and waved their flags. With most of its doors still hanging open, the train jerked into motion and pulled into the gusts of sleet wetting the black mouth of the station.

'And a merry fucking Christmas to you too,' said one of the guards, viciously jabbing the handle of his flag into the back of a passenger who clung to a swinging door.

These discomforts only intensified as the journey proceeded, yet to Gregory they were nothing compared with the misery in his mind and heart. Christmas was supposed to mark the closing of the old year and signal the coming of the new; it offered a festive respite from the rigours of winter and it celebrated the birth of fresh life and hope. For Gregory, however, this particular Christmas promised no more than the death of those things he held dear: his marriage, his career and his ambitions. He dreaded his arrival at Stowmarket and half-hoped the train was rushing its steaming cargo to some other, mistaken destination; anything to postpone his fate.

Two

Mary Pennistone leaned her forehead against her office window and stared without interest at the signs of Christmas to be seen in the windswept street below. Standing in Bloomsbury within the august shadow of the British Museum, Gilbert Street consisted on its west side of a dozen drab offices where business was conducted beneath naked light bulbs. In deference to the season plastic snow had been squirted on some of the windows, while others had been decorated with swags of limp paper-chains. Many of these offices had already closed for the holiday and were in darkness; a few were more brightly lit than usual where the inmates had gathered for drinks and, in one case, an impromptu dance. Christmas had come to Mary's building too. She could hear unaccustomed bursts of laughter escaping from the floor beneath where the staff party was getting under way in the production department, generally a temple of sober diligence.

A knock at her door announced the appearance of a figure clad in an ankle-length fur coat, whose white hair was protected by a cossack hat.

'Mary, my dear, I have come to say farewell and wish you a happy Christmas – if that's not a contradiction.'

'The same to you, Lionel. I hope you enjoy your holiday.'

'Oh I will, I will,' he said fruitily. 'In less than a couple of hours I shall be landing at Marrakech where they have never heard of Christmas, at least none of my friends have. I shall stand at the top of the aircraft steps and like a girl in a cake I shall burst out of my coat.'

He spun round and opened his coat to reveal a beautifully cut white cotton suit.

'Lionel, you are a ridiculous old fop,' she said fondly.

'As you know, I abominate Christmas and all it stands for, so I shall not be joining in the saturnalia in the production department, but that doesn't stop me giving you this.'

He buttoned up his coat, for which an entire species must have been made extinct, and reached into one of its pockets, producing an expensively wrapped parcel.

'Thank you,' she said, colouring. 'I'm so sorry, I haven't bought you anything. Since it happened, I've been so . . . You know, I haven't been able to think properly. I haven't even bought Michael a decent present.'

'Don't apologise,' he told her in a stern tone that took her by surprise. 'If you want to give me a present, then make use of this ridiculous festival and put the whole business out of your mind for the next few days. Get drunk, take Michael to bed and don't let him out, stuff yourself with Suffolk wholesomeness, but whatever you do, don't brood. It wasn't your fault. Everyone thinks it's his fault, but that's just part of the poisoned legacy they leave. You weren't to blame.'

He said these last words slowly, looking at her very directly. Instinct drew her eyes to the empty desk behind her.

'I know,' she said softly, 'but you can't help feeling guilty. Though, to tell you the truth, more than anything else, I feel angry.'

'So you should. You have every right to. She let us all down.'

He looked at his watch.

'I must fly, if you'll pardon the pun.' He kissed her lightly on the cheek. 'The season's greetings to all the pigs and the other members of your family.'

He raised his hat in a gallant gesture and tripped out, leaving his present on her desk.

She returned to her contemplation of the street below, a damp, bleak patch of the old Bloomsbury that was vanishing fast and giving way to a sleeker, slicker new Bloomsbury. It had taken less than a week for the crane wielding its metal ball to demolish the terrace where her office now stood, a purpose-built edifice which had won its architect a prize. With a sardonic sigh she ran her finger through the pool of water that invariably gathered in her window frame when it rained.

The noise from downstairs was growing positively riotous and she wondered whether she too had the gall to shun the party. She turned her back on the street and ran her eye over the stack that contained her year's work, nearly fifty books transmuted from typescript to print, from heaps of paper to smart hardbacks in shiny jackets. Arranged in order of publication, they looked solid and indestructible, concrete achievements that would withstand the march of decay and defy the oblivion of time. Yet none knew better than she just how ephemeral they were in reality.

She could not prevent her eye from flicking across the room to Liz's books. In their yellow, militant livery, they were books that had been going to change the world. Liz had despatched them from this office as if they were special agents, not mere books, each with its own mission to right some wrong. And yet, for all their pure-mindedness, how many innocent men had they freed, how many guilty men had they brought to justice, how much cruelty had they spared the suffering? These were of course tasks no book could hope to achieve alone, but Liz had expected it of her books; they had been weapons to her, and she had only been able to publish as a fanatic, a zealot fighting a holy war. As a result she had been disappointed again and again because her causes were never won.

Perhaps that had been the reason, or at least one of her reasons. The stupid cow!

Angrily she picked up her telephone and dialled her husband's office. After an officious delay, commensurate no doubt with his dignity and importance, she was put through to him.

'Michael? Hello, it's me. I can't face the office party so I'm going to get on the road straightaway. How soon can you leave? Maybe we can drive down together?'

Before answering, he paused for a heartbeat. In anyone else this barely audible hesitation would have been insignificant, but in Michael, who was effortlessly articulate, it was, as she knew from experience, the involuntary preface to a lie.

'Ah . . . it's pretty nightmarish here, as you can imagine. I'd better say I'll see you in Slaughterhouse this evening.'

They discussed the relative advantages of routes to Suffolk and rang off.

She was sorry they would not be travelling together, but what – or whom – was he concealing from her?

The pool of rainwater on her window sill started to overflow. She pushed the waste-paper basket against the wall to catch the drips. If the rain continued to fall as heavily her makeshift bucket would be full before Christmas Day had dawned. She left her office, kicking the door shut behind her without allowing herself to look at Liz's desk.

Three

Michael Pennistone, Mary's husband, examined himself, not without satisfaction, in the mirrored wall that ran the length of Brummel's, the world-famous Gentleman's Perfumery in Jermyn Street. He smoothed his hair, tightened the knot of his tie, and with a covert little movement turned sideways and studied the profile of his abdomen. He lived in terror of developing a paunch. Too idle to take any exercise, he was forced to maintain his youthful lines through a rigorous programme of semi-starvation. Christmas was therefore an even more anxious time for him than for other, ordinary people.

An assistant approached him, her manner showing the deference due to a spendthrift customer. She waited until he gave her the benefit of his attention and then offered him a heavy bottle with a spray operated by a rubber bulb.

'Would you mind?' he asked, gesturing with his finger in a circular motion.

'Of course, sir.' She smiled obligingly, put the bottle on the glass counter and squeezed the bulb gently while holding the inside of her wrist in the way of the fine spray that issued from the bottle's brass nozzle. She lightly rubbed the tips of her thin fingers on the network of blue veins that were gathered below the warm, white skin of her wrist, and then with a graceful waving movement of her arm she encouraged the liquid to evaporate. Michael watched this ritual with all the eagerness of a fetishist. Leaning forward and resting his weight on the counter, he advanced his large, handsome nose and lowered it over her trembling arm until the powerful black hairs growing out of his nostrils almost brushed her skin. He sniffed once, quickly, for fear the aroma would not please, and then, reassured, inhaled

9

again, this time slowly and languorously, sucking up the fragrance.

'Delicious,' he sighed. 'Quite delicious.' Reluctantly, he lifted his nose.

'And you,' he asked softly, 'do you like it?'

She smiled intimately. 'I think it's a most refreshing fragrance, sir. A very *elegant* cologne.' This was a woman who knew her job.

'I hardly dare ask what it costs.'

'Thirty pounds.' Her tone was noncommittal, but he could hear the challenge in her voice.

'This is only the tester bottle,' she added, turning to a shelf stacked with multi-coloured boxes. 'Let me show you the complete product.'

She took down a box designed in racing green with gold lettering, which read 'Ascot – the cologne of kings.' Despite this vulgarity, he was attracted to the bottle itself. Displaying no more than a discreet, golden 'A' on its side, it was shaped something like a whisky decanter, with a cut-glass effect and a large, glittering knob for a stopper. He weighed it in his hand, enjoying its opulent ponderousness. It would look handsome on his bathroom shelf.

'I'll have it,' he announced. 'Don't gift-wrap it. I'll take it in one of your ordinary bags.' He did not want to draw Mary's attention to his little extravagance.

He sighed, this time glumly. He was still stuck with the problem of Mary's present. She really was a most difficult woman, he thought with a touch of exasperation he did not usually allow himself. He had been fretting over what to buy her since the middle of November, yet here he was on Christmas Eve with scarcely an hour's shopping left, at least in shops worth shopping in, and he still had nothing to give her.

He had come to Brummel's, perhaps his favourite shop in all London, not so much for Mary's sake as to soothe and cleanse himself. He had got into the habit of wearing pungent colognes soon after he had begun his affair with Zara. At first, he had used them as a means of protection, fearing that Mary might detect an alien scent or body odour on him and his clothes. Zara favoured sweet, musky perfumes which had impregnated her whole room, its carpets, curtains and furnishings, as well as her clothes, her bed, her hair and every inch of her tawny skin. Whenever he left her, he would catch little whiffs of her distinctive odour emanating from his own body, and so he had taken to dousing himself in his own, countervailing perfume.

However, his precaution had rapidly burgeoned into an obsession as he discovered an entire world of body luxuries whose existence he had never dreamed of before. Now, more even than underwear, he loved to buy Zara things to make her smell sweet and exotic. He hardly ever came up to her room without bringing some new product for them to experiment with and they often passed whole afternoons in her tiny, sea-shell of a bathroom where he would oil and massage her, scrape and bathe her, powder, cream and perfume her. His pleasure in these sessions was becoming very intense; indeed, he had lately come to enjoy them so much they had almost taken the place in his desires of actual sex.

By contrast, Mary, he reminded himself, would have a puritanical loathing of such antics, which would strike her as virtual perversions.

'Your cologne, Mr Pennistone.' The girl held out a paper bag. He was flattered by the use of his name. 'Shall I put it on your account?'

'Thank you. No. Wait.' He had almost forgotten the real purpose of his being here in Brummel's. 'I have other things to buy.'

He sauntered without enthusiasm to a small counter at the back of the shop. It was labelled 'Pour La Femme', and displayed a selection of scents and other expensive fripperies which were designed for the gentlemen customers to buy their wives and sweethearts after they had satisfied their own, graver needs. He had long since stopped shopping here for Zara; the stock was too restricted, too primitive for their now recherché interests. Nonetheless, he picked over the bottles and packets on display. He toyed for a moment with a large globular sponge, which aroused a mild excitement in him as he imagined himself soaking it with soapy hot water and caressing Mary's back, she had always had a pretty back . . . but no, she was bound to have an ideological objection to sponges. They were certain to be a protected species, or else sponge fishers would turn out to be the victims of some diabolical exploitation.

Instead, he picked up a self-styled gift set, an assortment of completely uninteresting bits and pieces, which however was packed in a rafia basket and a luridly coloured kerchief. 'Hand-made by Peruvian Collectives', the label stated. (What was Brummel's coming to?) Surely that struck the right rustico-ethnic note? But did Mary approve or disapprove of Peru? Where did she stand on the matter of Peruvian peasants' rights? He could not remember.

Making a weary gesture he summoned the sales girl. As she approached he observed she had a pleasing swing to her walk; after Christmas he would find out her name.

'Does Brummel's sell such a thing as a gift voucher?'

He exposed her to his most boyish smile, and she smiled back.

'Certainly, sir. What value do you have in mind?'

'Forty pounds,' he said, and then remembering how unhappy Mary had been over Liz, he changed his order. 'No, you had better give me one for fifty pounds.'

With maudlin appreciation, he studied the girl's bottom as she went about the business of preparing his voucher. Outside, the rain fell on the street in great sheeting gusts, as if thrown there from some Olympian bucket. The prospect of Christmas at Slaughterhouse with all Mary's unspeakable relations was profoundly depressing. He glanced at his watch. Perhaps, after all, there was time to pop in to Zara and play Father Christmas.

Four

A hundred miles to the north Oliver Albion, Mary's nephew, boarded a train to start the journey that would bring him too home to Slaughterhouse for Christmas. The train was one of the self-drive, two-carriage local rattlers which plied between the north Norfolk coast and Norwich. As it pulled out of the station three boys, including the youngest Albion, broke into a high-pitched cheer and threw their caps in the air. Half a mile further on they pulled down a window and leaned out, making V-signs and sticking out their tongues at a fortress-like building which stood high above the line and commanded an unchallenged view of the cliffs, the long open beach below and indeed the entire North Sea.

'Sit down, for Christ's sake. Put your caps on. Don't put your shoes on the seats and, for once, try to pretend you aren't little yobs.'

These orders were issued in a tone of dispirited vexation by a young man whose authority was already annulled by the cigarette he had lit beneath a 'No Smoking' sign.

'It's a school tradition, sir. Like flying the flag at half-mast when someone's died. We always salute the school building on the last day of term.'

'You're new, sir. You wouldn't know,' chimed in another boy.

'I'm not bloody new,' the young man said sourly. 'And that was no bloody salute. Now why can't you be like young Carter here.' He pointed a yellowed finger at a fourth boy who was sitting opposite him. 'He's a credit to the school.'

Carter, suddenly the object of everyone's scrutiny, flinched.

'I wish you wouldn't swear, sir. I know my mother wouldn't like it. This was said with angelic sincerity by

13

the boy who had directed the most energetic V-sign at the now vanished edifice of their school.

'All right,' said the master, defeated. 'Just sit down and shut up.'

'But what shall we do, sir?'

'We're bored, sir.'

'How much further, sir?'

Exasperated, the young man stood up. 'Do what you damn well want. I'm going next door and I don't want to be disturbed. Understood?'

As he spoke, the train lurched, throwing him against the door. Sparks from his cigarette blew into his jacket. 'Bloody hell,' he muttered, banging his singed sleeve.

'I think this is a No Smoking carriage, sir,' one of the boys told him with disingenuous helpfulness.

'Oh sod off, Rogers.'

The boy opened his mouth to protest.

'I know, I know. Your mother wouldn't like it. Well, she isn't going to get it, is she?' He glowered at them and staggered through to the other carriage.

'Silly bugger,' said Rogers dismissively.

These pleasant exchanges took place under the jaded eyes of half a dozen other passengers, who were so used to sharing their journeys with hooligan children they showed no surprise at the boy's foul language or the master's desertion of his post. They stared emptily out of the windows.

With the exception of Carter, who remained in his seat, a large paper bag on his knees, the boys turned their attention to the driver. They talked excitedly of 'the dead man's hand' and pressed their faces against the glass partition, making themselves look monstrous. They tried to distract him by pointing with frantic urgency at his controls, but he was imperturbable and simply dropped the blind behind him, cutting them off from his view. They debated pulling the Emergency chain. Rogers produced a cigarette, which was passed round, one puff each. No one offered it to Carter, and he showed no interest in any of their pranks. He merely sat, nursing his paper bag.

This anarchic camaraderie was, however, most enjoyable to Oliver Albion. Their journey was bringing to an end his first term at Bitterley Hall, and he was thankful to see it finished. Ever since half-term in October he had been counting off the days until the Christmas holidays on a chart pinned to the inside of his desk top. Though some weeks had seemed interminable, the last one had sped by: there had been a school show in which masters tried to tell jokes and do conjuring tricks, a school feast where, for once, edible food had been served, and a carol service in the big hall lit only by candles. But on the very last full day, just as the trunks were being strapped up and put out in the gym for collection, he had been struck down by the so-called Asian flu that had been epidemic throughout the term. Not only highly infectious, it was a strain of flu that attacked without warning and inflicted on its victims an explosive and chronic diarrhoea. As a result, the school's laundry had been overwhelmed, the furnaces heating the boilers had required continuous stoking, and the already irascible matron had raged day and night for six weeks, curing her small patients by shouting them back to health. The headmaster had been forced to confer urgently with his lawyer and accountant.

By eleven o'clock on the final day of term the yard at the back of the school house was jammed with large cars and charabancs. Convoys of whooping boys were transported to the station, while rueful parents, already regretting the onset of the holidays, struggled to control their excitable sons and load their luggage. When the riotous exodus was complete, just four boys were left languishing in the sanatorium, too ill to travel.

'Well, thank you *very* much,' the matron snarled at her patients as the last car drove out of the yard. 'You at least have the satisfaction of knowing that my Christmas is ruined before it's begun.'

She studied their quailing faces, which were as white as their pillows.

'If you're not well enough to go home, you're not well

enough to talk. Or read, either,' she added viciously, snatching a book from Carter's hands.

For Oliver the discomforts and ignominies of being sick, the disappointment at having his sentence indefinitely extended, and even matron's spitefulness, were nothing compared with his terror at finding himself in the bed next to Rogers. He had in fact passed most of the term in a state of terror, which had only been relieved by brief interludes of commonplace fear. This was a new experience for him, for hitherto he had passed most of his life in carefree tranquility. At Bitterley Hall, however, he quickly learnt to be frightened of the masters, especially the headmaster with his black gown and leather-soled slipper. He also feared the matron with her iodine and scrubbing brush, and 'the Sergeant' who made the boys box until he saw blood. Oliver lived in perpetual fear of breaking rules he had not understood and being punished in ways that were as shameful as they were painful. And he feared all the boys who were older and bigger than he. Bitterley Hall had marked him, and the Oliver Albion who was about to return home for Christmas was very different from the one who had been delivered by his parents in September. Still, he had also learnt a thing or two which might prove useful in later life. For example, he had learnt how to disguise his feelings, hiding his fears and homesickness beneath a mask of callousness. He had learnt to show loyalty by bellowing in support of his school at hockey matches, even though he hated the game. He had learnt how to assume a look of innocence when he was guilty, how to look the other way when boys were being bullied, how to laugh at jokes that did not amuse him, how to speak up when it was politic and keep quiet when he knew he should protest. These were valuable lessons, all helping to promote self-reliance and make a man of him, which had been his father's much-stated purpose in sending him to Bitterley Hall.

Despite the great strides he had been making towards manliness, Oliver was in fact looking forward to a brief reversion to childishness during the holiday. As the train rattled closer to Norwich, he allowed his imagination to play freely over the pleasures of home, an indulgence he had not dared allow himself throughout the term for fear of breaking down in tears. He relished the thought of eating his favourite food, sleeping in his own bed, walking his dog, and wallowing in his parents' affection – or at least his mother's. Above all, he looked forward to Christmas Day and everything it promised.

Like many another, including his aunt Mary, his uncle Michael and the tormented Gregory, Oliver hoped that Christmas would give him a brief suspension of reality, a sweet interlude during which all the horrible parts of his life would disappear and all his worries be forgotten.

Five

'You'd be surprised, miss, how many do it at Christmas,' the sergeant had told her. 'Christmas and the first weeks of summer, they're the most popular times, if you see what I mean. Don't ask me why.' Mary had not been called 'miss' for years.

She had found Liz. The cleaners would have found her, but she had been early that morning. It was the first of many things that had made her angry. How could Liz, with all her principles, have put this on the cleaners?

'Is that common?' she had asked the policeman later, when the office was empty again. 'I mean, do many people do it with bags over their heads?'

'I've never seen one before. That takes real courage.'

'Is it courage, or cowardice?' she said.

'Well, it certainly took willpower. You imagine the strength of mind she needed to stop herself pulling them off.'

Liz had put two bags over her head, plastic shopping bags in the company's colours, with the company's initials printed on them. They had been designed for the promotion of some book. The company had killed her in the end. She had pulled rubber bands over her head and round her neck to keep the bags tight. They had cut dreadful purple weals in her neck, that long, thin neck which would have been scrawny if she had lived to be an old woman.

In the struggle against herself she had fallen onto the carpet, dragging her chair with her. When she began she must have been sitting at her desk because she had written the memo there and left all her correspondence in order. In fact, that was the first odd thing Mary had noticed, her diary and papers and the envelopes arranged on the desk with such uncharacteristic orderliness.

But why had she pulled off her sweater? Why had she wanted to be found half-naked?

Her memo – it could not be called a note, since it was not addressed to anyone and was completely impersonal, except for the last line – had hurt most. Why hadn't Liz written directly to her; surely she owed her that much?

Down in the basement, where her seniority entitled her to park, Mary sat in her car and read the memo for the thousandth time. Written in neat, almost laborious hand-writing, quite unlike Liz's usual frantic scrawl, were a dozen instructions concerning Motheba's book. The author (why *the author*? Mary knew Motheba nearly as well as Liz) – the author had to be shown all revisions to the typescript; the proofs had to be sent to a certain proof reader; the jacket had on no account to be anything but a plain design, using lettering only; and so forth. She must have known that Mary would deal with all these matters after her death, and yet her memo contained no reference to their professional complicity, far less their friendship.

And then at the bottom, in jagged handwriting, written perhaps at the last moment, were the words, 'too much suffering'.

Who, though, had endured too much suffering? Liz her-self, presumably. And yet she was not sure. If Liz had been suffering so badly, why had she not confided in her? Why had she betrayed their friendship by doing this?

Cramming the memo back in her bag, she set the car in motion and drove with angry recklessness up the ramp and onto the street. The rain fell out of a grey, dirty sky onto a Bloomsbury that would never be clean again. She could only hope that Christmas in Slaughterhouse would invoke a benediction on this evil year and bear a new life to replace this wasted one.

Six

At Colchester the congestion on Gregory's train eased as crowds of half-suffocated passengers, clutching the tattered remains of their Christmas shopping, staggered off the train into the soaking darkness of the afternoon. Gregory concealed himself in the corridor, masking his head in a newspaper until he was sure that no one he knew remained in the carriage, and then he took a seat. Though not by nature a devious person, he had recently entangled himself in a web of secrecy so complex he could hardly remember the truth himself or what he was hiding from whom. In almost every respect, he was no longer the man he appeared to be, or the man he used to be, or the man his wife and mother and friends assumed him to be.

For example, he showed every sign of being some sort of junior executive: he wore a dark suit, black shoes, white shirt and a trustworthy tie, his hair was cut short and he carried a black, leather briefcase. Admittedly, there was a threadbare, grubby look about him, suggesting that he was not a great success in his profession, but the uniform was unmistakeable. The fact that he was travelling from Liverpool Street station seemed to confirm the evidence: he undoubtedly toiled in the City at some lowly clerical task.

And until a month ago reality had conformed with appearance. Gregory had indeed been something in the City, a post secured for him by his mother. Mrs Burton was a widow living in frayed respectability on the mite left by her husband, from whom Gregory himself had inherited nothing except a genetic bias towards insolvency. She had but one string at her disposal, which connected her to an old regimental friend of her husband. She pulled it and to her amazement the puppet jumped and appointed her son to a desk in his stockbroking firm without even summoning him for an interview.

'Don't forget,' she told him as she brushed his new suit on the morning of his first day at work, 'that you're as clever as the rest of them. Not in an *intellectual* way,' she said, as if that were a facile, low sort of cleverness. 'You're not a bookworm, but I'm sure you have the makings of a magnate. Think big,' she instructed him, and pulled him down to give him the same loyal kiss with which she had despatched her late husband to Stowmarket station every morning for thirty years.

One afternoon the partner who had got him the job approached his desk and stood over him as he punched figures into his terminal.

'They tell me you are, um, most diligent, Burton.'

Gregory shot to his feet, surprising the partner with the great height he attained, for he was a very tall young man.

'Thank you, sir.'

'And your splendid mother. She is in good health, I trust?' He peered up at his looming protegé.

'Yes, thank you sir, she's in great shape. Very fit.'

Gregory might have been talking about a boxer he was training, but the partner, who had not been addressed as 'sir' since he left the army forty years ago, suspected the young man of mocking him. He withdrew hastily, muttering 'insolent young puppy' under his breath.

Gregory's prospects were not improved by this encounter.

Following the example of his father, he was punctual, hard-working, honest, respectful and smartly dressed. With these handicaps he could hardly hope to compete with his more business-minded colleagues and so his promotion began to lag badly behind theirs, just as his father's had in his day. Nonetheless, after a period of total incomprehension, he gradually learnt to make sense of the numbers he fed into the ever-gaping maw on his desk. He even began to take an aesthetic pleasure in the patterns they formed and the moods that seemed to overtake them so unpredictably.

Yet as understanding dawned on him so did a sense of revulsion. He slowly came to realise that whereas he was motivated in his work by the need to pay his bills, a desire to please his mother and a vague notion of self-respect, his far more successful colleagues were motivated by nothing short of raw greed. They sincerely, fervently wanted to be rich, and did not care how they got that way. He, on the other hand, could only say that he sincerely did not want to be poor. Unlike them, he did not pant for riches, and unlike his father he felt there was something wrong, as well as repellent, about their restless cupidity.

However, before these scruples could preoccupy him in any damaging way, he was diverted towards a different and all-absorbing interest. He fell in love – if *fell* is the right word for a revolution in his fortunes which was to lift him to a sphere of opulence equal to the dreams of even his most avaricious colleagues.

The object of his passion was a certain Rose Albion, the daughter of a farmer, whom he met in her local pub, The Sow's Ear at Slaughterhouse. Being a simple lad of limited sexual experience, he no sooner lost his heart to her than he yearned to marry her. But before proposing he agonised over his responsibilities to his widowed mother. He knew that if he were to marry, he would have to remain nearby and visit her often. And so by dint of subtle probing he ascertained that in the event of marriage Rose would be prepared to go on living close to Stowmarket – not a fate every young bride would happily embrace. From every point of view therefore she was the perfect mate.

Depending on how you judge these things, it will be to Gregory's credit, or the opposite, that only after he had satisfied his conscience with respect to his mother did he realise, with a pleasant shock, that he was contemplating marriage with someone who was eminently eligible for other reasons. Rose was, after all, an heiress, for her father owned a sizeable chunk of prime Suffolk farmland, to say nothing of assorted barns, buildings and cottages. Gregory did not need his desk-top computer to tell him that a thousand acres at a thousand pounds per acre added up to a nice round figure. Rose, the girl of his dreams, was a millionaire's daughter.

Rose was much quicker to make the corresponding calculations in relation to Gregory and his value as a husband. This was not because she was the more mercenary, though she was, but because she was preparing for the inevitable grilling she would face when she introduced Gregory to her father. For her own part, she was satisfied with Gregory's prospects, which however she did not exaggerate. They were sufficient to her purpose, and no more. For as long as she could remember, it had been her fixed ambition to marry someone who was literally and in the broadest sense 'something in the City', someone who did not stink of animal shit when he came home, who wore shoes not boots, whose neck was not red, who was, in short, not a farmer. She had no objection to muck and boots and red necks in themselves, but over the years these had come to stand in her mind as the badges, not of uncouthness, but financial insecurity. Throughout her childhood the family enterprise had been the source of continual anxiety and bad feeling, and so, much as she adored her father, she was determined she would not marry a farmer-husband. While she recognised that Gregory was hardly a whizz-kid and most unlikely to evolve into the magnate of his mother's fantasies, she convinced herself that he was professionally sound. He had a good, safe job with the prospect of regular increments and modest promotion, and he evidently enjoyed the protection of a senior partner. Life with him would not be adventurous, but it would be secure, and for that, as well as his elegant loftiness, she decided she loved him.

And so it was that Rose and Gregory were married one drizzling April afternoon in St Anthony's, the village church at Slaughterhouse, whose crumbling flint tower stood opposite the window of the bedroom where Rose spent her last night as a spinster, and whose deep bell, tolling solemnly, summoned her to the altar. She wore a simple white dress and veil, and carried a posy of wild flowers. A gasp rose from the congregation as she entered the nave, for she did look beautiful indeed. The ceremony was performed with impressive pomp by an elderly clerical cousin, the choir sang sweetly and the organist surpassed herself, playing the newly wed couple down the aisle with such reverberative gusto that an angel's wing, rotten with woodworm, was dislodged from the roof. During the exchange of vows Rose's mother sniffed a little and Gregory's mother wept operatically. Rose's father looked glum; Gregory Burton was not what he had had in mind for Rose, his headstrong, pretty Rose, but he consoled himself with the thought that none of his friends could stand their sons-in-law either.

At the reception he broke with convention: instead of making a speech, he dumbly presented Rose with the key to one of his cottages in the village. The advantages of being married to the daughter of a man of property were becoming evident from the very start. Speeches were made, large quantities of expensive champagne were consumed, the younger guests became drunk and randy, the older guests became drunk and randy too, and finally, after much foolishness, the newly weds were driven to Stowmarket station.

A fortnight later the honeymooners returned. Gregory resumed his vigil in front of his green screen and Rose set about turning the old pigman's cottage into a home. As far as the village was concerned, the new Burton marriage had already begun to merge into the fabric of mundane normality. But were they happy? Did they repent their impulsiveness? Did infatuation ripen into true love, or did it cool into disappointment and dislike?

The answer is they lived in bliss; their marriage was an ever-lasting honeymoon. They had sex almost every evening and went to bed early for the purpose. They also had sex, by day and night, in the kitchen, in the sitting room, on the staircase, in the bath, and sometimes, on hot, dark nights, in the garden beneath their apple tree. Gregory always caught the earliest possible train home, never loitering in the pub with his colleagues. They saved money, they tiled their bathroom and mowed their lawn at weekends. Rose got a job in Ipswich. They saved more money and tiled the kitchen. Gregory laughed at her feline jokes and did not notice how bad her cooking was; Rose counted the money he put in their building society and admired him for being handsome and tall. What more does happiness need?

But then one day in October Gregory's employers decided it would be prudent to trim an ounce or two of fat off their organisation. Gregory was one of the little adipose lumps they felt they could nip off painlessly – that is, without pain to them. The partner who knew Gregory's mother did not demur. The boy had been impertinent to him. What did he expect?

Since that awful day Gregory had not known an hour's happiness.

Seven

Ignoring Michael's recommended route, Mary took the Edgware Road out of the West End, turning off Kilburn High Road to cut through to the Finchley Road and the A1. This was the route she had used ever since she had lived in London and Christmas, she felt, was not the time to break with tradition. In defiance of the slashing rain people were crowding the pavements and pushing into the shops. She reminded herself she still had not bought Michael his present. It was only one o'clock but the rain and gloom were forcing drivers to switch on their side-lights.

Liz had died five days ago, yet Mary still could not think of anything else, a preoccupation she was starting to resent. She was surprised to discover that pity was not among the torrent of emotions aroused by Liz's suicide. Sorrow, grief and anger – these she felt intensely; but not pity. As much as anything, her thoughts were ruled by a baffled, bitter curiosity.

Why the sweater? She kept coming back to that as if it were the key to something. It was knitted out of a rich emerald wool and fitted very tightly; in fact, it was simply too small for her, but she had confided in Mary that she liked wearing it because it showed off her boobs. She never wore a bra. It had a high polo-neck collar, which she used to tug at continually, to Mary's annoyance. Mary suspected that she also liked wearing it because its collar concealed her long, attenuated neck, about which she was embarrassed.

Perhaps she had taken it off to leave her neck free for the rubber bands to grip tightly; perhaps she had yanked it off at the last moment, not caring how she looked when she was found. That had been Lionel's explanation, but it did not ring true to Mary. Liz was too self-conscious, too vain. Had she succumbed to vanity even in death, wanting to show off her breasts to the last? It was unthinkable – yet Mary thought it.

Had Liz imitated Motheba? That was another explanation. Motheba had been made to wear a bag over her head for days on end in prison. They had taken away her blouse and made her stand in her cell with a bag on her head, her wrists tied behind her back. Although she was a bank teller they called her a bar-girl and a go-go girl because she was half naked, and they had come up to her, unseen, and pinched her breasts or bitten them, or simply hit her. She was only a go-go girl.

This small, round-faced black woman, with huge eyes, had come to their office every day and whispered horrors into the office tape recorder. Her vocal cords had been damaged and she would never be able to do more than whisper. They had put a wire round her neck to lead her about like a blinkered animal, and sometimes they had pulled it too tight when they hitched her up in her cell.

She had arrived punctually each time, smiling, hanging up her coat and mouthing good morning to Mary. To do her work, she sat with Liz at her desk. She never cried, apart from once, though Liz cried at the end of every session after Motheba had left.

Her crime had been to be the mother of a teenage son who had gone missing in the bush. They said he was an anti-government terrorist and they wanted the names of the other members of his group. With the bag on her head they pushed her under water until she thought she was dead. She told them nothing because there was nothing to tell. After they released her she found out that her son had been killed weeks before, run over by a jeep that had not stopped. His watch was sent to her by the villagers who found his body. Telling this part of the story, she had cried.

'Who's going to buy the book? That's what I want to know,' the sales manager had asked, and Liz had nearly punched him. It was a crass question, and yet he was right, of course. No one would buy the book. Motheba was not a writer and her story was too terrible to read. It was not elevated by literary skill or illuminated by political insight; no one had heard of her country, no one went to sunbathe there, no one cared. Except Liz.

Liz cared. She cared passionately for all minorities, underdogs and victims. All humanity's miseries impinged on her, breaking her heart, rousing her anger. As a result, she was a superb editor and an impossible employee. An impossible companion too. There was no restraint in her, no discrimination. Reading the paper was a daily ordeal to her, and to anyone with her, for every edition punished her with fresh news of torture, disappearance, imprisonment without trial, famine made worse by obstructive politicians, and all the ordinary cruelties inflicted by people everywhere on each other.

'The world's a disgusting place,' she would say hurling the paper to the floor, 'and we are a monstrous species.'

'I am not a monster,' Mary would say, 'and you cannot feed all the mouths in Africa. Anyway, it's not our fault they're starving.'

'We are all to blame,' Liz insisted. 'We are human, we share the same earth.'

'Don't be so bloody pompous.'

'Look,' she said angrily, 'we live in comfort and prosperity. We live under the rule of law. We can expect to die in old age, for what that's worth. The climate is kind to us. Our enemies respect us and we have powerful allies. If there was a God, we would know he was smiling on us – give or take the odd rail crash. Therefore, it is our duty to help the rest, those more unfortunate than ourselves. There's a pompous phrase for you. And if we don't, surely it's all meaningless?'

'It's not your principles I object to, it's the fact that you take everything so personally. You're spiritually arrogant. You're a megalomaniac posing as a saint.'

'Oh sod it! Let's go for lunch.'

Liz was the liberal conscience gone mad. Guilt dictated that she lived in self-imposed penury. She rented a cell of a room at the top of a sordid house in the Angel – not Islington, where many of her colleagues were, for that would have been too middle class, too 'indulgent'. She shared a loo and was not permitted to cook in her room. She kept her walls undecorated except for political posters; she refused to buy furniture, relying instead on rubbish rescued from skips; and in winter she kept warm by the simple expedient of never taking off her coat, even in bed. 'If the cold gets unendurable,' she once told Mary, 'I let the bloke downstairs seduce me.' She gave away the bulk of her not inconsiderable salary, and allowed herself only one extravagance: she bought huge quantities of cheap, vulgar clothes. Her asceticism did not go as far as effacing her sexuality but in order to show solidarity with the under-privileged she cultivated a 'tarty' look, affecting chains round her ankles, slit skirts, black stockings and, of course, tight sweaters. Disdaining anything as bourgeois as a wardrobe, she kept her clothes in heaps on the floor and preferred to buy new ones rather than wash them.

Yet, for all this craziness, she was an unfailing spring of vitality. With her wild bush of chestnut hair, her big, happy smile and her raucous voice, she generated heat and light wherever she went. She was neurotic, but she burned with a life-giving energy, and everything dark and vile seemed to shrivel in her flame.

Nonetheless, she had killed herself. She had put out her own light. She had put the dunce's cap on her head and shown how stupid she was.

On the morning of her death Motheba came to the office as usual and Mary was obliged to break the news to her – one of the many pleasant tasks Liz had bequeathed. Mary only told her Liz had killed herself, not the manner of her doing it. Motheba flinched and her eyes grew still larger. Like everyone else, she expressed shock first, then guilt.

'It's my fault,' she whispered. 'I should never have told her all those horrible things. She was too sensitive, too . . . close to it.'

Mary told her not to blame herself; everyone felt guilty, but it was no one's fault but Liz's.

'It's strange,' Motheba said, 'we had got to the end of the worst part of my story. I had just begun to describe my release.'

'And it's Christmas,' Mary said. 'She was looking forward to seeing her boyfriend. Or so she told me.'

Motheba put on her coat.

'In prison nobody killed themselves, no matter how bad things were. We said to each other, if they want our lives they must take them, we are not making a gift of them.'

Exactly. So why had Liz given her life to the enemy? What right had *she* to quit?

Eight

With his head propped on a couple of pillows Michael lay on Zara's bed smoking a cigarette and listening to the rain rattling and splashing against her window. Her long chestnut hair, newly washed and glossily brushed, fanned softly across his hip and thigh as she bent over him and attempted to invigorate his dormant sex.

My God, he thought, idly running a hank of her hair through his fingers, my God, I'm bored. He glanced at his watch. It was time to leave. This must be the last visit. He would use the Christmas break to extricate himself.

Zara lifted her head from his lifeless groin and gave it a derisory flick.

'What's the matter? Have you gone off me?'

Why not tell her? He would not get a better opportunity. But telling the truth was not Michael's style.

'You are sweet and adorable,' he said, 'and you must be tolerant of an old man's little failings.'

'I know all about your little failings,' she said, 'and they don't include impotence.'

Lying down beside him, she took the cigarette from his fingers and put an ashtray on her stomach.

'My urchin charms no longer amuse you, and you're looking for an excuse to dump me. Go on, admit it.'

She transferred the ashtray to his stomach and rolled on her side to look him straight in the face. She also slid her thigh over him, rubbing him gently.

'My body,' he said, gesturing towards his still limp centre, 'has a finely tuned sense of responsibility. It knows, better than you and I apparently, that Christmas is a time for doing one's duty by wives and, for that matter, parents. You should be packing, not languishing here in debauchery.'

'What debauchery?' she said, prodding him painfully with her knee. She stubbed out her cigarette and allowed a cascade of sparks to fall on his skin. He brushed them off, gasping a little at the pain, but refusing to be provoked. If he was going to bring their affair to an end, he did not want to part from her on bad terms. He was looking forward to spending a few days alone with Mary after they got back from Slaughterhouse on Boxing Day; but when the holiday was over and Mary had returned to the preoccupations of her job, who could say he might not feel the need to call on Zara again. That too was a persuasive reason for keeping the girl sweet. Options – he was at his happiest when he had an abundance of options to manipulate and no commitments to bind him.

'Anyway,' said Zara, 'surely it's hypocritical to do your duty mechanically, just because you have to?'

'Nonsense. Duty is what keeps society civilised, and hypocrisy is what allows us to do our duty without going mad or becoming a nation of fanatics. Duty is a matter of making sure that the other person thinks he or she is being properly respected as a father, a wife, or whatever. Like everything else in human relations, it can all be done with mirrors. As long as the other person is content, it doesn't matter how the trick is performed.'

Zara stood up and stretched, pulling her arms straight above her head, her back towards him. She did nothing without calculating its effect on the spectator. He reached out and slid his hand round the slope of her hip. She pulled away, but turned to stand over the bed, the rufous triangle of her bush facing him.

'You're only inventing excuses for your own despicable behaviour.'

'Exactly. That's my point,' he said cheerfully. 'Our behaviour is bound to be despicable. We're a wicked, lustful species; that's the way we're made. You might as well acknowledge it and take provisions to see that others are not hurt too badly, if at all. Far from telling them the truth, we have a duty to protect our loved ones from the truth. Ignorance is bliss – now there's a truth if you want one.'

'You are the most amoral person I know.'

'On the contrary,' he said, running his fingers through her springy curls, 'I am the most moral person you know. I am a liar, a philanderer, an adulterer and a cheat, but I never deceive myself.' He leaned forward to kiss her belly. 'I never pretend to myself that my lies are anything but dishonest. I never try to excuse or vindicate my infidelities. Though I may lie to the world, I am always truthful with myself. I always know the right and wrong of what I'm doing.' He kissed the tops of her thighs in turn. 'I'm a strict moralist, you see,' he said, sliding his tongue down the crease of soft skin that marked the edge of her bush, 'without being remotely moral in my behaviour.'

He licked her again, pulling her onto the bed.

'Don't you ever feel guilty?'

He laid his cheek on her thigh and laughed.

'All the time. Constantly and continually. I am never free of guilt, but I've learnt to live with it. On the other hand, mine is the lowest form of guilt since it has no effect on my conduct.'

'Well, so far you've done nothing to be guilty for today,' she said testily, sitting up. 'I still think you've got tired of me, but now I know you won't tell me because you'll lie instead to spare my feelings.'

He caressed her thigh, saying soothingly, 'Zara, Zara, my tongue tells its own truth.'

She pushed his head aside and said, 'This is the only part of you I trust to tell the truth.' Lifting his inert organ, she held it up disdainfully between finger and thumb. 'And look what it's telling me.'

She dropped it onto his leg.

She left him and walked into the bathroom. He shifted across the bed so he could see her reflection in the long looking glass, and watched her as she sat on the loo and then looked at herself in the bathroom mirror, grimacing at her tangled hair. At the window, poised on tiptoe with her meaty buttocks jutting out, she peered down at the sodden road below.

The street lamp opposite, which had already been lit, threw a queasy orange light into the flat, but nothing could dim the vibrant glow of her pink skin. She was not tall and slim like Mary, but stocky and rounded, and her flesh seemed to be electrified by some thrilling energy of her own. Its name was of course youth. At twenty-two she had stopped growing, though over the course of their short acquaintance he thought he had detected a matronly amplifying of her hips and chest; nonetheless a juvenile vigour still flowed in her veins, keeping her eyes milk white and sapphire blue, her hair glossy and thick, and her skin fresh and radiant. Nature, as they both knew, needed no help from their fetish of oiling and perfuming.

With her sturdy hips and big round breasts and thick clump of hair, she personified female vitality. Even when she drowsed or lay supine in the bath her body oozed an irrepressible vigour, and this was what he hoped to draw into his own muddied veins. Her glowing flesh throbbed with life, and every limb and organ seemed fully flowered, bursting in readiness to receive and make new life. In a word, she was fertile. She shone with fertility; she was electrified by fertility; fertility sprang from every pore and nerve-ending and soft, membranous part. Yet, of all states of femaleness, the one he was most disgusted by, and most dreaded, was pregnancy. True, he longed to suck the life from her, to imbibe and ingest it, so that he too would glow, rejuvenated by the milk of her youth, but for all that he had no intention of planting life, his life, in her. He did not want to make a life with her, and he most certainly did not want to make a life inside her. His sexuality, despite its restless exertion, was in every sense sterile.

Zara was staring into the mirror once more, experimenting with a pair of trashy earrings. He was bored. Sadly, it had to be admitted that the company of youth was not to be enjoyed without enduring a certain measure of unavoidable inanity. At first he had feared she would become bored with him, since he was prepared to offer her little apart from sex and expensive gifts, but then it dawned on him that this was only arrogance on his part and that she required no more from their relationship than he did. They were both quite satisfied with brief, pungent bouts of decadence. In her way she was as sterile as he was, and they made a perverse match: he played the voyeur to her exhibitionist. She was never happier than when out of her clothes being admired, and if his method of admiring her was to rub oily stuff in her skin and buy her perfumes she could not afford herself, she seemed content.

But now he was bored with all that nonsense, and had begun to relish again the subtle, devoted attentions of his slender, clever, clean-limbed Mary, who was after all his wife. Forgetting Zara for a moment, he closed his eyes and conjured up an image of Mary in her bath, bending forward, her breasts snowy with suds, waiting for him to wash her back. Damn! He should have bought that sponge. It was not too late to buy one somewhere else. Equipped with a large sponge, even the barbaric bathroom in Slaughterhouse Manor might turn out to possess erotic possibilities.

Somewhat to his surprise, these uxorious musings began to induce an erection.

'Hello,' said Zara, returning to the bedroom and catching him unawares. 'So you do still fancy me. You naughty man, have you been looking at me through the keyhole again?'

She swung one leg over his hips and kneeling on the bed began to lower herself onto him. Poised above his erratic member, which was now stiff with desire and utterly indifferent to this sudden switch of object, she smiled down at him.

'I don't ask much of you, do I?'

'No,' he said, pulling her towards him.

She resisted, tantalising him, and then allowed him to feel the embrace of her slippery warmth, but only for an instant. Holding him down by the hips, she lifted herself off him. She was as strong as she looked.

'You must make me a promise.'

'Perhaps.'

'And you must keep it.'

'We'll see.'

She sank onto him and leant forward to give her breast to his eager mouth. Just as he had his lips on her nipple, she withdrew again, raising herself an inch above his heaving body.

'Promise you'll ring me from Slaughterhouse to wish me happy Christmas.'

'I'll try,' he panted, reaching up for her shoulders.

She pressed his arms flat on the bed. 'Promise.'

'It's so difficult to call from there. You've no idea. The house only has one phone and that's in the hall where you can be heard from every room.'

'You're a resourceful bloke. Do something. Go for a walk and find a phone box. Go to the pub. They must have a pub at Slaughterhouse.'

She settled on him again, squirming a little before starting a slow, kneading rhythm, which he joined with more urgency than he had intended; he did not like being taunted. She lay on his chest and, licking his ear, whispered, 'It's a test.'

She quickened their pace a little.

'It'll be a test of your chivalry.'

Unable to help himself, he moaned with pleasure, though in what he hoped was a noncommittal tone.

Abruptly, as his passion was becoming uncontrollable, she sat upright and uncoupled herself completely.

'Promise, promise,' she hissed fiercely.

'I promise,' he begged, and in doing so changed the nature of his Christmas in several ways.

Nine

Far away from these sordid goings-on, the train bearing young Oliver Albion and his school-mates trundled across the bleak Norfolk landscape towards Norwich. The long arm of the driver's windscreen wiper cranked to and fro, sweeping away thick eels of water with every stroke. Rogers and his mates, having smoked their only cigarette, and having grown bored with punching each other, were reading their comics and staring mindlessly out of the rain-beaded windows. Oliver judged the moment safe to move seats and join Carter.

In spite of the expediency he had learnt to adopt as his ruling principle of life at Bitterley Hall, he had made a friend. This was a real friend, whose friendship was in every respect a mistake, for it brought him neither protection, nor popularity. The friend in question was this same Carter, the boy with the paper bag on his knee, whom their master had been thoughtless enough to point out as a model of good behaviour. He might just as well have slipped the poor fellow the black spot.

Like Oliver, Carter had just undergone his first term; unlike Oliver, however, he seemed to have learnt nothing in the way of manliness and self-defence. He not only betrayed his feelings, but expressed them openly, almost theatrically. During their very first night, when the other new boys were burying their tears in their pillows, Carter had astounded the dormitory by sobbing and crying out, 'Mummy, Oh Mummy,' in a loud, anguished voice. He had mourned for a whole month, the tears flowing down his face in a continuous, unquenchable stream of hot grief. He would not dress himself in the mornings, or eat at mealtimes, or change into his games clothes, or work or read or sleep; he had only wept.

Behaving like this, Carter inevitably became a target for teasing, and he was an easily mocked figure for other reasons too, being large for his age, but seeming shapeless and boneless, like a well-fed caterpillar, and having a slow, insinuative walk. Yet he disconcerted his would-be baiters. When a gang of boys gathered to laugh at his ungainly body or to goad him into 'blubbing' by shouting 'Mummy, Oh Mummy' at him, he would look down on them and in his most imploring tone beg to know how they could be so cruel.

'What have I ever done to hurt you? Why do you want to see me cry?' he would demand, and the crowd would disperse, unable to face his naked vulnerability.

While the other new boys did their best to appear 'normal', hastily bleaching out of their behaviour any little oddness that might put their popularity at risk, Carter was flagrantly eccentric. Apart from anything else, he had opinions.

Most of the younger boys, and for that matter the older boys too, had not got beyond the stage of moronically hurling prejudices at each other by way of conducting a discussion.

'Norwich are shit. Arsenal are brilliant.'

'Don't be a dick-head. Arsenal are crap. Norwich are the greatest in England, Europe, the World, the Galaxy, the Universe . . .'

Oliver himself was an eager participant in these mindless contests, partly because he enjoyed them, and partly because he knew that blind loyalty to a football team was taken as a sure sign of being normal. Carter, on the other hand, disdained all knowledge of football, but he did hold proper opinions which, up to a point, he could defend in argument. For example, he claimed to be a Jacobite, something the others had never heard of before. He informed them that the present royal family were in fact Germans, foreign usurpers, and gave them a fervently inaccurate account of Bonnie Prince Charlie's adventures. The battle of Culloden, which he described in stirring detail, was evidently the greatest disaster in British history.

'We have been under the foreign heel ever since,' he told his astonished audience, and for a while 'Scots vs English' was the fashionable game during break, with a satisfactory correction of history on most occasions.

Notwithstanding Oliver's great desire to fit in and be accepted, he could not help being fascinated by Carter, and because as fellow new boys they often found themselves thrown together he even came to like him. After a few weeks he went so far as to risk being known as The Blubber's friend. 'The Blubber', a nickname referring neatly both to his formless enormity and his tendency to cry, had been bestowed on him by the razor-tongued Rogers, who was not seduced by his exotic ideas. Oliver however was fascinated by more than just Carter's potty views, for Carter knew things. For instance, he knew the names of the many birds that flew in the school's extensive grounds, and the names of the flowers and trees that grew there. He also knew a great many lurid facts about the reproductive methods of animals. He was especially illuminating on the habits of pigs; indeed, so extraordinary was his suggestion that the boar's willy was shaped like a corkscrew that for the first time Oliver, who was after all a farmer's son, doubted his friend's authority.

Oliver was also fascinated by Carter's fish, which lived in a big glass tank on a shelf above his desk. It was a goldfish, but quite unlike any goldfish he had seen before. It was large, with a body about the size of a mouse, and from its back, tail and belly trailed long, translucent fins, which fluttered and undulated in its slow wake like chiffon scarves. Its body was encased in little silver plates, and its fins were a milky-silver too, though they were so fine and filmy at their frilly edges as to be invisible. Its head, however, was capped with a grotesque outcrop of bright red lumps, giving it the look of a raspberry. Day in, day out, the fish maundered round its tank, making broken circles with lovely, idle, swirling movements, its mouth constantly gulping, its disc-shaped eyes constantly swivelling. Carter told him the name of its breed and listed its properties in some detail, but Oliver was only interested in the hypnotic motion of its rippling fins. It seemed so content in its glass case. Carter occasionally allowed him to feed it, a privilege he conferred on nobody else.

This very fish, temporarily contained in a plastic bag full of water and further protected by a brown paper bag, was what had been reposing on Carter's knee since the start of their journey from Sherringham.

Bored with comics, cigarettes and hanging out of the window, the other boys sprawled listlessly, taking up a seat each by lying across them.

'Let's see your fish, Blubber,' demanded Rogers.

Hesitating for a moment, Carter obliged by pulling off the brown paper bag and holding the fish aloft in its plastic aquarium. It swam in its customary majestic fashion, steadily circling, its fins drifting and fanning. There was nothing in its behaviour to suggest that it had any awareness of its unusual circumstances. It was utterly and obliviously at home in its transparent medium.

Rogers poked his finger into the bag, leaving a noticeably stretched dent in the plastic membrane.

'Please don't do that Rogers,' Carter pleaded. 'You see, it sends shock waves through the water. It's like punching the fish.'

This was too tempting for Rogers, who of course stabbed his finger once more into the bag, though more forcibly.

'What was that, Blubber. An upper cut or a right hook?'

Carter snatched the bag away. The fish swam imperturbably, its scales glinting in the light as Carter swung it closer to the window.

The other boy, eager to toady to Rogers, flourished his ball-point pen, making Carter lurch to and fro to avoid him. It was not long before his weapon made contact, piercing a small hole in the bag. Immediately, water spouted over Carter's lap.

'For God's sake, control yourself, Blubber. Look, you've wet yourself. Not very nice for the other passengers.' With an apologetic air, Rogers looked round the carriage.

40

Meanwhile quick-witted Carter had tipped the bag over, rendering the hole harmless but the boy simply pierced the plastic again. Water poured out freely as the new hole tore under the pressure. The fish still swam calmly.

'Help me, Ollie. Please, please, help me,' shouted Carter, running towards the toilet with the dissolving bag cradled uselessly in his hands.

Now, Carter's use of his foreshortened name shocked Oliver, for it had been agreed between them that they would only call each other by their Christian names when they were alone. Carter's was Fergus, which was innocuous enough, but Ollie was not a name to bandy about, because it was also slang for testicle. Though he was known as Ollie at home, he had so far managed to keep this shaming fact a secret at school, except from Carter to whom he had confided it as a token of trust.

Before Carter could reach the toilet door, Rogers had darted in front of it, barring his way. Water streamed over their feet. At last, the fish sensed danger, for it began to thrash and struggle in its shrinking plastic.

'Ollie!' crowed Rogers vindictively. 'Stay where you are, Ollie. Unless you want to lose your ollies.' The other boy laughed.

Oliver hesitated, loyalty and his instinct for self-protection fighting within him. The bag was now collapsed and the fish was suffocating in the clammy folds of plastic.

'It looks like sardines on toast for tea, Blubber,' taunted Rogers. 'Or does Ollie prefer fish paste?'

Oliver rushed at him and, seeing the fury in his face, Rogers dodged aside, letting them into the toilet.

'Fill the basin,' cried Carter. He stood behind Oliver, trying to ease the fish free.

Oliver pressed the cold tap, but found the plug was missing, long since ripped from its chain. Carter put the bag over the hole and the basin began to fill. Wrapped and immobilised, the fish looked like some exotic product in a delicatessen. Lying in a wrinkled pocket of the bag, it appeared to have shrunk and its fins were no more than shrivelled petals. It gulped, but did not writhe, as Carter began to peel back the plastic.

'This will kill it,' he said. 'The water's too cold and probably full of chlorine. I haven't got another bag.'

The basin filled and Carter liberated the fish, though he could not help tearing scraps off its fins. Once submerged, however, the fish revived instantly, its body swelling in the water, and its ripped fins unfurling. It could not swim, for the basin was too small and clogged with plastic, but it looked lively enough.

Yet Carter looked at it despairingly. 'There's nothing I can do for it,' he told Oliver, his voice trembling with tears. 'I haven't got another bag.'

'Can't we get one from somewhere?'

'It's spoilt now,' he said fiercely, the tears running down his face. 'I don't want it. They have murdered my fish.'

'I'm sorry,' Oliver stammered, 'I should have – '

Carter ran into the carriage. He took his macintosh down from the luggage rack and put it on to cover the wet patch on his trousers.

'The fish is yours,' he screamed at Rogers. 'Happy Christmas, murderer!'

Sobbing violently now, he dragged his case through to the other carriage. For once Rogers was dumbstruck. He and the other boys peered into the toilet where the fish was wallowing in its shallow puddle, seemingly at ease. Rogers shut the door on it.

'Jaws!' he said contemptuously. 'Still, it should give someone a scare.'

Oliver did not know what to do or say. He sat miserably at the far end of the carriage, leaving Rogers and his friend to snigger at the other. He wanted to join Carter, console him and ease his own guilt, but he did not dare. Surely they could have saved the fish? Perhaps one of the other passengers had a suitable bag. It wasn't too late to rescue it. If only he had stopped that idiot puncturing the bag. If only he had been quicker to face up to Rogers. And he could not face Carter.

The train pulled into Norwich station. Rogers and his friend ran off, shouting to him to tell the master they had been kidnapped. Oliver stood on the platform and watched Carter as he threw himself blindly into the arms of a large, clumsy woman, who could only be the 'Mummy, Mummy' so agonisingly invoked at the start of the term. Mother and son hugged each other passionately and wept. Then, slowly and still clinging to one another, they made their way towards the car park. Carter never once looked back at Oliver.

'Come on, Albion,' said the master, oblivious of all that had taken place, 'we've half an hour to kill. Let's get a drink.'

Ten

Out in Hendon and Barnet, where the city streets expanded into dual carriageways, the rain found room to operate on its natural epic scale, and it drifted in great grey sheets of shredding water across the shallow valleys dividing up these metropolitan villages. The drains were overwhelmed, the gutters had flooded, the pavements were continually sluiced with grey effluent from the traffic, and huge lakes, the colour of tarmac, were swelling on the level stretches of road.

The last time Mary had made this journey, Liz had been with her. It was in the spring. Michael and she were driving up to Slaughterhouse for Rose's wedding and they gave Liz a lift as far as Cambridge where she was to meet one of her authors. When they set out the weather was balmy and they decided to use Michael's convertible. He put the top down and Liz lay across the back seat, propping her legs on the folded hood. She pulled her skirt up to her thighs to let the sun warm them, and Mary noticed Michael adjusting his mirror to get a better view of her. She knew Liz despised him, but noticed that she did nothing to conceal herself; if anything, she exhibited herself all the more openly, undoing a button of her blouse.

As they rolled along, luxuriating in the freakish warmth and enjoying the rare sight, for them, of grey giving way to green and concrete yielding to grass and leaves, Liz denounced what she called 'the pastoral myth'. The deeper they penetrated the countryside, the more it offended her.

'Don't let all this fool you,' she said, lighting yet another cigarette and waving vaguely at the landscape.

'It may look green and pleasant, but the bottom line is that it's just a factory floor like any other. And the richer the farmer – I beg your pardon – the agri-businessman, the lower his wages. Especially here in your precious East Anglia. Did you know that more farm labourers claim supplementary benefit than any other kind of worker?'

As it happened, Mary did know this, but Liz was relentless and would not rest until she had tried, judged and damned the farmers for their crimes against nature and humanity alike. All was greed, cruelty and patriarchism and Liz was marching to fight a new holy war.

Despite her thighs and the undoing of a second button, Michael was irritated by Liz's hectoring. To divert himself, he concentrated on pushing his car as fast as the road would allow. Their speed alarmed Mary, but only stimulated Liz who shrieked above the roar of the engine, her hair flying in the slipstream and her cigarettes trailing showers of sparks. It seemed to Mary that Liz was like a monstrous child and that she and Michael were her long-suffering, bewildered parents. The simile was strengthened by the fact that Liz's parents were both dead and Mary, who was childless (not barren, but untried), had informally adopted Liz in the office, treating her by turns as apprentice and protegée until she had outgrown the need for patronage. Not that Mary was old enough to be her mother, for only ten years separated them, but she found that Liz persisted in making her play the adult to Liz's juvenile, a role she did not repudiate. Where Liz was rash and inflammatory, Mary was cautious and politic; where Liz was clear-sighted and convinced, Mary equivocated and acted the devil's advocate; and where Liz was crass and egocentric, Mary forgave and hid her wounds. As the younger, and therefore more worldy-wise of the two, Liz did not hesitate to condescend to Mary, often treating her as if she had no opinions or history of her own. Nothing infuriated Mary more than this condescension.

'You seem to forget,' she shouted over the noise of the car and Liz's harangue, 'that my family are farmers. In fact,' she added, turning to face Liz directly, 'I always wanted to be a farmer myself.'

'You're joking,' Liz said, genuinely shocked by this revelation of her mentor's unsavoury past.

'When I was a little girl, I used to help my father all the time. I dreamed of taking over the farm when he was old and I used to watch him, hoping for signs of senility so he would have to retire. By the time I was fourteen I could have run our farm on my own.'

Liz sat forward, poking her head between the two front seats to hear Mary more clearly.

'So what happened?'

Michael chipped in. 'She was usurped by her oafish brother.'

Mary smiled fondly at him. Although she disapproved of the enmity that lay between her brother and husband, she liked to hear Michael defending her cause so vehemently.

'It's true,' she said, putting her hand on his knee for a moment. 'My ne'er-do-well brother, the dashing Tom, father of this afternoon's bride, pulled the prodigal son trick. After drinking himself stupid in the army for five years, he suddenly woke up one day and realised he had no money and was never going to be a general. So he came home and told my father he'd seen the error of his ways and asked to be taken into the farm. There was much rejoicing, of course, and the fatted calf was killed, literally in his case. The fact that he didn't know one end of a shovel from the other and had never shown the slightest interest in the farm before didn't seem to worry anyone. He just moved in and that was that.'

'What did your father say to you?'

'He told me to go to university and find something else to do.'

Liz exploded. 'The pig!'

'You haven't met Tom's wife,' Michael said, 'she's got bristles on her chin and, though I've never seen it, and never want to, I shouldn't be surprised if she had a little curly tail.'

'Don't be horrible, Michael. No, father's not a pig, just incredibly conventional. I don't suppose he'd ever met a woman farmer and he couldn't conceive that such a species might exist. As far as he was concerned, women on farms were wives, not farmers. My mother never so much as collected an egg and I don't think she owned a pair of boots. Mind you, he'd have been thrilled if I had married a farmer, especially a local one. That's what he most likes about Tom, really: the fact that he's given him a dynasty.'

Unseen by Liz, Michael shot Mary a look that was both resentful and malicious. Liz, sucking fiercely at her cigarette, was too concerned with the iniquity of mankind to observe the frailty of a single specimen.

'Why are men so bloody crass?'

Michael smiled. He was not the man to fight for a cause, certainly not for one so forlorn as the honour of his sex.

To Liz, all men were pigs in their relations with women – apart from her current lover, who was however only the exception proving the rule. And then, usually within a couple of months, he too would be unmasked and denounced as yet another pig who couldn't see beyond his own prick. The pattern never varied, but nor was her sense of idealism ever diminished. The mantle of the great hoped-for god was passed from mortal to mortal, and although each turned out to be as unworthy as the last the mantle itself remained divinely pristine. Meanwhile, she placed no restraint on her sexual dealings with these 'pigs', going to bed with whomever she fancied and earning for herself the title of the 'office bike'. (Or so Mary had heard her described by one of the lads in the post room. She had told him, very sharply, to get on with his work and had been derided as the 'office dike' for her pains.)

'And yet, despite everything,' Mary said, 'I still think of Slaughterhouse as "home".'

'It's such a grotesque name.'

'Ah, but they use their pigs to produce the most delicious home-cured ham,' said Michael provocatively. 'That's one of the few good things about going there. The ham and the bacon.' He put his fingers to his lips and kissed them in an epicure's gesture of delight.

'Don't be disgusting. I didn't realise it was a *pig* farm.'

'In my day father only kept a couple of dozen sows,

but nowadays Tom has nearly two hundred, I believe. Of course, he doesn't kill them himself. They're sent to the abattoir.'

Liz shivered in horror as if Mary had confessed that the family business was running a concentration camp.

'Why aren't you a vegetarian?'

'Their conditions aren't that bad, not like a real factory farm. It's too old-fashioned, which probably explains why Tom isn't a millionaire. From what I've seen, his pigs have a short life but a merry one.'

'How can you say that?' Liz shouted. 'It's well known that pigs suffer dreadfully in any kind of confinement. Just because they can't protest to their MP doesn't mean they're not under terrible stress, you know.'

'Oh get off your soap box, Liz.' Mary turned round and grinned at her. 'It's too nice a day to be harangued.'

'You've shocked her,' said Michael. 'She thought you were a nice, decent liberal, and now she discovers that in reality you're no better than an animal torturer.' He turned for a moment to address Liz. 'You should see her when she's at Slaughterhouse tucking into her bacon and kidneys and cutlets at breakfast while the butcher's lorry loads up the porkers outside in the yard. You can hear them squealing and kicking, but she doesn't turn a hair. They're a hard breed, these Albions.'

Mary laughed. 'Do shut up, Michael.'

In her scheme of things, anomalies, contradictions and changes of mind were to be expected; indeed, they defined human behaviour. But Liz did not laugh; she scowled. To her, such aberrations were unbearable. Hers was a black and white world, peopled with heroes and villains, whose motives were either pure or impure, but never mixed. She could not stomach inconsistency: opposites had to be reconciled, or forced to fight until one emerged the victor. In her kingdom there was no room for honourable tories, scurrilous saints, well-meaning farmers or rurally responsible colleagues who ate the flesh of maltreated beasts.

'From this day forward,' she muttered grimly, 'I'm a

committed vegan. And I shall never insult pigs again by using "pig" as an insult.'

They drove on without talking. Mary darted a covert smile at Michael, who reciprocated. She closed her eyes.

Suddenly, Liz leant forward again, extending her long neck, and in her most earnest voice asked, 'May I come with you to the wedding? I'll go on to Cambridge this evening. I can easily put John off. Please let me come.'

She was a child pleading to be allowed to stay out of school an extra hour. But fond though she was of Liz, Mary had had enough of her for that day and, without considering her request seriously, she said no, it was out of the question. Michael added that she wouldn't enjoy herself. 'You may think I'm contemptible,' he told her, 'but compared with the rest of Mary's relations, I'm charm itself. You'd loathe them.' Yet Liz persisted, almost begging them to let her meet the family. Hoping to ease the awkwardness, Mary tried to strike a lighter note, 'Georgina – that's my sister-in-law – would never speak to me again. Her catering is always very precise; that's to say downright miserly.' Liz seemed close to tears, but Mary did not relent, and the remainder of the journey was passed in an uncomfortable silence.

When they dropped Liz at Cambridge she did not thank them for her lift or introduce them to her author, who was waiting for her with evident impatience at their rendez-vous. He was conspicuously handsome and greeted her with a kiss on the lips. 'Perhaps it's time I wrote a book,' commented Michael.

This Saturday drive produced two extraordinary results. The first was the black eye which Liz brought to work the following Monday. In point of fact, it was an ugly *mélange* of mauve and purple, but its most sinister aspect was Liz's refusal to talk about it, or even admit to its existence. The second was that Liz developed a minor obsession with Mary's family. By dint of systematic questioning, she made herself an expert in its history and current events. Like a fan of some soap opera, she followed the humdrum doings of 'The Albions' with avid interest, and demanded to be brought up to date whenever Mary had some contact with Slaughterhouse – which however was not often.

One morning in December, Liz said to her, 'Among the many advantages of being an orphan is the fact that you don't have to spend Christmas feeling guilty. Oh God, I remember how awful it used to be. Everyone makes everyone else guilty. If you don't see your parents, you feel guilty about neglecting them. If you do see them, you feel guilty for not loving them enough, or they feel guilty for not loving you enough, or you all feel guilty and get drunk and come away feeling worse than ever. Well, I'm free of all that now. No more guilt for me.'

She paused.

'I expect I'll be staying with John at Cambridge this year,' she added lamely, and Mary sensed she was angling for an invitation to spend Christmas with Michael and herself. She said nothing, but mused on the idea for a few days. She even asked Michael who, retaining a clearer memory of Liz's springtime thighs than her acerbic opinions, said, 'Why not? We orphans must stick together.' However, before Mary made up her mind, Georgina rang to say that Mary's father had suffered a stroke. He had been lucky, and had only lost the use of his hand, his left hand at that. He was a bit confused of course, but that was only to be expected. There was no need for Mary to come rushing down. Georgina knew how important her work was, but she wondered if Mary and Michael would like to stay for Christmas. Mary said yes immediately. She then rang Michael. She was very well aware that for all his talk of home-cured ham and hand-made sausages, he hated Slaughterhouse and she was tenderly grateful to him for agreeing straightaway, without a trace of demurral in his voice, that they must go. The whole question of Liz's invitation went out of her mind.

Two days later she found Liz in their office with her head tied up in a bag like a Christmas present and her breast as bare as a plucked turkey's.

No more guilt for *her*.

Eleven

When Gregory was made redundant, the news was broken to him by the manager of his department. To soften the blow, he spoke to Gregory in a tone so rich with optimism he made his downfall sound more like a promotion. He was bound to find a new job straightaway, he said, it was just a matter of spreading the word. Lucky bugger that he was, he would probably be offered something with twice the salary for half the work. Redundancy was merely another way of saying golden opportunity.

It was only when Gregory was sitting once more at his own desk that the reality of his situation struck home. He had been given the boot and in four weeks' time he would be out on the street. The thought of Rose's reaction to his news terrified him, and he immediately decided to postpone telling her until he had actually got his new job. That way he would be able to present this amusing little setback as the origin of his good fortune.

And so he said nothing. As the month of his notice went by, he scanned the newspapers, followed up his colleagues' tips, took the advice of his superiors, made appointments and attended interviews. He did all the things he ought to have done, and met with nothing but disappointment. Meanwhile, he worked with his habitual conscientiousness until the last minute of his employment and even worried about taking longer than an hour for his valedictory lunch, a jolly event at which he bought everyone large drinks and was rewarded with a clinging good luck kiss by the manager's secretary. Thus, despite his best efforts and the sustaining faith of his manager, it was an unemployed and prospectless Gregory who drunkenly boarded his train home to Stowmarket on the last Friday of his last month as a magnate-in-the-making.

He had already decided once more to postpone telling Rose about his situation. Deceptiveness was turning out to be a far more complex and shameful vice than he had foreseen. Lies, he was beginning to discover, had a horrifying tendency to reproduce themselves on the scale of vermin. It seemed that one lie needed at least two others to keep it secure, and then these two needed another two, and so on; meanwhile, the truth showed no powers of resistance and merely offered itself up as so much meat to these maggots. By temperament and out of principle, Gregory was a truthful person and he loathed himself for his lying.

He was a little consoled by the knowledge that he had a month's money and a valid season ticket in his pocket, assets which would enable him to devote all his time and energy to finding a new job during the next three weeks before Christmas. Surely he could not fail? Rose might be a little annoyed when she heard about his duplicity, but she would be thrilled by the dynamic advancement of his career. This would be his real Christmas present to her.

The following Monday he kissed her goodbye as usual and took his usual train to Liverpool Street station where he hit his usual platform on the run. He sprinted to the nearest public telephone and hogged it ruthlessly while he rang all the numbers he had marked in the jobs sections of no less than four newspapers. After an hour's work he had succeeded in securing one appointment. Being zealous, he arrived at the address early, only to find himself back on the pavement within a minute; a mistake had been made, the post was already filled. It was to be his only appointment of the week. Exhausted, he caught his usual train home.

He did not sprint to the telephone on Tuesday, though he walked purposefully. On Wednesday he strolled, on Thursday he dawdled, and on Friday he didn't bother. Instead, he wandered ouside the station and smoked cigarettes in a café and read the sports pages of his newspapers. Later, out of sheer boredom, he rang the number of one of the prostitutes selling herself from a sticker next to the station phone. 'Feeling Naughty?' it said, 'Ring Suzette.'

A warm, elderly-sounding voice replied, calling him 'dear' and explaining that she was only the maid. Madam would be there in an hour or so. She had a lovely full bust and could give him a nice whipping for twenty pounds. Did he want to make an appointment?

Gregory did not want a whipping, nice or otherwise, and Rose's was still the bust that monopolised his desires, but the old lady's wheezing tones had conjured up such a welcoming picture of tea-cosies, gas fires and snoozing cats that he was tempted for a moment to swap the cold street for the homeliness of Suzette's boudoir.

During the last week he had discovered just how cold the streets could be. Once he had made his phone calls his days held no purpose except to wait for his train, and so he walked, taking himself on expeditions to parts of London so strange to him they might have been in Chicago or Bombay. He found that he had involuntarily joined an army, an army of the damned. Conscripted by poverty and failure, it was an army whose ranks were filled by men and women of all ages, and even children, an army with no qualifications of fitness or talent, which only fought itself. It was an army in a permanent state of mutiny against officers who had long since deserted, and it continually marched the streets with nothing to do, no money to do it with, and nowhere to go. It marched on a very empty stomach and its soldiers had neither hope nor ambition in their knapsacks.

That December was cruelly cold. During the days it rained and snowed by turns, and at night it froze. To be on the streets for any length of time was, therefore, to be alternately soaked and chilled to the bone. Gregory was of course lucky, for he had money in his pocket and could go to places where warmth and dryness were to be bought for the price of a cup of tea or a pint of bitter. He was lucky too because his clothes were clean and respectable, allowing him to stay unmolested in places where shelter was free – libraries, galleries, museums and churches. But Gregory's restlessness and curiosity drove him back onto the pavements and he soon learnt where the other, unrespectable divisions of this army gathered in search of sanctuary from the weather, the law and probing eyes.

He was horrified to discover heaps of living bodies bundled in plastic and piled like sacks of garbage in doorways and alleys and basements. Beneath bridges and in dead ends he found whole settlements made of plastic, cardboard and bits of car junk. He came upon people grilling themselves over gratings at the back of office blocks and scavenging among the rubbish bins behind expensive hotels. He saw them camping on waste ground near the river where there was lumber and flotsam to burn.

Wherever he walked he was conscious of others walking beside him, going from nowhere to nothing. Unlike him, they shuffled and plodded, their heads drooping, their shoes falling off their feet, their clothes perpetually sodden, their flesh blue with cold and black with dirt. Only the completely mad, of whom there were surprising numbers, strode out smartly, as if drilling on the barrack square.

He was shocked to see how many beggars patrolled the streets. One afternoon a boy, no more than seven years old, with a terrible sore on his mouth, darted in front of him, holding out his hand. Gregory put a fifty-pence coin in his palm. The boy looked at it with disgust and then spat on him. On another occasion a woman holding a baby, or at least a baby-shaped bundle, followed him down Gray's Inn Road, whispering and pointing to her breast. He gave her a pound coin and without a change in her beseeching expression she peeled off to follow another man. As the Christmas frenzy approached its climax, more and more beggars clustered round the big stores, menacing the shoppers.

He was shocked to see schoolgirls selling themselves on street corners, and still more shocked to see men buying them. The girls stood on the kerbsides behind Kings Cross station wearing tattered mini-skirts and beckoning to the cars that drove past and splashed their sticks of legs. The men took them into side streets and pushed their damp heads down to suck. Gregory saw one man reading a newspaper while a girl was bending over his flies.

By the end of the week his shoes had split and fallen apart under the strain of his incessant tramping. He bought two new pairs, one for marching in and one for changing into when he was on the train in the evenings. During the day he carried his 'office' shoes in his brief case, together with certain reports, computer print-outs and other businesslike documents which he sometimes drew out and studied with a frown at weekends when Rose was in the room. But she seldom asked about his work and the fiction of his usual life proved easier to protect than he had feared; indeed, he was not called upon to tell a single direct lie. This was a comfort to his conscience, though it was a great sadness to his heart that Rose's interest in him seemed to be dwindling.

On the second Monday of his shadow life he did not bother with papers or telephoning, but made immediately for the streets outside the station and resumed his pilgrimage. Only in the zealous urgency of his pace did he resemble the Gregory who had leapt from the same train a week earlier.

Nothing in his background or education had prepared him for what he was witnessing on the streets of London; he had no idea the city held so much suffering. He was shocked as he had never been shocked before, but this had the effect of galvanising both his heart and his head and releasing in him powers which were all the more vigorous for having lain dormant until then. He only had to see someone in distress to see an injustice, and he found that injustice roused him to anger and guilt in equal measure. He was infuriated by the sight of suffering on every street corner and behind every building, and at the same time he felt that in some impalpable way he was to blame. Although as yet lacking any kind of philosophical or practical remedy with which to right these terrible wrongs, he was determined to find one. His few days on the streets had turned him into a crusader.

One notion was clear to him, one principle that shone luminously through the vapours of his perplexity, and that was: where there was need, he ought to give. This principle struck him as unarguable in its logic and radiant in its simplicity; it created a perfect union between morality and action. If he saw a man in need, it was his duty to help him, and the best way was to give him what he needed. He had a mission!

Hitherto, he had been slipping coins to beggars and buying cups of tea for those who asked him, but only on a spontaneous and random basis. Now he understood where his duty lay: it was to give, and to give all he had. This was suddenly revealed to him one morning while eating a fried egg in a café in Hackney. Without hesitating, he put down his fork and ran from the café in search of someone in need. Not ten yards away he came across a woman huddled for warmth in a doorway, blowing on her purple knuckles. He pulled off his gloves and thrust them into her hands, striding away before she could respond. By the end of the day he had managed to give away his scarf, his sweater and even his overcoat. He told Rose it had been stolen on the train and she passed no comment as he set off the next morning to combat the snow and sleet in his thin raincoat.

From that day he dedicated every hour in London to charity, and he gave with a simple purity that would have satisfied the most literal Christian. He fed the hungry, clothed the naked, gave money to the penniless, supplied drink, not always wisely, to the thirsty and brought warmth to the frozen. Once he had learnt the trick of it, his giving became as frenzied as it was prodigal, so it was not long before he had used up his meagre resources of accessible cash. The small sums of money he had allocated to each day of his redundancy were usually spent well before noon, and he was often forced to pass the rest of the day in hunger and thirst himself, shivering in a shirt beneath his raincoat.

As a result, he was forced to give away things rather than cash, and he began to take clothes into London each morning, smuggling socks, shirts, sweaters and trousers out of the house by hiding them in his briefcase. He gradually emptied his drawers and cupboards, leaving behind just enough items to prevent Rose from becoming suspicious. Once again, he was saddened to see how small her interest was in his welfare, for she did not appear to notice this dire contraction in his wardrobe. Finally he took to selling his few valuables in order to raise a little cash. He pawned the cigarette lighter Rose had given him the previous Christmas, and he pawned his father's regimental cuff-links, a deed which, he knew, would break his mother's heart if ever she learnt of it.

Careless of ridicule and indifferent to cold and fatigue, Gregory scoured London for people on whom to vent his charitable urges. As often as not his advances were misunderstood and his offers taken for insults. Women thought he was molesting them, men thought he was propositioning them, and children thought he was abducting them. Sometimes he was attacked and his money stolen from him before he could give it away; sometimes he was attacked, in place of thanks, by the very people to whom he had just given his money. Wherever he went, he was abused and harassed, but no one could deter him. He wanted neither gratitude nor respect, only the chance to go on giving. He was the spirit of Christmas gone berserk.

His mission came to an end as abruptly as it had begun. On the Monday before Christmas he saw a man being robbed in Cecil Court. The muggers punched him, tore off his coat and ran away, leaving him lying on the pavement in a pool of watery blood. Two or three people stepped over the body before Gregory could reach him. As he knelt beside him, eager to patch up his wounds and get him to hospital, he remembered he had no money and no way of obtaining any. He could not raise the price of a sticking plaster or a cup of tea, far less the fare for a taxi. He had nothing left to give, no cash, no clothes, no possessions. He realised he did not even have the strength to lift the man. With an effort, he rolled him over, cutting his hand on a broken bottle. His blood mingled on the pavement with what turned out to be red wine. He took off his raincoat and wrapped it round the man, who sat up and hiccupped. 'Christ!' he said, 'you look terrible.' He reached into his shoe and pulled out a squashed wad of money. 'Let's go and get a drink. You need one.' He gave Gregory back his raincoat and, supporting each other, they lurched down the street towards Leicester Square.

At that point he knew he had failed. He had failed in his mission, he had failed to make money, he had failed to give it away, he had failed his mother's ambitions and and he had failed to keep faith with his wife. Christmas lights twinkled from every house and shop window, while the nation ran about in a frenzy, heaping up things to give itself. This was done in the name of one who had given his life to save the species from its worldly nature. And what had his, Gregory's, giving achieved? Nothing, and less than nothing. It had not made the slightest difference to anyone: the army of the destitute had not been reduced by a single man or woman, and the sum of London's suffering was undiminished.

Sitting on the train, his head in his hands, Gregory finally despaired. The darkness gathering outside was nothing to the darkness in his soul.

He felt a deep, anguished need for some spiritual principle that would unlock these mysteries, but none was forthcoming. At his school the Christian teaching they had received had been of the apologetic, be-nice-to-your-neighbour variety, in which neither God nor Christ had played much part. He could not honestly say he believed in God; and if God was not to be believed in, where did that leave Christ? Had He been duped by some cosmic con-artist, or was He merely mad? And if there was a God He must be mad too to allow all this suffering.

Somewhere between Colchester and Ipswich the Stygian night of his despair darkened to utter blackness when he realised that in his orgy of giving he had neglected to buy a present for Rose. He had nothing to give her but lies.

It was at this moment that Roger Musson, best man at his wedding and erstwhile colleague in the City, sat down opposite him, smiling with seasonal cheer.

'Hello, Gregory,' he said. 'How's tricks?'

Gregory wept.

Twelve

Liz's funeral was sparsely attended.

In the chilly gloom of the crematorium, the chaplain told his skeleton congregation that they were gathered to mourn the sad passing of Elizabeth Rebecca Fisher.

Hearing her called Elizabeth, a name Liz herself had never used, Mary suddenly felt for the first time that Liz was truly dead; she was no longer Liz, her red-headed, infuriating friend, but Elizabeth, the deceased. Nor had she known before that Liz's middle name was Rebecca. Was she Jewish? It was possible, and if so she was being dispatched from the wrong place with the wrong rituals to the wrong God. But then what did it matter? Liz had, after all, been an atheist.

Lowering his head, while dropping his voice to its most sonorous timbre, the chaplain exhorted them to rejoice in the memory of her many achievements, to grieve the loss of so much promise, and to struggle to understand the torment that had led to her last, tragic decision. Above all, they were not to judge either Elizabeth or themselves. It was God's function, he told them, to sit in judgement, and He was all-merciful.

But Mary did judge. Who but Liz was responsible for putting them through this misery and embarrassment? Whose fault but hers that this earnest, asinine young man was doing his silly best to give some dignity to an occasion which she had rendered irretrievably absurd? It was fine for her, lying smugly in her coffin, unseen and uninvolved. She was probably laughing her immortal head off.

Yes, she would judge. But was hers a just anger as Liz's had evidently been? No. She was forbidden her anger, for that was God's prerogative. Did God feel guilty too, as she did? He was vengeful and jealous, so they were told, but was he also capable of guilt? Or had He granted himself the divine privilege of perpetual blamelessness? Surely He was occasionally ashamed of what He had done and left undone? After all, every father feels a twinge or two of guilt regarding his children. Was He, our Father in Heaven, the exception? Could He put his hand on his heart and say in all conscience that He had loved this daughter enough? Why then had she stuck her head in the eternal sand?

As the chaplain called on them to kneel for a moment in a silent prayer, Mary heard muffled sobbing. Craning her neck while trying to retain a posture of prayerfulness, she was astounded to observe the post-room boy – he who had referred to Liz as the office bike – bent over his pew in an agonised spasm of grief. These were the first tears she had seen shed for Liz.

Mary herself had cried at the time, but more out of shock than grief, and when she had cried later it had been out of frustration. She had wanted to get hold of Liz, shake her and ask her why she had been such a bloody fool. The boy, however, appeared to be weeping true tears of lamentation. Furthermore, he was the only member of the congregation to be wearing black: from what she could see he was wearing a dark suit and white shirt with a proper, funerary black tie. He had brushed his hair, not something he did habitually, and had flattened it against the sides of his head in oily slabs. His eyes were reddened and sore. Had he loved her? Surely not.

One evening in November, coming back to the office late and using her key, Mary had looked through the glass panel in their office door and seen Liz lying naked, her toes on the carpet, her back flat on the desk, her arms wrapped round her face, her hair tumbling down, and her hips raised invitingly to this youth. The highest point of her white body had been her red bush, burning like an autumn bonfire among the dead leaves of her papers.

His trousers were round his ankles, but he had not taken off his leather jacket. Was he so careless of her beauty, so nonchalant towards her radiant sexuality, that he could not be bothered to undress? Or had she, in her greedy eagerness, hustled the poor lad? At all events, it seemed that he had burnt himself in her red flames, leaving a wound that was still raw.

And what had she felt for him? Was he more to her than 'a good screw' (her invariable phrase)? Had some tangled, turgid romantic plot involving the priapic office boy driven her at last to wrap up her life in a bag as if it were so much garbage? And where was John the don, the Don Juan of Cambridge, the handsome, brilliant kisser of editors on kerbsides; where was he? Had egghead and beefcake been made rivals for the fair lady's favours? Which had won? Deserting her today, perhaps John had deserted her earlier; perhaps her red pelt had been just one more quarry to add to *his* bag. Or maybe he was unable to get his head together to keep this final date. Even if this youth had not respected her in life by taking off his clothes, he had at least put on the correct ones at her death.

Well, the lady was for burning now, and no one would be seared again in her red fire. She had extinguished herself and soon she would be ashes – hair, skin, juice, flesh – all ashes.

Mary came from a burying family. The bodies of her Albion ancestors had been lowered unscorched and intact into the Slaughterhouse graveyard. Her grandparents, her mother and an infant sister she had never known occupied a plot to the south of St Anthony's, out of sight of the house, and in due course they would presumably be joined by Tom and Georgina, Rose and her husband, whatever he was called, little Oliver, and even herself. Michael, on the other hand, would probably make more fashionable arrangements for his disposal. And her father – how long would it be before she was weeping at his grave side?

After a few bars of piped music a pair of purple curtains opened behind the coffin and Liz's body slowly rolled out of view. No ceremonial top hat with black ribbons for her; no stylish send-off, no slow cortege, no lines of weeping neighbours, no grieving family, no husband, broken but brave, no children, white-faced and dry-eyed, no lover masking his tragic feelings, no colleagues to honour her professional feats, no friends to get drunk over her memory, no photographers to snap the bereaved, no flowers heaped on the banks of raw soil, no funeral director bowing low over her open grave. No grave.

For only the second time since Liz's death, Mary wept.

On the steps of the crematorium she composed herself and looked up to see the chaplain waiting for her. She turned abruptly to avoid him and bumped into the post-room boy. He blew his nose with disgusting fluidity into a large white handkerchief, the only item of his costume, apart from his shirt, that was not black.

'I want to say goodbye to you,' he said, putting out his hand and then withdrawing it before she could shake it.

'Goodbye. Why?'

'I can't work in that place any more,' he said, his teeth gritted. He clenched his hand into a fist and held it up in a gesture of frustrated rage.

'You saw us that evening, didn't you? It gave me a bleeding shock I can tell you. Nearly put me off my stroke.'

He laughed abruptly, his voice cracking.

'Liz never noticed. She was deaf and blind when she was on the job, if you know what I mean. That's where she liked doing it,' he said wonderingly, 'on the desk. Wouldn't go anywhere else with me. It had to be the office or nowhere, and always on the desk. Bloody uncomfortable, I can tell you. I got fed up with it. I was always worried about getting caught, though she didn't seem to give a toss who found us. But it wasn't that. She never looked at me during the day, couldn't even remember my name sometimes, then at night, when the place was empty, she used to ring down to the post-room and by the time I got upstairs she would be spread out on the desk, starkers. We hardly said a word to each other. In the end I hated it. I told her we had to stop and the next time she rang down I told her to bugger off. In the morning I came into the office and found out that she was, that she . . .'

63

He began to cry.

Mary put out her hand to comfort him, but he pushed it aside.

'I admired her, the stupid cow,' he said, 'but I never understood her. Did you?'

'Not really, Dave, no.'

She had remembered his name, but she wondered if her use of it had been clumsy, making too pointed a contrast with Liz's negligence.

He looked round awkwardly, seeming not to know how to bring their conversation to an end.

'She really rubbished herself, didn't she?' he said at last.

'I suppose she did.'

He sniffed, looking round again.

With an abrupt jerk of his head he nodded to her.

'Cheers,' he said gruffly and walked off.

There had been flowers on her desk the day before she died, a huge, vulgar sheaf of red carnations in a cellophane wrapper. Liz had used an office waste-paper bin as a vase, filling it with water which mixed acridly with her cigarette stubs. She had not arranged the blooms but simply shoved them in a clump into the tin basket and stood it on her desk. Who had sent them? There had been no card. In her struggle to kill herself, she had knocked the bin to the floor where the water had left a grey, marshy stain on the carpet. Her torso was spattered with ash sludge too. She had indeed rubbished herself; and yet the carnations lay scattered about her corpse, still fresh and fragrant, as if to compensate for the burial she would not be given.

Thirteen

Whenever Oliver Albion was asked by some fatuous adult what he intended to be when he grew up, he would unhesitatingly reply, 'A farmer,' and the adult would beam indulgently and say, 'Just like your Dad,' as though the coincidence might not have occurred to the boy. In truth Oliver never devoted a moment's thought to the future and his answer was not the result of identifying with his father, but a desire to bring the conversation to a quick, acceptable end. Yet in recent weeks he had given much anguished thought to his father, and it was his face that Oliver saw looming out of the gathering darkness as his train sped towards Stowmarket. He tried to imagine his father welcoming him home, but the mask beyond the window remained expressionless, its eyes blank and staring.

Anguish had not played much part in Oliver's brief life. Indeed, the story of his early years had been one of painless progress from birthday to birthday, a quiet, agreeable journey which fulfilled its modest timetable of attainments and suffered no serious delays. He grew up to be a carefree, amiable boy who, confident of being loved, dispensed his own affections with casual largesse. This enviable state of affairs trundled on until the time of his eighth birthday in March when, quite without warning, his little engine was suddenly derailed.

The immediate cause of the accident was Rose's wedding outfit, or rather its cost. Her mother, Georgina, had insisted that her dress be hired, an economy which Rose regarded as spiteful and humiliating. By way of minimal revenge, she demanded that her accessories, shoes, gloves, underwear and so forth, should be bought for her. If she had to go up the aisle in second-hand rags, she declaimed bitterly at lunch one day, she could at least be allowed to wear her own knickers. Any compromise on this matter would, she said, make her feel squalid.

Thus, it was over the momentous issue of a pair of silk drawers that the Albion marriage committed itself to civil war.

Whenever battle was joined, and it was usually during meals, Georgina would asseverate, with more passion than originality, that they were not made of money, that far too much of their hard-earned savings was already being spent on 'this' wedding, and that Rose was being downright selfish to expect them to indulge her in childish extravagances. Tom, for his part, argued that since his daughter was only going to get married once at his expense (*his* expense, not *theirs*, Georgina noted grimly), she must be given the best. The next time she could bloody well pay for herself, but if she had set her heart on silk knickers for this wedding, silk knickers she would have.

Oliver was disturbed and frightened by his parents' meal-time war. As often as he could he fled the sniping and shelling at the dining table and took his dog across the farmyard to the farrowing house where family life among the sows and their piglets was orderly and tranquil. No one attempted to block his withdrawal.

To his mind this arguing over the price of dresses was beyond reason; the issue was too trivial and not worth the bloodshed. But he had not yet learnt that the language of love, though difficult to speak itself, translates readily into the language of money. In his simplicity, he assumed that when they talked of costs they were referring to money, to actual cash in a literal bank. He had still to grasp that love between parents and children is never freely given but is always bargained for and exchanged on terms. He had yet to discover that the transfer of love, like property, is subject to all sorts of arrangements – mortgaging, letting, sub-letting, even squatting, though seldom the final relinquishing of freehold; nor had he discovered that love has its fraudulent side too, that love can be embezzled and swindled, signatures forged, cheques drawn where funds do not exist and promises of repayment made in order to deceive. It certainly did not occur to him that when his mother insisted that they could not afford Rose's fancy underwear she was also giving notice that Rose's borrowing facilities on her fund of maternal affection were being closed down, and that when his father insisted that Rose should be pampered on this one occasion he was in fact announcing that his paternal investment in the property hitherto known as 'Miss Albion' was to be transferred to the newly named 'Mrs Burton'.

All this was beyond Oliver's ken. He only knew he was frightened by his parents' hostility for each other, by the gap which had suddenly divided them. He wanted nothing so much as the restitution of their old unity, the double-sided whole in which he had been snugly encased, like a walnut between their two welded shells.

But worse was to come, for he gradually realised that his own name had become entangled in these battles, that he had in fact replaced Rose as the subject of their dispute. As a result, he was consumed with guilt; for evidently he, not Rose, was the cause of this war. *He* was responsible for all this bitterness, all these horrible feelings.

The battles were now fought over the question of his next school and for the first time, though by no means the last, Oliver heard the dreaded phrase, 'making a man of him', a transformation which could apparently be effected only at a boarding school.

His mother, he gathered, was not opposed to manliness in principle, merely to its being thrust on Oliver at too tender an age. But his father bellowed that it was high time he was severed from her apron strings; high time he was toughened up and generally prepared for life's hardships. He was willing to compromise by allowing the boy to be sent to Bitterley Hall, despite its reputation for artiness and its decadent preference for soccer over rugby. Further than that, however, he would not bend.

As frightened children will, Oliver took to eavesdropping on his parents' rows and when they began to argue about his own immediate destiny he glued his ear still tighter to the keyhole. It was therefore only a matter of time before he paid the eavesdropper's penalty by overhearing things that were not only painful, but also intolerable to live with because they could not be shared or discussed.

One evening a few days before Rose's wedding, when he was thought to be in bed, Oliver stood at his customary post behind the dining room door and exposed himself to the following muffled exchange.

'What makes you think we can afford to send him to Bitterley Hall? Do you know how much the fees are? Eight thousand a year, and that's not counting extras. We've never had that kind of money, and we certainly don't have it now. I'm not blind, you know. I can see what's happening on the farm. I read the newspaper. I listen to the news. No one's making any money out of pigs at the moment.'

'We've had his name down since he was born. The boy is going, and that's that.'

There was a short silence and then his father added, 'We're giving Rose the best, and so we must do the same for Oliver.'

'What are you talking about? We can't afford her silly wedding in the first place. You accuse me of spoiling Oliver. What about your spoiling Rose? She has you round her little finger.'

'A girl deserves a good wedding, and a boy must have a good education.'

'My God! Which century do you think we're living in? Anyway, it's nonsense. Rose had an excellent education in the state system and so will Ollie if we leave him there.'

'Oliver must go away. It's a family tradition. My father was sent away to school and so was I. The boy must go.'

'You hated it.'

'It did me no harm.'

'Is that the best you can say for it? Is that why we're

68

sending him away from home, why we're spending all this money? Just to do him no harm?'

Oliver heard the heavy noise of his father's footfall and he shrank away, preparing to flee down the corridor. But then he heard the thump of a log being thrown onto the fire and he edged back to the door.

'I'm not arguing with you; I'm telling you. My mind is made up. It's a question of being fair. We owe it to the boy.'

'We don't owe him this.' Oliver could hear his mother's voice shaking with sobs, a most unfamiliar sound. 'Let's give him a slap-up party when he's eighteen and then they'll be all square.'

'Don't be ridiculous, woman. He must be properly educated, and that won't happen as long as he hangs around here, being mollycoddled by you. Can't you understand that?'

'I understand *you*,' his mother suddenly shouted. 'I understand you very well. You're a hypocrite. You've never loved him as much as Rose. Why don't you admit that you just want to get rid of him? You can't even admit that to yourself, can you?'

These extraordinary questions were followed by the noise of some violent activity, a chair, maybe a table being shoved against the wall. His mother made a small cry, though whether of pain or shock Oliver did not wait to discover. He ran to his bed and lay in the darkness and silence thinking about his father. Could it really be true that his father wanted to get rid of him? What had he done? Surely his mother must have got it wrong; but why would she say such a thing? Although no one was there to see it, more than an hour passed before he stopped trembling in his sleep.

If there is one great distinction between the child and the adult mind, it lies in the child's capacity to give love the benefit of the doubt. Adults are forever fretting over the quantity and quality of love they receive, but children refuse to accept they are unloved until the evidence becomes too brutal to ignore. True to type then, Oliver, though greatly distressed by his eavesdropping, was not willing to accept

69

what he had heard at face value. His father, he told himself, was worried about the wet spring and Rose's wedding, but these were temporary aggravations that would pass. And so for the next week or two he made it his policy to keep out of his father's way. This was not difficult since Tom was seldom to be seen in the house or the yard, and in the absence of any new sign of his father's dislike for him, Oliver began to put his faith in the future: things would be better in the summer.

Soon after the wedding his mother broke it to him that they had finally decided to send him to boarding school in September. There was nothing to worry about, she told him, Bitterley Hall was very nice and it was on the seaside not far from Cromer where she had lived as a little girl. On a hot day in May during half term she drove him to Norfolk and showed him the school itself, which proved to be a large empty house full of beds and desks. The atmosphere of the tall, echoing rooms was not unlike that of their dining room at home, and Oliver was indeed cheered by the nearness of the sea whose postcard blue coloured the outlook of all the windows at the front of the house.

'The boys are always in sight of the sea,' enthused the headmaster, patting Oliver on the head and beaming at Georgina. 'It is their constant companion, whether they are at work, at play or at prayer.' He chuckled complacently. 'I am sure the little man will fit into our community most harmoniously. What is he, would you say, sportsman or scholar?'

'A bit of both, we think,' Georgina replied.

'I remember your father well, Mrs Albion,' the headmaster said, taking her arm and leading her onto the terrace. 'A fine man, and still sorely missed, they tell me, at the yacht club.'

Despite appearances, the headmaster was no fool. If there had been any doubt as to Oliver's enrolment at Bitterley Hall, it was quashed by this single, unctuous remark. Georgina looked out across the spanking waves, smiled sadly and sighed.

'Is sailing on your curriculum, Mr Peach?'

'Indeed it is, Mrs Albion,' said the headmaster, ripely. 'We do not live in Nelson's county for nothing.'

For Oliver, the whole day passed in a whirl of confusion, none of it unpleasant, and some of it positively enjoyable. After taking their leave of Bitterley Hall and its chivalrous proprietor, they drove into Cromer where Georgina, breaking all precedents and principles, gave Oliver £5 to spend in the amusement arcade. She pointed out to him the site of her father's old office on the high street and dragged him to the graveyard where he was buried. While she cried, Oliver sat on the tomb in the sunshine and tossed green stone chippings into an urn. Finally, they bought a pair of dressed crabs for Tom and set off home. Oliver slept for most of the journey.

As a result of this excursion, Bitterley Hall was invested with more or less harmless associations and although he did not relish the thought of being parted from his parents or from Elsie, his dog, he was not frightened by the prospect of this new era in his history.

He was therefore utterly unprepared for the shock of separation when it finally came. Saying goodbye to his parents in the school yard was not too bad. His father shook him by the hand and wished him good luck. His mother, unable to speak, gripped him in a sudden and violent hug, discarded him with equal violence and stumbled to their car. Then they were gone and he was sucked into a chaos of new faces, new rules, new rituals and new fears which allowed no opportunity for reflection and kept his feelings in a state of frozen shock. On his first Sunday, however, after prayers and letter-writing, a period of free time was announced: the boys were at liberty to wander the grounds, read in the library, or amuse themselves as they chose. Oliver chose to weep. He found a concealed corner behind the boat-shed and sat on the shingle, hugging his knees. He stared out to sea, which was grey now, and howled.

This Sunday retreat grew to be a habit with him. During the weekdays he mostly managed to control his tears, but the emptiness of Sunday mornings broke him. He learnt to hate the sea. It became the symbol of his miseries, the prison wall he was forced to look at every day, the blank calendar that measured out his endless sentence.

Yet he was a resilient boy and did not succumb to the melancholy of homesickness for longer than a month or so. Apart from his Sunday morning lapses, which were to continue throughout the term, he lived, as we have seen, more in terror than sadness. Among the many sources of his fearfulness one of the first to manifest itself was none other than the kindly seeming, head-patting, beaming Mr Peach who beat him savagely for taking an apple from the pantry.

'You are being chastised,' Mr Peach told him between strokes, 'to teach you that thievery is abominable and deception unworthy of a member of Bitterley Hall.'

However, this honourable beating did not completely crush him, and as the weeks went by his natural buoyancy asserted itself and he developed a wary composure. He was sustained by two things: one was his unpolitic friendship with Carter, the other, strangely enough, was his father, or rather his image of him. Mothers, however intensely they were thought about in private, were not much talked of; fathers, on the other hand, were frequently mentioned, for they were the totems of status, mystical figures concerning whom the boys boasted and, if necessary, made up lies.

It was Rogers who set the tone of the competition.

'My father's worth half a million,' he drawled one day during morning break, 'and he says he'll be a millionaire before he's fifty. What's yours worth, Carter?'

'I haven't got a father,' returned the ingenuous boy.

'That makes you a bastard then, doesn't it?'

'No, it doesn't, actually,' said Carter patiently, without a trace of rancour. 'My father died when I was a baby. I'm as legitimate as any of you.'

Rogers, seeing that his insult was in danger of back-firing, rounded on Oliver.

'I've no idea what my father's worth,' he said frankly, but

in a lofty tone which he hoped would suggest a wealthiness beyond the reach of mere, vulgar arithmetic. Oliver may have been terrorised, but he was not without resources.

'He's a farmer, isn't he?' demanded Rogers sneeringly.

'No. He's an agri-businessman,' Oliver corrected him with sudden inspiration. 'And if you knew anything about the price of land' – which Oliver did not – 'you would know what eight hundred acres is worth.'

Rogers was silenced.

'A bloody fortune,' added Oliver with sufficient aggression to mask the fact that he had not named a specific figure.

Rogers remained silent.

Rogers senior, the millionaire-in-the-making, had hitherto been a mythical figure of insuperable power, the mere invocation of his name being a spell capable of crushing every contender. The discovery that his, Oliver's father could be pitted against this titan, and come away from the contest with honour, shocked Oliver at first and then filled him with exhilaration. Knowing that the name of his father could now be deployed as a bastion to protect him from at least some of the school's malign forces was deeply consoling, and it gave rise to a whole chain of fantasies which accrued an ever-more virile magic as the weeks of his expulsion from Slaughterhouse stretched into months.

During his first nights at Bitterley Hall the slightest, most transient memory of home, flickering into his mind before he could quash it, had been enough to unplug his tears. But in time he devised a way of drawing solace from home without provoking its mournful reflex: he translated his parents and the rest of the personnel at Slaughterhouse into more or less mythical figures whom he played with in his imagination, sharing with them a series of endlessly repeated rites of consolation.

His brusque and bristling mother he converted into an almost abstract field of force which simply emanated warmth, affection and a sensation of digestive well-being. But it was his father who underwent the most extreme transformation

73

in these home-sick reveries. While the detestable sea surged and sucked in the blackness below his dormitory window, Oliver would busy his mind with fantasies concerning a father inflated into truly heroic proportions. He conceived him as a king ruling over a farmyard kingdom with a noble palace, a city of sheds and corrugated iron, a province of fields and woodland, an army of tractors and a loyal population of pigs. And standing beside this colossus-king was of course Oliver himself, princeling and beloved heir to the throne, resplendent in his own sparkling crown and brandishing his own irresistible sword. Almost every night this fantasy-father would take him by the arm and speak to him man-to-man, confiding that he was obliged to go on a long journey and begging Oliver, his only begotten son, to rule in his stead as Prince Regent.

Thus, Oliver was able to arrange a most satisfactory negation of the horrible thing he had heard at the dining room door.

And now, on the last day of his term, with the gates of Eden standing open to receive rather than eject him, his spirits soared and forgiveness filled his young breast. Joy, optimism and good will, the very elements of the Christmas spirit, shone in his eyes. Surely his father, his comrade and champion, would welcome him home?

The face beyond the train window, hovering in the darkness, remained impassive.

To quell his doubts, Oliver turned to his escort and said, 'My father's thinking of buying a new boar. A Large White. Do you know anything about pigs, Mr Tupper?'

'Pigs?' said the young master, somewhat surprised by this enquiry. 'All I know about pigs is that I shall be very glad not to be eating the school's so-called sausages.'

Then, feeling that he should not be inculcating disloyalty, he added, 'Mind you, I've known some swine in my time.'

Oliver smiled tolerantly at this example of official wit.

'My father,' Oliver continued inexorably, 'says that Large White boars serve better than any other breed he's tried.'

'Serve?' said Mr Tupper, baffled.

'Yes sir. You know, like in biology lessons. The boar *serves* the sows.'

'Good God, Albion. Kindly keep your agricultural smut to yourself.'

'Yes sir.'

They fell silent.

With ever mounting excitement Oliver stared out of the window, watching for the landmarks that brought him closer to home.

Mr Tupper, seeing that Oliver was preoccupied, took a stealthy swig from the bottle secreted in his suitcase. This year, as usual, he was spending Christmas in Sevenoaks with his sister and her husband. They were teetotallers.

Fourteen

Driving past Bury St Edmunds's monstrous and misleading skyline, with its five towering beet silos and its fecund chimney stacks pouring smoke into the grey, saturated sky, Mary was overcome by despair. The granite spear of St John's steeple looked to her like a missile aimed at heaven and the strains of 'O Come All Ye Faithful', relayed from King's College, Cambridge to her car radio, rang in her ears with all the conviction of an advertising jingle. The fellowship of Christmas and the consolations of returning 'home' were the necessary myths in which she had placed her faith, hoping they would somehow requite her for Liz's death, but now their magic seemed to be shredding into a void where even self-delusion could not flourish, becoming as nebulous as the smoke dissolving into Bury's graceless firmament. Suicide was a labyrinth with death at its centre, but trapped within its lightless passages were other victims – family, friends, lovers, acquaintances – who would neither die nor escape, yet were doomed to grope forlornly after the riddle of the dead one's motives, guided by nothing except their guilt. Mary knew she stood inside the entrance of this maze and could feel the tug of its magnetism.

At the first opportunity she left the A45 and enmeshed herself in a different maze: the tangle of streets and lanes that connected the villages strung out between Bury and Stowmarket, at whose centre, according to her private projection, lay Slaughterhouse. As she picked her way along the network of crooked lanes, her spirits were gradually raised. She had entered the topography of her childhood, her father's kingdom, and she no longer had to give her mind to navigating. A deep, unerring instinct reeled her back into a landscape which was more felt than seen, a place so familiar as to be mysterious when picked apart and deliberately studied.

As a child she had always felt they had entered their home territory when they passed Miss Shotcombe's house, a gaunt, red-brick villa, whose narrow windows were permanently blinded by shutters and grimy curtains. According to village gossip, Miss Shotcombe was a lunatic, her sanity having cracked the day her dog, a poodle, had been killed by a Spitfire crash-landing in her meadow. Since then she had neither washed nor left her house, or so it was said. Nobody had seen her since 1941, except for delivery boys and roundsmen who claimed to have glimpsed her blackened face and rancid hair. On the side of her house the date of its construction, 1910, had been picked out in cream-coloured bricks. Mary's father used to tell her that it had been built in his honour, for that was the year of his birth.

Beyond her house, which still seemed to emanate a crazy presence – surely Miss Shotcombe was dead by now? – stood the shattered trunk of an oak tree. Over the centuries it had lost all its limbs to lightning or gales, yet each spring it had produced a punkish crest of shoots from the rim of its hollow torso. Neither dead nor alive, it had prevailed throughout her childhood in this flourishing state of moribundity. Her childhood eye had seen a malevolent visage, gnarled, bearded and cruel, in its bark. The face was still there, and it had lost none of its baleful power.

The road turned again and in the crook of this bend, quite separate from the village or any farm, a quartet of cottages huddled together, seemingly for comfort and safety, the outer two leaning inwards like drunks. Once they had belonged to her grandfather and had housed his labourers and their families; now they comprised a single residence used only at weekends by a pair of nancy-boys (her father's description) whose collection of whimsical teapots had been shown in a magazine. The far cottage, closest to Slaughter-house, which currently served as a wine store downstairs and a spare bathroom upstairs, had been the home of an ostler turned tractor driver. His name was John, but behind his back he was called 'Lenin' because one evening in 1945 in a moment of drunken dementia he had talked of joining the union. Nature had given him a long and joyless face, but he rendered it all the more lugubrious by wearing a walrus moustache. Whenever he spoke to Mary or any member of 'the governor's' family, he tapped the peak of his cap with his forefinger in a furtive, rueful gesture. Perhaps, after all, he had nursed mutinous longings.

She was in sight of the village roofs now, their profile dominated by the martial-looking block of the church tower, and as usual she shocked herself with the snobbish pleasure she took in the fact that the land to left and right of the road, as far as the eye could see, belonged to her family.

She turned off the road, parking on a patch of scrub beside the massive, dilapidated structure of an old tithe barn. This ruin had not been put to agricultural use since the war and the village had unofficially adopted it. On summer nights courting couples sought its privacy and its dubious protection from the weather, and on summer days the village children, many of them the living products of the barn's moonlit hospitality, played among its weeds and smashed tiles. Her brother Tommy had once found a condom here and had held it up, lank and dangling, for her inspection. He told her they were called 'freddies' which made them laugh for a whole afternoon. Freddy was the name of their father's cowman, an earnest, righteous bachelor of thirty-five who, with childish condescension, they assumed had never seen a 'freddy' in his life, far less made use of its function – whatever that was, for it remained inscrutable to them.

Smiling at this memory and feeling a rare pang of affection for Tom, she walked beside the barn and opened the gate to stand on the edge of her father's field. It had been recently ploughed, perhaps that same day, for the furrows at her feet still had a steely sheen from the action of the ploughshare. Away to her left the village lay in the cleft of its little valley. Smoke and mist were mixing in the four o'clock gloom and lights had already begun to prick out the pattern of its streets, shops and cottages. She could make out the farm, which stood above the village immediately behind the church. She could see the rawboned outline of the Dutch barn, while the house itself, a white plane looming through the thickening grey, was partly blacked out by the spreading silhouette of the yew in the churchyard.

Looking back on the field, she found that the whole expanse of its ribbed surface was speckled with white flints. Despite centuries of stone-picking, these fields still threw up their primeval crop of rock; it came out of the ground as eternally as sand from the sea, or dust off the desert. The village rested on foundations of flint, its roads were bedded in flint, its houses were dressed in flint and their garden walls were built of flint, the church was faced with flint and all its doors, windows and buttresses were decorated with knapped flint. Millions upon millions of tons of flint had been gathered to give the village bones of flint, a whole skeleton of flint, yet these stones continued to rise out of the ground, like a stony sweat, oozing forever through the skin of its soil and petrifying beneath the great, open, flint-coloured Suffolk sky.

She bent and picked up one of these stones, which her father had cursed all his working life. Its white rind was intact except for a single slate-blue chip, and it had a humanoid form with four limb-shaped parts and a nodule for a head. She rubbed the mud off it and took it to the car. It was time to go home.

Fifteen

As a boy Michael Pennistone had dreamed of becoming a hero when he grew up; he had craved adventure and adulation in equal portions. He saw himself spilling patriotic quantities of enemy blood, scaling virgin peaks and bringing to book Interpol's most wanted men, deeds for which he would be rewarded with statues in the public parks and the love of insatiable women. However, not even the vaguest shadow of these dreams came to pass in his adult life. The world, or at least that part of it which he had chosen to inhabit – Wardour Street and the rat-runs of the public relations business – offered no openings for heroism. It was certainly thick with villains, but instead of being the targets of lion-hearted young men they were the ones who were honoured and adored. There were maidens too, plenty of them, but those he came across who appeared to be naked and in distress did not wish to be rescued from their dragons by penniless junior executives.

His childish dreams were crushed by these disillusionments and he was driven to slake his thirst for excitement at a very different spring, which he had discovered in the meantime. He became hooked on sexual adventure and the dubious adulation it sometimes aroused. At the age of eighteen he had been taken by a schoolfriend to a brothel in Soho where an Italian woman smelling strongly of cigarettes, high-octane perfume and her last client, had exchanged her wondrously hairy parts for two pounds of his birthday money. Thereafter, it was not so much women's bodies he craved as the sensation which had burst in his head that first time in Dean Street as 'Sophia' had allowed him, with a weary sigh and a demand for an extra ten shillings, to claw at her breast and suck her long, purple nipples. There had been a wild hammering in his temples, his mouth had dried, his pulse had beaten in his chest like galloping horses and his erection had rocketed into shape. He sought that sensation as if it were a drug.

He embarked on a career of promiscuity and by the time he was in his mid-twenties his ability to secure willing women was very nearly the equal of his satyriasis. Like most lechers, he was no friend of women; indeed, he almost hated them for possessing something which, no matter how often he took it from them, still remained theirs. Yet his sexual experience did give him a certain confidence when in their company and this put them at ease, smoothing the way towards intimacy. He also learnt the trick of laughing freely with women. He had no sense of humour himself, only a sharp, cold eye for the ridiculous, but he had observed that women warmed quickly to men who made them laugh and so, in lieu of actual jokes, he supplied the laughter alone. He perfected a melodious tenor chuckle which was as charming as it was false.

Otherwise, he had no secret, no magic strategem for getting women into bed. He had made the discovery that his looks, which were handsome enough in a thin-lipped, aquiline way, were virtually irrelevant to his sexual success. Women did not have to be seduced. All that was necessary was to make his desire blatant and one woman in three would find the urgency of his demand irresistible. Some yielded passively, as if obeying a command; some cried out in their passion, as if he were submitting them to torture; some shocked him with their erotic artfulness and some bored him with their sentimental pleas for kindness. He did not care what their response was, he only concerned himself with achieving that moment when the woman offered her breast to his greedy teeth and the blood rang in his head. He was indifferent to the woman herself, he only wanted to sink himself in the oblivion of her body. That was his fix.

He made another discovery. Sexual ecstasy does not linger in the memory, capable of being relished anew in tranquillity. Sex, for him anyway, was ashes as soon as it was done. The milk he sucked from those frantic breasts was the bitter milk of addiction.

Yet as time went by this compulsion eased and he learnt to temper the rage of his fornication with a touch of dalliance. He added fetish and ritual to his needs. He became obsessed with preserving his appearance of youth and lavished no less attention on his own figure and clothes than on those of his women. Professional success enabled him to buy a flat in Kensington in a newly built block of steel and glass units, and he filled it with furnishings and objects that were brand-new. He abhorred antiques and despised anything which retained the patina of time. He would have nothing in his flat that was not sleek and steely, whose lines were not sharp and clean, whose surfaces were not polished, shining and smooth. The same went for the women he brought there. They had to be as pure as stainless steel, with no trace of age or experience blemishing their faces and bodies.

And when a flawless girl unbuttoned her white blouse in his mirrored bedroom and showed him her immaculate breast, the old hammering would thud in his head and his potency, less zealous now than in the past, would rouse itself. As he advanced on the girl's faultlessness, his sluggish weapon aloft at last, he knew the joy of losing himself for a moment in sheer sensation. He would bury his head between her snowy thighs and feel that after all his life had some meaning.

As to the girls, they passed in succession through his flat, sometimes taking away a handful of fresh, scented bank-notes and sometimes, in special cases, a strand of pearls. But they never left behind any stronger sign of their visit than their glossy hair left on his satin pillows.

Then he fell in love. Or he came as close as a committed, lifelong narcissist is capable. He met Mary one evening at a reception beneath the glass ceiling of the ballroom in the Belgravia Hotel. Though she was a little old for his taste, being all of thirty-one, she fascinated him from the first instant his cold gaze raked her slim, tall figure. He stared admiringly at her clear complexion, her long, graceful neck and the smooth chignon in which she had gathered her auburn hair. He stared longingly at her elegant movements which seemed to promise a softer voluptuousness beneath the cool poise of her social manner. His judgement of women, as we have seen, hardly extended beyond the physical, and in this respect he was thrilled beyond even his jaded expectations by Mary Albion. And when, some nights later, she shook out her chignon and bared her girlish breast to his hungry eye, the throbbing in his skull was as explosive as it had ever been in the heat of his youth. But on this occasion he also attended to the woman's personality and found Mary's in every way agreeable and entertaining. He was bewitched by her intelligence which was lucid yet docile, sharp but tender. He realised with a self-pitying pang how lonely he had been during his years of venery. He realised he deserved to be loved and invited Mary to marry him.

She accepted without prevarication and within a month she joined him as his wife in his steel box of a flat. She softened its pitiless walls with books and because they were newly published and clad in glossy jackets he welcomed them.

She confounded her friends (he had none to be confounded) by displaying every symptom of happiness. When they questioned her about her choice of husband, like many a bride before her, she could not provide a wholly coherent answer. He was handsome, wealthy and successful, qualities not to be sneezed at; he was ardent in bed and considerate in his other dealings with her; he had a dry sense of humour, which she appreciated, and if he was a little vain and self-absorbed, as she conceded, he was also his own man. She did not tell them that she also relished his conservative outlook, for it made a refreshing contrast with the messy radicalism rife in her office. Nor did she tell them that his sexual intensity had caused her to enjoy her first orgasm. She spoke banteringly about his rakish past, but was wise enough not to enquire too pressingly how he had acquired the expertise which was giving her so much joyful pleasure.

For nearly four years they delighted in the felicities of a busy marriage. Michael contained himself in fidelity and remained captivated by her sweet, sharp-witted sensuality. Mary learnt to value his possessiveness, finding it more protective than restricting. Indeed, she was the most glittering and subtle of his possessions. They both had careers to pursue and ambitions to fulfil, and their marriage became a charmed haven to which they gladly retreated after the turmoil of business. The doubting condescension of her friends was humbled during these years as their own long-standing marriages collapsed, scattering children and misery as they fell. Mary and Michael began to assume the probity of an institution, and people thought their mutual devotion almost freakish in its constancy.

This happy era came to an abrupt end on the morning of Mary's thirty-fifth birthday. Lying on the bed amidst a foam of tissue paper, the straps of her new silk négligé slipping off her polished shoulders, she declared she would like to have a baby. Michael was appalled and said so. She insisted with more force than he expected. Voices were raised, doors were slammed, tears were shed. Her birthday failed to be the frolicsome occasion it had been in previous years.

Michael hated her baby, even though its conception was still abstract. This homunculus would destroy her beauty and steal the love she had for him. He loathed the thought of her perfect body being desecrated: her drum-skin stomach would balloon like a water melon, her breasts would become grossly pumped up and riddled with blue veins, milk would ooze from her nipples and she would stink. He had seen and smelt a pregnant woman once, and it had made him sick. As for birth itself – the splitting, screaming and bleeding – it was insufferable. And once born, the demon baby would be Mary's loved one, and he would be discarded.

That night he lay beside her and stared grievingly at her sleeping form. She seemed suddenly to have aged. Even as he watched, her body was shedding the bloom and resilience of youth. Soon it would sag and wrinkle and crumble. He could already see death inscribed on her flesh. Worse still, her senescence was a ghoulish reminder of his own mortality, for he was three years older than she. He could not look at her without smelling death on her skin – his death.

Sex with her was inconceivable. He would be raping a corpse, but a corpse capable of bearing life in its withered womb. He could not enter her without creating the monster that would kill them both.

The next morning Mary promised she would defer her pregnancy for a year and something like their old pleasantness was restored. Yet for him the shadow of death continued to hover over their marriage. His desire for Mary gradually declined and it was only a matter of time before he cast his steely eye in the direction of another body, one which was uncontaminated by the threat of death in life. Zara became his mistress during that summer. Meanwhile the unsuspecting Mary, without realising what she was doing, compensated for the child he was refusing her by half adopting a substitute. That child was Liz.

Sixteen

By the time Mary drove into the farmyard darkness had fallen and rain was sleeting through the valley. There were no lights to be seen around the farm except the faint glow of heater lamps in the roof of the farrowing house. The wind was blowing too hard for her to hear either pigs or men in any of the buildings. The front of the house was unlit, but a single light burnt above the back porch, its fly-blown bulb radiating a tallowy halo.

She ran into the porch and felt a surge of nostalgic affection for its clutter of boots and coats. The door into the house had a battered brass knob which rattled loosely on its spindle. Its noise was an echo of her childhood, of the countless times she had flung open the door, burying the handle on the other side still deeper into the plaster of the scullery wall. She switched on the light which picked out the white, plucked carcase of a turkey lying beneath a wire mesh safe. Though drawn and dressed, its head was still intact, the scarlet crop lolling over the lip of the dish.

Pausing for a moment to prepare herself, she opened the door into the kitchen, carefully turning off the scullery light.

'We were expecting you much earlier,' said Georgina, her sister-in-law, pointing crossly at the big clock on the wall. 'I suppose you want tea now. You'll have to make your own. I've got to collect Ollie from the station.'

Notwithstanding these curt remarks, she took two thick-rimmed mugs from the dresser, tore the lid off a large, black teapot and hurled a teabag into it.

Mary said nothing. She was too irritated for either speech or movement. Every time she came home to Slaughterhouse she resolved to make fresh efforts to like Georgina, or at any

86

rate to be patient with her and remain calm. In the car she had vowed for the hundredth time that she would overlook her irritating ways and concentrate on her undoubted virtues. Yet here she was, less than a minute after her arrival, gritting her teeth to stop herself quarrelling with the woman. She knew that Georgina's greeting had not been unkindly meant, despite its brusqueness, but every syllable she had uttered, every gesture she had made with her graceless, flapping arms had infuriated her and sapped her good intentions.

However, reminding herself that it was the season of forgiveness and sisterly love, she cranked her face into a smile.

'I can look after myself,' she said. 'Please let me. You go to the station.'

This small Christmas gesture was rewarded. Georgina permitted herself the rare luxury of a fleeting smile in reply to Mary's. Her shoulders sagged and for a moment she leaned wearily on the sink. Then, with an abrupt movement, she rallied and filled the kettle, firing a violent jab of water into its spout as if to flush out any insects that might be nesting there.

'Sit down,' she said. 'You've had a long journey and I mustn't be too early at the station.'

Why not, wondered Mary, watching Georgina as she looked guiltily at the clock's looming face.

Georgina was squat and rotund. She exaggerated her dumpiness by wearing clothes whose colours were derived from mud – browns, duns and sludgy mauves. Their cut was based on the same principle as the bicycle cape: they hung shapelessly from her short neck and seemed designed for no other function than to keep out the rain. Her small face was encumbered by a long, heavy jaw and her habitual expression was one of frantic preoccupation. Why had Tom, Mary's handsome brother, the village Lothario, chosen this woman? That was a question Mary had puzzled over, without result, ever since the day, twenty-five years ago, when he had first brought Georgina into this very kitchen to meet his family. She had not been pregnant. She was neither rich nor socially illustrious; she was not humorous, brilliant or eccentric. Perhaps she simply had a loving heart? If so, she kept it locked up and hidden.

Georgina's most conspicuous trait was haste. Whatever she was doing, she behaved as if she were criminally behindhand with it. Her implacable timetable appeared to be divinely ordained. Wherever she toiled she was pursued by her merciless Taskmaster whose finger forever pointed at His watch and whose horrified eye forever stared at a neglected cobweb, an overlooked smudge. All her frantic movements and each of her few words were designed to appease Him and show her uncomprehending family that she served a worthier cause than theirs. Indeed, other people were hardly human in her eyes: they were muddy boots, unwashed coffee cups, coats not hung up, newspapers not put away; they were mouths waiting to be fed and clothes demanding to be washed; they were needs to be serviced and rubbish to be disposed of; above all, they were work, continuous work. Unlike ordinary mortals, she did not have time to sit around watching television and chatting. Nor did her higher calling permit her to indulge in everyday pleasantries, such as saying hello to the sister-in-law she had not seen for eight months. It was not a question of manners, but of priorities, and hers were always far more pressing than anyone else's.

'You can take up your dad's tea,' she said. 'It will save me the job.'

Making these little economies of energy was constantly on her mind; an ounce saved here was an extra ounce to spend there.

'How is he?' Mary asked.

'Worse than he pretends. Worse than he knows. It was his own fault. He'd been overdoing things. He wouldn't listen to me, of course. No one does. And now look what he's landed me with. I have to wait on him hand and foot. He's as bad as a child to look after.'

'How much damage did the stroke do?'

Georgina poured boiling water into the pot and slammed on its lid.

'Go and look for yourself. He's lost the use of his left hand and he says he can't see with one eye. Don't ask me which; it changes every day. And he's even more cantankerous than he was before.'

'What does the doctor say?'

'Doctors!' snorted Georgina. 'The specialist has given him a pill to take, and Dr Trollope says he must rest. But who's going to make him rest? That's what I'd like to know. I can't spend all day amusing him. I've put the television in his room, but he says he can't see it. He's in and out of bed all the time.'

She poured a mahogany-coloured fluid into the mugs.

'I can't deal with him,' Georgina added, despairingly. 'I've done my best, but he's impossible.'

Her words were accompanied by a low throbbing noise, somewhat like a double bass. Mary looked behind her to find a pair of bulging, watery brown eyes staring at her. An aged black Labrador with a grey muzzle lay in an armchair next to the Aga. It writhed a greeting with its head and neck, but made no effort to stand up. Mary stroked its ears which had the effect of making its tail beat faster. A little cloud of dust rose from the cushion with each stroke. Mary had noticed a pungent smell in the room, defying even Georgina's deodorant regime, and now she had located its source.

Georgina herself regarded the animal with extreme distaste.

'It's high time the wretched thing was put down. She stinks to high heaven, as you must have noticed, and she can hardly walk. But, officially, she belongs to Ollie so we can't really – you know – put her to sleep while he's away at school. Especially during his first term.'

'That isn't Elsa?'

'Elsie. Yes it is. She's twelve.'

'Isn't she Tom's dog?'

'She was. She's no good with the gun now, so he gave her to Ollie.'

Mary remembered this same dog as a lithe and glossy

juvenile capering round her brother's legs, always in trouble. Now she was a senile wreck.

Georgina glanced anxiously at the clock and, in haste once more, banged the mugs on a tray, together with a plate of biscuits. Mary watched as she aligned the mugs against the edge of the tray, both handles in parallel, and tried to square up the biscuit plate. It was part of God's curse on her that He had designed a world which was not composed of straight edges. In His impenetrable wisdom He had inflicted on her a crooked creation, riddled with bends and curves, a creation that could never be made neat and tidy.

'I'm late now,' she said in an accusing tone. 'You'd better take his tea up before it gets cold.'

Mary picked up the tray and turned to the door leading into the hall, but Georgina pointed to the door back into the scullery.

'We've put him in the old cook's attic. For the time being.'

A hint of embarrassment had crept into her voice, but she expunged it immediately. 'I can't be expected to run up and down those stairs all day. This house isn't run for the convenience of old men in bed, you know.'

'I suppose not,' Mary murmured, too surprised to say more.

Georgina led the way, turning on the light in the scullery and then a second light which illuminated the steep stairway to the so-called cook's attic. As soon as Mary put her foot on the first step, Georgina was gone, slamming the back door behind her.

In her imperious schedule there was no more room for goodbyes than hellos.

Seventeen

As luck would have it, Gregory's train from London and Oliver's from Norwich pulled into Stowmarket station at the same time.

Long before his train drew to a halt, Oliver jumped down and ran beside it. Unusually, he wore his cap squarely on his head, in the approved manner. This was out of deference not to Mr Tupper, but to his mother who would have come to collect him. He did not expect to see his father at the station; he would be too busy.

Mr Tupper hung his flushed face out of the window, watching the progress of his charge along the rain-soaked platform.

'Goodbye, sir,' panted Oliver. 'Have a nice Christmas. See you next term.'

'Farewell perfidious Albion,' shouted Mr Tupper, holding up his bottle in a salute. 'May your Christmas be a damned sight merrier than mine.'

But Oliver was out of earshot. He pounded over the bridge and pushed his way through the crowd on the opposite platform as they struggled with their cases and parcels in the sleeting darkness. In his haste Oliver did not notice Gregory's gangling form. Nor did Gregory notice him, for he was engrossed in solemn conference with his old colleague and best man – though the title seemed singularly unfitting at that moment. This excellent fellow was talking earnestly and solicitously to Gregory, who for the most part remained silent, his head drooping a little lower with each word confided in his ear.

When they reached the steps at the entrance of the station he took Gregory's limp hand and shook it warmly.

'Don't despair,' he said in hearty tones, 'you'll get another job in the New Year. A much better job, I expect, knowing you.'

He laughed, but Gregory's gloom was not relieved. The best man put a hand on his shoulder.

'My advice,' he said kindly, 'is to forget all about it for the next few days. Have a bloody good Christmas and put it out of your mind.'

He shook Gregory's hand again. 'Love to Rose,' he said and with a wave strode out of the station yard.

These interesting remarks had been overheard by none other than Georgina, his mother-in-law, who was of course collecting Oliver. In her economising way, she did not waste words greeting Gregory, but simply barked at him, 'What was that? What did he mean, "another job"? Why *another* job? Gregory, answer me.'

She stamped her foot.

But Gregory, the son-in-law of whom she had never really approved, whose job in the City she had never accepted as a proper job for a man, and whose mother was such an unspeakable embarrassment, Gregory said nothing. He was too dejected to mouth even the emptiest politeness to his mother-in-law, of whom he, in his turn, was mightily afraid. He could do no more than nod his head, then shake it, and stumble in the direction of the car park.

Meanwhile, Oliver had run past her, not seeing her stumpy figure amid the crowd. Now he ran back up the steps, shouting, 'Mum, Mum, here I am.'

Without imitating the high theatricality of Carter's reunion with his mother, he nevertheless threw his arms around her and plunged his head into the voluminous folds of her waterproof. If he had possessed the strength, he would have lifted her up and carried her to their car.

Georgina was immediately diverted and Gregory was forgotten – for the moment.

Oliver was her one indulgence, her sole luxury. He was the only maverick element in her life; he was the only member of her family on whom she smiled. For his sake and his alone, she was even willing to suspend her dreaded timetable. While never lapsing so far into idleness as to sit down, she was prepared to desist from her duties long enough to hear one of his fatuous jokes or play the dupe in one of his transparent conjuring tricks. For him she would make snacks outside her official eating hours, a privilege no one else was ever permitted. In short, for Oliver she would do anything. He was her vice.

And so it was that, on her side anyway, their reunion on the steps of Stowmarket station was more emotional than might have been expected. She was forced to use her handkerchief. Having recovered, she looked briskly at her watch and bundled him into the car. As they made their short journey home she attempted to extract from him some account of his experiences at school. But, though cheerful in tone, his answers were quite uninformative. Concerning those subjects she most dearly wanted to hear about – his health, his happiness, the efficacy of his winter underwear, the wellbeing of dear Mr Peach – he said not a word, though he did treat her to a blow-by-blow account of the Bond film they had been shown in the san. He also told her that, despite their illness, they had been forced to read for *two* hours a day. He reported this outrage in shrill tones, but made no mention of all the other outrages from which he had truly suffered. He told her nothing about his homesickness, of the beatings and bullying, of his fears and hatreds. He told her nothing about Carter or the murder of his fish.

In return for her questions, he asked some of his own. How was Elsie? How was grandpa? *How was Dad?* Her answers were no more satisfactory to him than his had been to her. He did not want to hear about Elsie's disgusting ailments, nor grandpa's peculiarities. He certainly did not want to hear about his father's embattled relations with his feed supplier. What he wanted to hear was that they were all longing to see him. Still, he was liberated from Bitterley with the eternity of a three-week holiday in front of him, and it was Christmas Day tomorrow.

Eighteen

Back at the station yard, at the far end of the carpark, a solitary car stood in darkness. Inside, Gregory sat with his head leaning against the steering wheel. He too had been using his handkerchief, though he was the victim of very different emotions from Georgina's. Nor was his recovery half as rapid. The crisis he had been dreading for more than a month had finally broken. He had only told the best man about the loss of his job, not his disastrous crusade, but that was bad enough. He was exposed as a liar and a failure. He was finished.

Yet even as he languished among the rubble of his marriage and career, he was suddenly visited by the second of his bolts of visionary understanding. This lightning flash not only illuminated his blasted landscape, allowing him to see it once again in the light of optimism and good faith, but it also galvanised certain elements which had hitherto lain inert and sterile, and in that catastrophic instant a new form of life sprang into existence.

He did, after all, have something to give, something of which he had a limitless and exclusive supply – himself. His very self and being. To start with, he would donate those of his organs and parts which could be spared. His kidneys, for example. It was sheer selfishness to hang onto both when he could get along perfectly well with only one. His cornea could go too. A single eye had served Nelson quite adequately. Testicles? Two seemed a great extravagance. All those yards of intestine, surely a length could be lopped off without damage to his system. A touch of indigestion was a small price to pay. And there was his bone marrow, he could give away tins of the stuff. Also his skin tissue, an entire hide, and of course his blood, gallons and gallons of blood. The beauty of these resources was that so many were self-replenishing. Yes, he was a walking factory of transplantable goodies; he was Father Christmas and all his presents wrapped up in one.

As soon as the holiday was over he would go to the West Suffolk Hospital and volunteer himself for distribution. Rose would understand. She would help him. He lifted his head from the steering wheel, dried his eyes and blew his nose. First, however, he had to explain the last four weeks to her. His spirits sank again at this prospect, but he gathered his courage and set off towards Slaughterhouse.

As soon as Rose saw him standing in the doorway of their cottage, she knew her worst fears were about to be realised. Bedraggled, shivering, haggard and, above all, guilt-ridden, he made a pathetic picture, but she felt nothing but contempt for him. The meaning of his increasingly bizarre behaviour over the last few weeks was quite clear to her now. His furtiveness, his bouts of abstraction, his refusal to make love to her, the removal of his clothes and precious things to London, combined with the news just telephoned by her hysterical mother that he was looking for a new job, all pointed to the same, banal explanation: Gregory had found himself another woman.

She had never seen anyone so pregnant with confession. Still rooted to the doormat, his tattered macintosh dripping water, Gregory stared beseechingly at her and began to move his ashen lips in preparation for speech. Before he achieved utterance, Rose intervened.

'What's her name?' she demanded. 'Not that I want to know,' she added, angry with herself for having made so clichéd an opening. 'I couldn't care less what your little tart is called.'

She strode into the kitchen and then reappeared instantly.

'Oh Gregory,' she said in a softer tone. 'You haven't really given me a chance.'

Gregory was utterly confused by her outburst. Tart? What tart? For a crazy moment he thought she must be referring to the woman who had promised him a nice whipping.

He continued to move his lips soundlessly as he struggled to make sense of what Rose was saying. This must be Georgina's work. As usual she had got the wrong end of the wrong stick.

Defeated and exhausted, he threw his macintosh in a corner and sank into his chair, his head between his knees.

'What has your mother been telling you?'

'Don't be a wimp, Gregory. You might as well tell me the whole sordid story. We've got Christmas to get through, don't forget. Now who is she?'

'I honestly don't know who you mean,' he moaned.

'The girl you're moving in with. All your clothes and stuff have gone. I'm not blind, you know.'

To her astonishment, he sprang from his chair with a look of joy on his face. He wrapped his long arms around her, tears pouring down his cheeks.

'No, no,' he cried, 'it's nothing like that, nothing at all. I've given those things away. *Given* them. It was my mission. Do you see?'

Rose saw nothing.

Gregory proceeded to stammer and gibber his way through an account of the last four weeks, giving great prominence to the revelation that overcame him in Hackney. He strode round the room, his tears coursing freely down his face. As he spoke, he added obscurity of gesture to his incoherence of speech by flinging his arms violently about him, sometimes pointing dramatically in the direction of heaven, sometimes wringing his hands in an agony of despair, sometimes showing Rose his outstretched palms as if to unveil signs of stigmata. He finally crashed the vehicle of his story at the point where he had realised that his giving had helped nobody. Abruptly, he fell silent and dropped to the floor, his long limbs as inert as a puppet's.

Rose had understood hardly a word. All she knew was that throughout the tangle of his narrative there had been no mention of any girl. It is a measure of the power of sexual possessiveness that when Rose heard that Gregory was not an adulterer, as she had feared, but merely a nutcase, she was overwhelmed with jubilant relief.

'Gregory, darling Gregory,' she cried, her voice echoing in the hollowness of their near-empty cottage. 'I am so happy. I thought you were leaving me for someone else.'

She sat on the floor beside him and stroked his gaunt, tear-stained face.

'You mustn't worry about me any more,' he said. 'I have a plan.'

But before he could tell her about his programme for philanthropic self-butchery, she kissed him passionately and began to unbutton his dank shirt. A month without sex is a long time for a red-blooded girl of nineteen. Gregory did not resist. He too had missed their amorous pranks, and in any case it was his duty to make these last days of his intactness as agreeable as possible for Rose. Having been shorn of a limb, he would probably find it difficult to achieve their present carefree proficiency. Indeed, he could not foresee how sex might be managed at all once he was one-armed, one-legged and one-eyed, to say nothing of being leeched, flayed, disembowelled and half castrated. This vision of his dilapidated self caused his passion to wane, but Rose's eager caresses soon revived him.

While his clothes steamed on the fireguard, they lay on the hearth rug and recaptured their old, newly-wed bliss. Later, they fell asleep in front of the fire with smiles on their faces. Still naked, Rose smiled because her beloved Gregory was once more in her arms. Gregory smiled with the satisfaction of one whose plans were shaping up perfectly.

Nineteen

Stepping as quietly as she could, Mary let herself into the attic room. It was small and coated in white emulsion and contained little more than a metal-frame bed, a bamboo table, chair, a chest of drawers and a scrap of rug covering the linoleum. A paraffin heater stood in one corner exuding sickly fumes. The room was furnished and decorated just as it had been in the days when the maid slept here, next door to the cook. The shade of the bedside lamp had been turned up so as to cast the light against the white wall and shield her father's eyes. He was sleeping motionlessly.

His mouth hung open and she could see the gummy gaps between his few yellow teeth. His moustache, now a dingy white, was ragged and matted. His skin appeared to be a yellowy-grey colour and cruelly withered, but maybe that was only an effect of the light. He lay on his side, leaving his left shoulder and arm exposed. His wrist with its pale patch where he usually wore his watch looked frail and wasted. But his hand, she noticed, had lost none of its enormity. It lay on the sheet like a bludgeon.

She put the tray on his table and went to the window. Cupping her face against the glass, she looked down into the yard but could see nothing. Somewhere Tom must have been at work, but there was no sign of him. The yard was lightless and silent, except for the agitated whimper of the wind. She wanted a cigarette.

She looked back at the bed. Her father was drooling now. His stroke had turned him into an old man and she, his daughter, could not contemplate him without disgust.

She decided to leave him and, taking her cup, crept towards the door.

'Is that you Georgie? Where the hell's my tea? Who's that?'

She turned and found him sitting up, his head thrust forward. His pyjama top was unbuttoned and she could see the scrawniness of his rib cage.

'Who's that?' he repeated, staring directly at her, but seeming not to see her.

'It's me, Mary,' she said foolishly.

'Don't lurk in the corner, girl,' he said, turning his head from side to side. 'Come and kiss your old dad. I'm not a corpse yet.'

She moved towards him and he suddenly caught sight of her. He smiled and opened his arms wide in his old gesture of welcome. However, his left arm only jerked in a feeble spasm and then sagged back onto the sheet. Mary sat on the bed, and he gripped her with his right arm and kissed her heartily.

'It's lovely to have you home again. I've missed you.'

He picked up his lifeless left arm and dropped it.

'Can't do a thing with it. That quack Trollope says I'll recover the use of it, but what does he know. He's even more bloody senile than I am, and he hasn't even had a stroke. Where's the tea?'

He peered blindly at the table. She put the mug in his hand.

'God, Georgie makes a pissy cup of tea. I can't train her. She's so mean, I think she uses the same teabag all day. Though it's got a good colour,' he said in a puzzled tone, holding out the mug and its dark brown tea for her inspection. 'I can't tell if my taste buds are knackered or it's her bloody awful cooking, but everything she gives me tastes of cardboard.'

He hugged her again.

'You're looking gorgeous as usual. That husband of yours must be good for you, after all. Where is he? Downstairs I suppose, swilling my best whisky.'

'He hasn't arrived yet. He'll be here soon.'

'Good. Send the bastard up with a drink for me. At least

he knows how to mix a decent drink. Georgie's whisky tastes worse than her tea. I'm only allowed one a day and even then it's all ice and water. One a day. Christ!'

He looked helpless for a moment and rubbed the top of his head.

Mary pulled up the chair and sat beside him.

'How are you, Daddy?'

She surprised herself. She had not called him Daddy for years, and lately she had managed to strip Dad, her usual style of address, of any filial warmth that might have clung to it. But his affectionate greeting had taken her by surprise. She was also bewildered by his contradictory mix of vitality and enfeeblement.

'I'm angry, Moll,' he said, automatically following suit by using her childhood name. 'I've never been so angry. This fucking stroke has finished me.'

'You seem fine. I mean, better than I expected.'

'Better than Georgie told you, is what you mean. She's got me just where she wants me at last; under her thumb.'

He writhed with irritation, and then smiled.

'Don't misunderstand me: I'm grateful to her. She's looked after me like a nurse. She even sleeps next door, you know, in the cook's room. There's more to that woman than we realised. She's as clumsy as a duck, and tight, God is she tight, but for all that she's not a bad old stick. Ugly as sin, of course.' He gulped his tea, and spat it back. 'Put that down,' he said, giving her the mug and rubbing his head. 'They all say I'm going to improve, and I expect I will. Trollope's arranged for a girl to come in every day and give me physiotherapy.' He pronounced the word as if it were a disease itself. 'She makes me wave my arm about and wiggle my eyeballs. I do it to please her. She's very pretty. But it's not the point. I could have another stroke any day.'

He rubbed his head, whipping his hair into a matted nest.

'Don't do that, Dad,' she said gently. 'You'll wear a hole in your head.'

'I've got to keep it warm.'

'Shouldn't you wear a hat or something?'

'I can't wear a bloody hat in bed. Lying here is humiliating enough without making a spectacle of myself.'

He lay back and seemed to lose sight of her for a moment. Then he sat up and looked round in his blind way.

'Tell Georgie to make some of that cat's piss she calls tea.'

'You've just had your tea. You didn't like it. I put it down for you.'

'Typical. I don't know my arse from my elbow at the moment. *And I hate it.*'

He said this with terrible feeling, glowering at her.

'I could be chopped down again tomorrow, but I don't intend to let that happen.'

'What do you mean?'

'While I was in hospital I saw a couple of chaps who'd had second strokes,' he said, ignoring her, 'and I swore I wasn't going to end up like them. The poor buggers were shitting themselves and staggering about on those fucking frames carrying their little rubber bags. These were grown men and they couldn't say their own names or scratch their own arses. Not me. Never. I can put up with being old, though God knows it's no fun, but I refuse to go back to being a baby. I'd rather die now than fall apart, bit by bit. You can understand that, can't you Moll?'

He did not wait for her to reply.

'I always thought I'd go out like a light, bang. One minute I'd be standing with a drink in my hand and my eye on some girl's bottom, the next I'd be flat on the floor, a goner. But that's a fantasy isn't it, every silly bugger's fantasy. This is death, this is how it really happens.'

He shook his useless left arm in her face and his great lump of a fist flopped to and fro like the head of a dead animal.

'Thanks to the miracle of modern medicine we all have to die by inches these days. That hospital's full of poor old sods who should have been dead years ago. They're longing to go, most of them, but they're not allowed to. Oh no, they've got to stick it out until they're too blind, deaf and daft for life to be any use to them. Half of them are so pumped up with drugs they might as well be dead, and the others don't have lives worth living. No one visits them, they just sit staring at the telly, whether it's switched on or not. No thank you. I'm not going to end up like that. I shall make *arrangements*.'

'What on earth are you talking about?'

'Nobody knows how to die any more. Nobody knows what it's for.'

He leant his head back against the rails of the bed.

'But you mustn't take any notice of a morbid old fart like me,' he said closing his eyes. From long experience she recognised the expression on his face as one which indicated the working of some deeply submerged craftiness.

Then he opened his eyes abruptly, turned his head and looked at her as if for the first time.

'Hello Moll,' he said smiling broadly. 'How lovely to see you. Is it Christmas?'

Surely, this was play-acting.

'Tomorrow. Tomorrow's Christmas Day.'

'We must get moving.' He threw back the bedclothes, but took no further action. 'Ollie will be back soon and we must get him his present. The boy should have his own gun. Tommie had one at his age. Georgie says he's too young, but she always talks bloody nonsense. If he's old enough to go away to school, he's old enough to have a gun.'

'I expect Georgina's bought something for you to give him.'

'She snores, you know.' He jerked his thumb towards the wall. 'I hear her at night, snoring like a pig. She cries too, in her sleep. I bang on the wall and she stops. Your mother used to grind her teeth, but nothing would stop her. I used to prod her in the ribs. She'd say sorry, turn over and start again. You've never heard such a noise. It's a wonder she had any teeth left. How are you, Moll? How's business?'

'All right. Fine. It's always slow at Christmas. Everyone seems to be drunk or in America.'

'Don't worry. I'm going to make us all millionaires. We'll expand this place and then we'll all be as rich as bloody Croesus. You must persuade Tom. He's always been an imbecile when it comes to money. Have you seen him yet? He looks dreadful.'

As usual, stroke or no stroke, conversation with her father had left her feeling bewildered and apprehensive. For the third time she was forced to ask him to explain himself.

'Rich,' he said. 'Don't you want to be rich?'

His chin dropped on his chest and he fell asleep. Or at any rate he shut his eyes and would not open them again.

Without making any effort to be quiet this time, she left the room.

Twenty

Oliver ran into the kitchen, shouting, 'Elsie, Elsie! Where are you, girl?'

With a painful effort the dog rose from her cushion and tottered stiffly toward him, wagging her tail so vigorously she could hardly remain upright on her bowed legs. Her grizzled lips puckered in an unmistakeable grin. Oliver knelt beside her, put his arms round her neck and covered her wrinkled face with kisses. Georgina looked on with revulsion, but did not demur. Instead, she urged him to say hello to his 'Aunty Mary' and began to unpack his dirty laundry, expelling a lachrymose sigh which spoke in bitter protest of the distinction between aunts, who could afford to loll about in other people's kitchens, and mothers, whose travails were never at an end.

'Hello, Aunty Mary.'

'Hello, Oliver. Is it nice to be home?'

She regretted this foolish question as soon as it had left her lips.

'Yes, thank you, Aunty Mary,' he replied with robotic politeness.

He studied her keenly for a moment; she was, after all, his only aunt and he was always hopeful that she would exhibit some interesting foible or disability. Rogers had an aunt he boasted about who had a glass eye, which she polished with a special velvet cloth. As usual, however, he was disappointed by Mary's lamentable ordinariness, but he consoled himself with the thought that, according to his mother, she was 'well-off' and should therefore have brought him an expensive present. His 'Uncle Michael' was a different matter; he looked forward to seeing him because his father invariably referred to him as 'that shit',

even in Oliver's hearing, and his mother, who admittedly condemned everyone for something, condemned him as 'a swank' for wearing flowers in his buttonhole and smoking cigarettes. This was the stuff of true uncles.

'Where's Dad?' he asked.

Georgina was not deaf to the anxiety in his voice.

'Out in the yard somewhere. Go and tell him that Aunty Mary's arrived at last.'

'Come on, girl,' said Oliver to his dog and whistled at her. He held open the door and she hobbled in front of him.

Outside, the cold air was made all the sharper by the wind which lashed round the buildings and rattled the corrugated iron roofs. Elsie plodded beside the boy, picking her way among the potholes.

'Poor old girl, you're stiff aren't you?'

He stopped to pat her, and she sat down immediately, thankful for the rest. Her ears flapped in the wind. Oliver looked up into the black, turgid sky and wondered what would happen if Joseph and Mary were to ride their donkey into Slaughterhouse. Would they be turned away from The Sow's Ear, which was an inn, after all? Would his father allow them to have the baby here on the farm? He could be born in one of the old pigsties, which had proper mangers, or perhaps it would be better to put him in the farrowing house where he could be kept warm under a lamp like the piglets. There was no star in the sky, but there was a shepherd nearby, old Sid, who lived next door to Rose. Not that he would be watching his flock, nor washing his socks; he would be watching telly. And what about the wise men, the three kings? Michael, with his buttonhole, Mary and gormless Gregory would have to take the parts; they were not very wise or regal, but at least they had come bearing gifts.

At the entrance of the farrowing house, where a single, feeble bulb burned in a glass protector, he found the pale corpse of a squashed piglet lying at his feet in the mud. It must have been thrown there by his father when he made his afternoon rounds. Rats had already begun to gnaw at its shrivelled belly. Elsie sniffed at the tattered umbilical cord, but Oliver pushed her head away. The sows were always rolling on their offspring, and some days there would be two or three corpses piled at the door, but his father refused to bring in the farrowing crates that imprisoned the sows and stopped them moving about. Oliver loved him for that.

If Joseph had not found a warm place for Mary to give birth, if there had been no room even in the stables, the baby might have died out in the cold and they would have had to bury the pale, bloodless little thing, just as his father buried the piglets. Then there would have been no Christ, no Bible, no verses to learn before breakfast, no sermons from Mr Peach on Sundays . . . no Christmas; nothing but a cold piglet corpse for its mother to cry over.

He pushed open the heavy sliding door, its bare metal stinging his fingers with iciness. In front of him was a long central aisle with a narrow gulley running down the centre of its concrete floor. On either side stood a series of pig pens, like box pews, with heavy wooden doors secured by sliding bolts. Within each of the first few pens to the left and right a soft glow radiated from the heater lamps, while the rest of the shed lay in darkness. Every inch of its surface was powdered and crusted with white dust from the meal fed to the pigs; long skeins of whitened, thickened cobweb dangled and fluttered from the beams, and the walls of the pens were capped with flaky ridges of hardened meal. All this filmy chalkiness glimmering in the semi-darkness gave the place a ghostly air which made him nervous, but he took courage from the sweet-and-sour smell of dung and moist straw.

He found a sack, also whitened and clogged with meal, and laid it on the concrete floor for Elsie. She dropped onto it immediately, arranging her arthritic bones with care. Using a bucket as a platform to look over the walls, he moved down the aisle in search of a farrowing sow. The first couple of pens were occupied by gross, watchful sows whose time was close. Their heads in the straw, they looked up at him with their bright little yellow eyes, but did not shift their positions. He dragged his bucket to the third pen.

'Is that you, Oliver? For Christ's sake stop that racket.'

He had found his father.

His voice came from the other side of the aisle. Seeing a door with its bolt drawn, Oliver tiptoed across the concrete. His father was inside the pen, kneeling in the straw opposite a sow whose swollen, reddened teats were feeding a litter of eight or nine blind and bloody piglets.

'Hello, Dad,' he whispered. 'Can I come in?'

His father beckoned to him and pointed to the corner nearest the door.

'Sit there. Where's Elsie?'

'On a sack. She's asleep.'

'Keep her out.'

A deep convulsive tremor coursed like a wave across the sow's flanks. She drew up her hind leg and Oliver could see the mucus dribbling from her scarlet, out-turned vulva. She seemed to stop breathing and her body trembled. Her piglets scrabbled in the straw, punching at her soft udders with their snouts. The sow lifted her head, twisting her neck in an awkward, pained movement. She made a low grumbling snort. Her vulva expanded. More blood and liquid oozed from it. Her tail thrashed and the head, shoulders and forelegs of a piglet suddenly emerged. Another spasm and it slithered onto the straw, scraps of bloody matter and membrane clinging to its pink, bullet-shaped body.

'The runt,' his father said. 'This is the last.'

The piglet, which was indeed smaller than its siblings, lay motionless for a moment, and Oliver wondered if it were dead, but then it shuddered and drew its first breath. Immediately, it set about the business of fending for existence. Struggling against the stalks of straw, it fought to stand, but was brought down by its umbilical cord, which was still intact. It found its feet again, jerked against the cord and was tumbled over. At its third attempt, the cord slid free and the piglet staggered forward without falling. Coming up against its mother's buttock, it stabbed frantically with its snout hoping to make contact with her teats. Frustrated, it moved on, but in the wrong direction, embarking on a doomed journey round the vast island of her body.

His father scooped it up tenderly and placed it next to a teat, where it sucked furiously for a brief instant before being pushed aside by one of its bigger sisters. His father replaced it, and this time it managed to keep possession. Abruptly, the rest of the litter fell asleep in a twitching, quivering heap. The runt slept too, its cord already drying into a little stalk.

Oliver stood up and his father bolted the pen door behind them.

'You've grown,' his father said.

'Aunty Mary's here. Mum told me to tell you.'

'Have you seen your grandpa yet?'

'No.'

For some reason his father looked pleased.

'I have to look at the weaners and the gilts. Do you want to come?'

Together they walked across the yard towards the fattening shed, Elsie limping after them. In the darkness his father took his hand and held it. Oliver joyfully whistled the tune of 'Ding Dong Merrily On High'.

Twenty-one

In her unceasing efforts to appease the great Taskmaster, Georgina made it her practice to prepare her meals the day before they were required; indeed, under ideal conditions, .she would have cooked, served and washed them up without allowing anyone to spoil her system by eating them. Meals had little to do with nutrition, and nothing to do with pleasure; they were rituals invented by an unjust society to spoil children, indulge adults and punish her. She herself seldom ate during family meals and never sat down. Christmas lunch was of course an occasion when the Taskmaster would look down on her with special pitilessness, and so her labours that evening were undertaken with twice their usual velocity.

Along the walls of the kitchen stood a row of tall, glass-fronted pine cupboards and from one of these Georgina, insecurely balanced on a chair, snatched a dozen dinner plates, side plates and soup bowls. They belonged to a Crown Derby dinner service of innumerable pieces, which Mary's mother had bought at an auction not long after the war. Mary noticed that most of them were chipped or cracked and clumsily glued. The author of this vandalism was all too obvious as Georgina tossed the china onto the table below her. She submitted the cutlery and glassware to the same brutal treatment, heaping the whole lot on a broken-down trolley, which she trundled towards the door. Without saying a word, she waited impatiently for Mary to open it for her.

Mary followed her down the flagstone passage and through the tattered baize door that led to the newer, Victorian part of the house. Using the trolley as a battering ram, Georgina forced her way into the pannelled dining room. A fire had been laid in the huge marble fireplace, but it had not been lit. Georgina's breath issued in dense plumes from her nostrils as she puffed her way round the long, oval mahogany table, laying places. Mary attempted to assist, but every knife she put down was realigned, every glass repolished and replaced. Wherever she stood herself, she was in the way and Georgina, still silent, simply pushed her aside. In the end, she gave up and sat shivering on a chair by the door.

'Who's coming tomorrow?' she asked.

'Well, there's the two of you,' Georgina said, accusingly. 'There are three of us, not counting your dad, who may or may not honour us with his presence depending on his mood. Rose and Gregory are walking up after church.' She pronounced Gregory's name with a violent sniff of disapproval. 'And we've had to invite his mother, who will no doubt drink us out of house and home. I just hope she's sick after she leaves, not before. And of course my sister is coming – you remember her? – and Basil and their little girl, Alice. That makes twelve, if we include your dad.'

Mary did remember her sister, who had amazed everyone at Tom's wedding by proving to be as beautiful as Georgina was ugly. Nor had nature relented, for as the years had gone by Georgina's ugliness had ripened like stilton, while her sister's beauty had only bloomed, leaving her lovelier with each birthday. However, the balance was somewhat redressed by her husband Basil who, though not actually ugly, was one of the most repellent men Mary had ever met.

'That turkey will just have to do,' Georgina said angrily. 'Eight pounds is surely big enough. We're not made of money, contrary to what your father imagines.'

'He says he's going to make us all rich. But things aren't that bad, are they?'

'He's a sick man and he doesn't know what he's saying. We'll cope. We always have.'

She banged a pair of decanters onto a salver in the centre of the table.

'It's Tom I'm worried about,' Georgina said. 'He seems to have taken your dad's stroke very badly. He's very low at the moment. He won't talk to me, but I can see he's suffering.'

Mary was struck by a flash of rage. She stood up and paced in agitation beside the lifeless fireplace. Tom was always the focus of everyone's concern; the world had been worrying about Tom ever since he had been born. This was typical: her father has a stroke and Georgina fusses over its impact on Tom.

What right did he have to the word *suffering*. Motheba had suffered. People who had been raped and tortured, they had suffered; people who had been imprisoned for decades, people made to stand in their cells with bags over their heads, people who had not seen a smile or talked to their families or eaten a proper meal from one year to the next, they had endured true suffering. But here was Tom, ensconced in his manor house, petted by his devoted wife, free to come and go as he chose, with nothing more agonising to fret over than how to spend his EEC subsidies; what did he know of suffering?

And yet, she thought, sitting down again, if Tom could not lay claim to true suffering, what about Liz? 'Too much suffering,' she had written. What had she meant?

'What has Tom to worry about?' she demanded in exasperation. 'The wolf is not exactly at the door, is it?' She gestured ironically at the table, which was now glittering with glass and silver.

'Your father drives him too hard.'

'For God's sake, Georgie. He's a grown man. He doesn't have to do everything his daddy tells him.'

'Your father has a very strong character,' she said, thumping the last of the wine glasses into place, 'as you well know.'

Mary understood this last remark as a pointed reminder of the family theory, promoted by Tom and endorsed by Georgina, that the real reason for her, Mary's, leaving the farm when he had returned from the army was that she and her father were both too domineering and obstinate to work together.

'He's a sick old man. You said so yourself. Surely he's the one we should be thinking about. He may be dying.'

'I doubt it,' said Georgina briskly at the door. She switched off the light, leaving Mary in darkness.

Mary was too angry to move. Georgina's petty frugality was irritating, but her anger erupted from a deeper, older source. As soon as Georgina had spoken the fatal spell, 'We must worry about Tom,' Mary had been rushed helplessly back into her childhood and all its turmoil. Twenty-five years snuffed out by a single remark. She was angry with herself for losing her carefully prepared equilibrium so quickly, and for gasping in the airlessness of their primitive conflicts without being able, after all these years, to import any fresh oxygen of her own making to breathe.

She was angry that her powers of creativity were too feeble to bring new life to the claustrophobic sameness of their family behaviour. She felt it was a failing in her that she was unable to break up this dance of death and help them all to hear a new tune. But whenever she set foot in this house, her home, she felt the whole fabric of her adulthood – her work, salary, reputation, mortgage and marriage – had been snatched from her at the door, as if it were no more than a grown-up costume she had only been allowed to wear to a party.

Sighing miserably, she stood up and felt her way across the hall towards the baize door. Fumbling in the blackness, she heard a scream. She tripped in the passage, bruising her knee on the flagstones, and ran into the kitchen.

Michael, debonair as ever, was leaning against the back door, while prodding his rolled umbrella in the direction of a small pig which was rooting among the bags of potatoes and sprouts on the floor.

'Hello, darling,' Michael drawled. 'I was just explaining to Georgie that I found this little fellow out in the pantry. As soon as I opened the door he nipped in as if he lived here. He's having a grand time, isn't he?'

The three of them stared down at the pigling, which certainly was enjoying himself. He was a weaner, perhaps twelve weeks old, with a low, long body like an affable pink missile. He appeared to have stepped straight out of the pages of a child's story, for a mischievous twinkle shone in his eye and his tail was coiled in a perfect corkscrew. Quite undaunted by his domestic surroundings, he sniffed at the kitchen floor with vivacious curiosity, occasionally breaking into peals of excited grunts.

With an expertise that took Mary by surprise, Georgina picked up a large tray and used it as a board to corner the pig. She shouted fiercely at Michael to open the door. He complied with a languid gesture and she shepherded the animal into the pantry, slamming the door behind her.

They heard her yelling in the yard for Tom.

'Hello again,' said Michael, putting his arms round Mary. He kissed her with passionate warmth, so much so that she thought he was making a sexual overture. The noise of the back door being opened broke them apart.

Georgina was followed into the kitchen shortly afterwards by Tom and Oliver, who jubilantly told the story of their returning the weaner to its pen as if it had been a feat of Homeric ingenuity and comradeship. The adults exchanged tepid greetings and Georgina dismissed them to the sitting room, or 'office' as she called it.

Despite owning a house possessed of half a dozen rooms that would have made pleasant sitting rooms, Georgina and Tom chose to confine themselves during their rare moments of leisure in a dark and obscure chamber at the back of the house, next to the kitchen.

'Why should I have to walk half a mile just to sit down?' had been Georgina's querulous reply when Mary had once asked her why they no longer used the front drawing room of which her mother had been fond.

'Not that I ever get time to lounge about,' Georgina had added sharply, in a tone implying that such a question would only have occurred to someone who was an incorrigible lounger-about herself.

At night this small room was lit by a single bulb of frugal wattage which hung from the centre of the ceiling and conjured up the cosy atmosphere of an interrogation cell. By day such light as would have struggled through the murky panes was blocked by an enormous roll-top desk. Following the practice of his father and grandfather, Tom worked here at the farm's accounts and correspondence.

A pair of logs smouldered meanly in the brick fireplace, emitting more smoke than heat.

'Can't you do anything about that chimney?' Mary asked Tom. 'It seems to be getting worse.'

'If you don't like it,' Tom told her bluntly, 'you can always go upstairs to your bedroom. You won't find any fires up there to bother you.'

He laughed sourly.

Michael caught Mary's eye and made an expression of desperation, which she ignored. She went to the window intending to draw the curtains and as she stood by the desk she noticed it was heaped up with unopened envelopes. Many of them were clearly bills, while others bore the official insignia of the Inland Revenue, the Ministry of Agriculture, the bank and so forth. It was her turn to catch Michael's eye and indicate her disturbing discovery to him, but he appeared to be preoccupied by a spot of mud on his trousers.

Michael was in fact preoccupied by a need far more urgent than cleanliness. He craved a drink – to be precise, a whisky and soda. This desire was made all the sharper by the gleaming presence of an unopened bottle of Bells sitting within arm's distance on an oak chest and sharing a tray with a syphon and six cut-glass tumblers of heroic dimensions. He was generally a man of unabashable aplomb and in any other house he would not have hesitated to make his wishes known, but here at Slaughterhouse his confidence always failed him. Frustrated, he turned his thoughts to other disturbing topics, notably Zara's preposterous and infuriating demand that he should ring her from this Colditz of a house. He would have ignored it if he had not feared that she would exact some mortifying revenge.

A violent crash announced that Georgina had made her usual forced entry through an unresisting door.

'I hope you all like sardines on toast,' she said, though

the oily smell of fish mixed with the acrid tang of burnt bread told them that their likes and dislikes were already irrelevant.

'We'll be having a big meal tomorrow so there's no point in gorging ourselves tonight.'

'Delicious,' murmered Michael, who abominated sardines.

'Ollie's already eaten his,' she told them. 'He was starving. We pay all those fees and they don't even feed him.'

Michael stared thirstily at the whisky bottle, hoping Georgina would notice. She didn't.

'I don't think he believes in Father Christmas any more,' she said in a confidential tone.

'Well, of course he bloody well doesn't. He's not a baby,' said Tom.

'I know, but he still wants to put out a glass of sherry and a mince pie next to the fireplace.'

She smiled weakly at Mary and Michael, as if to apologise for these childish whimsies.

'He's a bloody clever bugger if he can get down that chimney,' said Tom, laughing harshly. 'He'll singe his arse and come out as black as a nigger.'

Mary knew he only used the word 'nigger' to annoy her.

'Ollie's coming in a minute. Be nice about it, Tom. Don't spoil it for him. He's so excited.'

Georgina left the room and a minute later, with something of his mother's demolitionist style, Oliver broke in carrying a tray with the ceremonial sherry and mince pie. He was followed by the halting Elsie, who made directly for the fire and lay down among the ashes at the front of the hearth. Michael watched the progress of the sherry bottle with the keenest interest.

'Mum says can you please get me a glass down, Aunty Mary?' squeaked Oliver, more than a little self-conscious under the cheerless gaze of the three adults.

Mary did as she asked, taking a small sherry glass from the corner cupboard which hung above the oak chest. In taking it from her, Oliver somehow contrived to drop the sherry bottle, then the glass itself, which shattered, and finally the mince pie. Before anyone could stop her, Elsie, notwithstanding her stiffened joints, darted among the shards and bolted the pie.

'You clumsy little fool!' Tom shouted at him, raising his hand. 'Why must you make a balls of everything? If that dog's eaten any glass, she'll die, and you'll have killed her.'

Oliver ran from the room.

Tom, very red in the face, glowered after him.

'What is the matter with the child?' he said, and stormed from the room himself. Mary and Michael could hear him in the kitchen shouting at Georgina to get a cloth and clear up the mess.

During the mêlée Michael had retrieved the sherry bottle, on which he had continued to maintain a firm grip.

'Well, cheers!' he said to Mary, taking three new glasses from the cupboard and filling them.

'One for Father Christmas. One for you and one for me.'

'Michael! How can you?'

'It's Christmas, is it not? The season of good will and merry-making. Cheers!' he said again, pouring himself a second glass.

Outside in the dark Oliver ran across the yard, careless of the mud and potholes. He hauled open the door of the farrowing house and ran down the aisle to the pen with the newly born litter. Sinking into the straw, he began to cry. He put his face in his hands and howled.

He cried out of humiliation and hatred for his father and self-pity: he cried because he had failed his father and spoiled their new friendship. He cried for the loneliness and homesickness, the fear and unhappiness of the last twelve weeks. He cried with relief at being home again and dread at having to return to Bitterley. He cried for Carter and his fish; he cried because if only he had saved the fish, he would not have broken the glass. He cried because it was Christmas; he cried because he was crying.

And when he had recovered a little and looked around him, he started to cry again. The runt was dead.

Twenty-two

Lying in her bath, Mary reflected without much affection on Georgina's wintry personality. Despite the day, there was not a single Christmas decoration to be seen in the house, not so much as a sprig of holly. In her mother's time a magnificent tree used to be erected and decorated in the drawing room, and as Christmas Day approached a great heap of presents would be gathered beneath its branches. She had not looked in there yet, but surely Georgina would have kept up that tradition for Ollie's sake. Poor Ollie. Why was Tom so hard on him?

The bathwater, which had never been more than luke-warm, was cooling fast. The bath itself had rusted and she could feel its roughness on her back. The rubber plug was perished and cracked, and the water was dribbling down the waste pipe. Georgina's hospitality extended no further than a rind of coal tar soap and a small hand towel. Michael would not be able to play his usual bath-time games. She put her foot on the plug and heard the trickle cease abruptly; she lifted it, and the noise began again. Everything was draining, ebbing, emptying. What stage of the month was it? A week to go. No life in her; just another dead egg.

The wind outside smacked the window, rattling the glass in its petrified putty and shaking the old frame. If it had been daylight she would have been able to see the twisted branches of the old oak in the park straining against the gale. But now the darkness had turned the window into a black hole in the wall, making her feel uncomfortably exposed.

Should she ask Michael to draw the curtain for her?

She liked him to look at her in the bath. She felt confident of her sexiness then: naked, but not altogether vulnerable; exhibited by the water, but protected too by its warmth and soapiness. In the bath she felt clean and young – flawless – and she had lived long enough with Michael to know how beguiled his libido was by the purifying slipperiness of soap. Her breasts rose above the water like atolls ringed with a surf of suds; they were south sea islands, the haunt of mermaids. She would like to be a mermaid herself, a beautiful blonde mermaid, the dream of sex-starved sailors, the heroine of lewd ballads.

If Michael did come in he would avoid looking at her. Nowadays, he preferred to observe her covertly, through half-open doors, by way of mirrors, through cracks and gaps. For all she knew, he was even now peeping at her through the keyhole.

She could hear nothing from the bedroom next door. He was probably lying on his bed in his dressing gown and smoking. Wrinkly and rubbery it was, like a snake sunning itself in a thorn bush. If she touched it, would it stir? Would it uncoil itself for her? What must it be like, she had often wondered, to have this fifth limb sprouting in front of you, so hard and muscly, and then to have it burst and melt back to a little rubbery thing again? Everything dies back in the end.

She was not a passive woman, certainly not in the office, but as a lover she was passive. She liked to lie and be looked at and have love made to her. And afterwards if he kept his hand there – that's all he had to do – a deep glow would persist until she fell asleep. But he never did. As soon as he finished he got up and went to the bathroom to wash himself as if he had been contaminated. And he would not look at her. His eyes, so hungry before, guzzling every inch of her, became blind. The light died. Nothing lasted.

She turned the tap to warm the bath, but it ran cold. She would have to get out and put on her nightdress, which was plain, long and thick to combat the unheated room and unaired bed.

Was this grim, cold, loveless place her home? Home was where your childhood had been, and then when you had children of your own your house became home. But she had no children, and it looked as if she never would, not unless she was willing to lose Michael. What a choice: either a barren wife, or a single mother. Liz, for all her life-enhancing qualities, had always sworn she would never have children. Pregnancy murders your figure, she used to say. My boobs are small enough without having them sucked to nothing by some greedy brat. They were small, her breasts, it was true, but beautifully round, like apples, and her nipples had been pink almost as though she had rouged them. Dust now. Dust blackening Gilbert Street. Why had she taken off her sweater? Why had she done it? Breasts, after all, were life: they were sex and milk and comfort. Why flaunt them in death?

The water was cold now and she was shivering in the draught from the ill-fitting window, but she could not bring herself to leave the sanctuary of the bath.

She could never do what Liz did; even at her lowest moments, she had never considered suicide. Indeed, given her powers of obstinacy and perseverence, she would probably survive to a grand old age. But what was grand about it? Without children, what was it but a feat of futile endurance? She would decline into an old woman who would not die, an empty life cursed with longevity. Is that what her father had meant? The thought of his death terrified her, yet a part of her, the disappointed mother perhaps, relished the prospect of his enfeeblement. But it would be Georgie, not she, who would have to look after him in his second infanthood. Georgie, crabbed, miserly, dried-up Georgie, was mother to them all.

She stepped out of the bath at last, rubbing herself vigorously with the threadbare towel. In a final gesture of provocation, she walked naked into the bedroom, but Michael was not there. She pulled on her nightdress and stood at the window listening to the tolling church bell as it summoned the village to midnight mass. Georgina would be down there somewhere, cleaving the night with her torch. No Christmas star stood over Slaughterhouse; or if it did, its gleam was shut out by the clouds. She threw open the window and searched

the invisible landscape for a prick of light, a sign of life. But the darkness was absolute; only the baying wind made itself known.

Reluctantly, she got into her dank bed. Just as the tolling ceased she heard the sound of another bell, within the house – the light ping of a telephone being put back on its cradle. When Michael came into the bedroom a minute later, she played dead.

Down in the village the main street was momentarily busy as the last customers tottering out of the public bar of The Sow's Ear mingled with the worshippers hurrying towards St Anthony's. Huddled beneath their umbrellas they made their way along the pavement beside Rose and Gregory's cottage and those who glanced through the badly drawn curtains could not help but see the naked pair sprawled dormantly in front of their fire. It was fortunate that Georgina's route to church did not take her past their window. Puffing heavily, she was the last member of the congregation to enter the damp, candle-lit nave.

The church bell was silent. The great south door boomed as it was closed by the verger. The clock struck midnight and the service began with a resonant chord from the organ.

'God rest you merry, gentlemen,' Slaughterhouse sang in quavering unison. 'Let nothing you dismay . . . O tidings of comfort and joy, comfort and joy.'

It was Christmas Day.

Christmas Day

One

Imagine yourself standing on the grassy knoll behind
Slaughterhouse Manor, your spirits soothed by the gentle
bleating of the Albions' black-faced ewes. Look down the
hill and allow your eye to wander at its leisure towards the
village. Allow it to stroll, so to speak, over the stag-heads of
the old oaks in the meadow and past the noble edifice of St
Anthony's tower, with its pantomime gargoyles and harmless
battlements. Send it past the pall of yew trees blackening the
graveyard, across the cottage roofs and chimneys set like
gnarled ribs in the crooked spine of the Street, down the
serpentine drawl of the Crow's valley towards the old mill
rotting into its silted pond, and on towards The Sow's Ear
whose swaying sign overhanging the road has marked the
boundary of Slaughterhouse for three centuries. Imagine
yourself enjoying this pleasant contemplation on a crisp
Christmas morning when happy invention can easily peep
into cottage windows and see the smiling faces of village
children as they tear open their presents. On such an occasion
it would be just as easy to imagine that Slaughterhouse had
lain thus since Domesday, mouldering in tranquil obscurity
as Christmas after Christmas passed; a guiltless, guileless
place whose destiny was to idle through history, merely
gathering the comfortable wrinkles of antiquity.

It would be easy to imagine this, and it would be utterly
mistaken.

History leaves its scars on villages like Slaughterhouse in
secret, silent places, and teaches its people to close their
faces and sour their hearts with cynicism. When everything
is taken from you, year after year, the only defence is to
learn how to grudge, to grudge even speech. Give nothing
away, and then you will lose only what is extracted from

you by force. That is the lesson to be learnt from the drawn curtains, locked doors and low roofs of Slaughterhouse.

Look again at the perpendicular splendours of St Anthony's east window, and guess its date. Late fourteenth century, you say confidently, because you have already perambulated the church, pottering round the nave with the vicar's guide in your hand and smiling at the rustical charm of the gravestones. Late fourteenth century; just so. Yet there is nothing in the elegant branching of that tracery to tell you how bitterly the villagers worshipping in their new church hated the Prior of Bury St. Edmunds, their landlord; nothing to tell you how joyfully they greeted the news of Wat Tyler's confrontation of the boy-king Richard II on the meadows of Mile End. Nevertheless, that is the case. Once they heard that the king had given his blessing to the punishment of traitors, the Slaughterhouse peasants wasted no time in joining the angry throng that marched on Bury and stormed the Abbey. Slaughterhouse men and women were among those who flushed out the Prior and cheered as he was tried, condemned and executed. They were part of the exultant crowd that stood on Angel Hill, in that summer of 1381, and shook their fists at the Prior's head spiked on its pillory near the Abbey gate.

Look at the war memorial, raised by local subscription in 1921 and now causing a continual traffic hazard by standing at the centre of the Street immediately in front of the post office. It bears the names of six men who sleep in the bosom of the Lord, so the inscription assures you, having made the supreme sacrifice on the fields of Flanders. However, if this was the flower of Slaughterhouse youth it was a low, creeping, ignominious bloom, for the inscription fails to tell you that three of these heroes did not answer the call of their country so much as the call of their bellies. Having had their pay stopped one day because it was raining and no work could be done on the farm, they decided to join the army to get a square meal. Warm and well fed for the first time in their lives, they gained a few pounds and even a little height at the Colchester barracks, before proceeding to their fate in the trenches.

They travelled thither under the hapless command of Captain Christopher Albion, who in his turn had answered the call of his mother, a remorseless distributor of white feathers. He was the youngest of the village volunteers and the first to die. His name, by virtue of alphabetical precedence rather than rank, heads the roll-call of glory incised on the memorial.

Now, stand with the post office behind you and look back towards the Manor. You must lift your head, of course, and appreciate that you are looking at a landscape in reverse, one that was not designed for your point of non-vantage. That part of the village skyline for which the Albions are responsible is no longer dominated, as it once was, by the edifice of the big house and its showcase of trees. They have been overshadowed by the lumbering profiles of more recent erections – the gangling struts of a Dutch barn, the inverted cone of a feed silo and the shanty-town roofs of pig units. Naturally, these agricultural carbuncles do not disfigure the outlook from the Manor; they are only visible to the village. As they say, it's the ugliest house in the street that has the best view.

Not that Slaughterhouse Manor is ugly; on the contrary, the actual Manor is a virtual cliché of country-house charm. Built in 1755 out of local red brick, it is a small masterpiece of elegant comfort and mellow proportions, a house in which Jane Austen herself might have felt at home. The original owner also indulged in some minor landscaping: he laid a drive with serpentine curves to disguise the modest scale of his meadow, or 'park' as he liked it to be called; he sited the oak trees whose shattered torsos still ornament the view from the bow-fronted drawing room; and below the portico with its two slender columns he designed a terraced garden, complete with a pond and a whimsical summerhouse in the shape of a pagoda. The house remained a gentleman's residence for the next century and a half, suffering no modifications more radical than the addition of a cast-iron conservatory. Then, just after the Great War, the Manor was demoted into a farm by Albert Albion, Mary's grandfather and the first Albion to call himself a landowner. He built a quadrangle of flint barns, stables, cowsheds and workshops round a cobbled yard at the back of the house. As if to atone for this utility, he ornamented the front of the house by planting a wisteria beside the portico and now, once a year in May and June, its festoons of drooping purple flowers mask the entire façade from the eaves to the terrace.

However, a beautiful house does not make for beautiful occupants, any more than an ugly one makes for ugly occupants. A graceful environment does not confer grace, a well-proportioned building will not induce balanced thinking, and there is no wisdom to be sucked from old bricks. We are the children of time, not place, and even the most eccentric of us is shaped and worn by the winds of history.

Two

At Slaughterhouse Manor Christmas Day began as all Christmas Days should, with a child waking at a painfully early hour and leaping out of bed to open his stocking.

As the church clock struck six in the darkness outside, Oliver crept fearfully past his father's bedroom, eased himself down the staircase and slipped into the kitchen. He warmed himself at the Aga for a moment and helped Elsie as she clambered painfully off her chair. He went through to the office, which smelt pleasantly of leather and wood smoke, a smell he paused to savour and explore. Elsie plodded after him, one of her back legs twisted by the seizure of her hip, and flopped once more in the hearth where the embers of the previous night still radiated a little heat. Oliver threw on a couple of logs and blew a flame out of the ash.

He noticed that the mince pie allegedly left out for Father Christmas had been eaten, apart from a few plausible crumbs, and the glass of sherry was empty. Perhaps, after all, his father had drunk it. He liked sherry.

Hanging from a nail in the brick fireplace and bulging misshapenly was one of his father's long green shooting socks. He lifted it down and began to draw out its contents. He knew that most of the little parcels would hold nothing more interesting than tangerines and sweets, but he undid them slowly, feeling them first and weighing them in his hand, and was careful not to tear the paper which he flattened out and put in a pile. Christmas only came around once a year and its rituals were not to be rushed. Among the makeweights were a couple of promising packets. The first contained a watch-calculator he had asked for, though it was a more expensive version than he had been expecting. The second was far larger but rendered enigmatic by Georgina's clumsy, piecemeal wrapping. What could it be?

Georgina hated the whole business of present-giving. It struck at the very root of her code of life. Frugality and Christmas were not merely incompatible, they were enemies. However, convention had to be respected, and Tom's wishes had to be fulfilled. He left her in sole charge of the family's presents, even his own to her, but this most unwanted responsibility did at least give her a chance to impress him with the ingenuity of her thrift. She solved the Christmas problem by dispensing a single, universal gift – home-made marmalade.

Every January she boiled up gallons of a lurid, orange-coloured emulsion and sealed it in jam jars, and every December, just as the surface of each jar was ripening into a furry scab of mould, she wrote her victims' names on the paper caps and drew holly leaves in green ink beside them. This was her sole concession to the debauchery of Christmas wrapping.

As always, the only exception to her policy was Oliver. Although she could not resist padding out his stocking with a couple of miniature jars of marmalade, she had long since recognised that the boy had to be bought an orthodox, commercial present. In letter after letter he had begged for something called a Death Racer, claiming to be the only boy in the school to lack one, and hinting that his deficiency was rendering him a laughing stock, almost a pariah. This Death Racer, she discovered in Stowmarket's toyshop, was a device similar to a pair of binoculars but with a moving three-dimensional image which showed soldiers scoring points by gunning down terrorists, or spacemen annihilating aliens, or divers destroying sharks, depending on your choice of game. Georgina opted for the sharks, thinking their connection with natural history might at least be educational, and with a shaking hand signed a cheque that would have financed enough marmalade for ten Christmases.

Her money was not wasted. When Oliver tore apart the cocoon of brown paper and discovered he had indeed been given a legendary Death Racer (he had exaggerated their prevalence at school, for they were in fact rare and highly prized) he sank back on his heels, dazed with satisfaction. Seldom do fantasy and reality mesh; this was such an occasion.

He was eager to show off his new possession, but had been placed under the strictest injunction not to wake Mary and Michael. His father would be dressed by now and making his tea in the kitchen or working with Fred in the yard. He did not want to see him. His mother would be down soon, but she would be too busy. No, there was only one person who would certainly be awake and welcoming at this hour, and that was his grandfather.

At the top of the attic stairs he saw his mother's bed was empty, so he pushed open the door and found his grandfather sitting up in bed, his eyes open and his teeth in place.

'Happy Christmas, Grandpa. Look what I've got.'

The old man stared at him, but saw nothing. Oliver held the Racer in front of his unresponding face.

'Where are you, boy? Don't hide.'

He reached out his enormous hand and made contact with the Racer, which he inspected and put to his eyes thinking it was a newfangled kind of binoculars. He swung round and pointed it in the direction of the yard.

'Now, where's that fool Fred? We don't want him cutting any corners just because it's Christmas Day, do we?' he said jovially, but all he could see was a school of sharks swimming towards him. He threw down the Racer, more convinced than ever that his faculties were deserting him.

'What did you score?' Oliver asked. 'I've scored eight hundred and forty already, but that's nowhere near the record. Weatherby's scored one thousand seven hundred and eighty-two, or so he says. No one believes him. He's a total prat, so how could he?'

'What do you call that thing?'

'Death Racer. Do you want another go?' Oliver held it out to him.

'No, I do not. I'm racing to death quite fast enough on

my own. Death Racer! Good God! Whatever happened to guns and catapults and bows and arrows?'

'I wouldn't mind an airgun,' said Oliver with pointed wistfulness. 'I could shoot rats and things round the farm with an airgun.'

He wondered where his grandfather had put his present, which by tradition was the most generous of the day. The old man was fumbling repeatedly under his pillow, but pulling nothing out. He knocked the Racer to the floor and began to rub his head. This was Oliver's cue to leave. He might have persisted a little longer if he had not forgotten to bring his own present, an unlovely and unreliable leather purse which, like all his other presents, he had laboriously cobbled in craft class. As it was, the old man's agitation was disturbing him: he was still polishing his head and staring about him blindly, spittle dribbling from his lip. It was clear that his gropings beneath the pillow were not going to be productive, so Oliver retrieved his Racer, intending to leave the room. As he stood up, the old man suddenly caught sight of him, as if for the first time.

'There you are. Why are you hiding under my bed? You're not frightened of me, are you boy?'

Oliver, who was frightened by now, shook his head.

'This is only nature taking its course,' he said, gesturing at his dilapidated torso beneath the sheet, 'but I'm the same person inside.' He tapped his head. 'More or less.'

'Come here.'

Oliver edged towards the bed. The old man leaned towards him and pinched his cheek, gently shaking the flesh between his fingers.

'Yours is as fresh and firm as an apple. But look at mine.' He plucked at his own sagging, tallowy cheek, which was frowzy with unshaven bristles. 'We are all rotting away. Even you. From the moment we're born we start to fall apart.'

He took Oliver's hand and pulled it towards him.

'Touch *my* cheek. Feel it. No one likes touching old people, but it's only decay, as I keep trying to explain to your mother. You can't catch it, because you've bloody well got it already.'

He laughed shortly. There was a little yellow slug of rheum in the corner of his eye, which disgusted Oliver, but his cheek, when Oliver's reluctant fingers finally made contact, felt soft and abrasive at once, like a piece of tanned leather with the bristles still attached. He pulled his hand away quickly.

The old man opened his mouth wide. 'Look,' he said pointing. Oliver did not want to look inside his mouth, but he took his arm again and pulled him closer. 'Look.' He moved his tongue and his top teeth fell down, grinning horribly beneath his chafed, naked gums.

'I'm like a baby. No teeth of my own, just empty gums.'

Oliver pulled back and the old man let him go, pushing a finger into his mouth to set his teeth back in place.

'You'll have to make a new start for us. We're depending on you. We need new life – youth. Don't worry about school. It'll soon be over and then you can get to work on your farm. I won't live to see it, but I'm going to arrange it for you.' He tapped the side of his nose twice. 'You won't disappoint us will you, Ollie? Do it for your Dad's sake.'

Oliver said nothing and the old man's focus seemed to fade. His head sank back on the pillow and his hand resumed its rotary polishing, though slowly now, somnolently. Oliver ran from the room, shouting up the stairs. 'I'll get Mum.'

He burst into the kitchen where Georgina was scraping burnt toast over the sink.

'Hello, Mum,' he said breathlessly. 'Happy Christmas and thanks for the Racer. It's really brill. Grandpa's going bonkers. Has he bought me anything or hasn't he?'

'You'll see,' she said, delivering a kiss on the top of his head with the force of a mallet banging in a tack. 'Happy Christmas, Ollie.'

Three

When Georgina reached the attic she found the old man asleep. With a practised movement she extricated his teeth from his sagging mouth and dropped them into the glass of water by his bed. They lay at the bottom, magnified and distorted, a pair of pink jaws gaping like some crustacean. She pulled up his sheet and folded it over, squaring it precisely as she tucked it in. He did not stir. At the window she scanned the blackness for a sign of Tom, to whom she had not yet spoken that morning, but there was not a glimmer of light to be seen. She stumped down the stairs to the kitchen.

Such Christmas cheer as she had permitted herself at the beginning of the day vanished as soon as she confronted the turkey to be cooked for lunch. Out in the gelid scullery, beneath the glare of a naked bulb, it looked as appetising as a cadaver on a pathologist's slab. But Georgina was not concerned with tastiness; to her, the turkey corpse simply represented yet another labour in the Augean stable of her housekeeping. What she saw was an entire month's food reduced at a single sitting to nothing but grease and garbage and filthy plates. What she saw was a heap of cold bones to be boiled into one of her rancid soups which she would force herself, out of sheer parsimony, to drink to the very last grey drop.

Thus it was that Michael, always an early riser, discovered her in an attitude of sadistic menace as she contemplated the turkey's defenceless fundament while holding aloft a packet of instant stuffing. He took the tool of her violation from her. Liar and adulterer he may have been, but when it came to cooking he was a model of probity.

'Georgie, my dear,' he drawled, caressing her with his

most velvety smile, 'I'm sure you have a thousand and one things to do this morning. Why don't you let me take some of the burden from your shoulders? May I help you with the cooking?'

Georgina did not approve of Michael and she certainly did not intend to share with him the kudos for producing the most important meal of the year. Nor did she want Tom to think she had been shirking her duties. On the other hand, Michael was an excellent cook and his assistance would leave her free to do other tasks.

'You can peel the potatoes,' she said curtly.

'I'd love to.' His smile was inflexible. 'Are you sure there isn't something else I can do?'

'We'll see.'

She pointed towards the kitchen.

'There's a sack under the sink and the peeler's in the drawer.'

Still smiling, he made a mock-gallant gesture indicating that she should enter the room before him. Overwhelmed by the insistence of his charm, she momentarily bared her own teeth.

Michael took off his jacket, rolled up his Turnbull and Asser sleeves and began to whittle the peel from the potato. Georgina watched him, her mouth slightly agape; she was mesmerized by the artistry and economy he brought to a chore which she always performed with clumsy wastefulness.

'Go, go,' he commanded. 'Shine the light of your smile in some other place and leave me to my work.'

He pointed sternly at the door with his potato peeler.

She looked at him doubtfully. Teasing always confounded her: having only a stunted sense of humour she could never tell whether she was the butt of banter or malice. On this occasion, she decided his 'chaffing' (her word) was benign.

'Make sure you don't drop any peel on the floor,' she said, by way of thanking him, and left the room.

It was as well she did not suddenly turn her head while closing the door, or she might have seen his chivalrous smile snapping shut faster than a salesman's case.

At the back door she pulled on her boots and set off across the yard, picking her way through the mud and potholes with unconcealed disgust. Mud had been her enemy ever since she had married Tom, and her hatred of it grew more intense with each winter. She was not on amicable terms with nature and shunned it whenever possible, but she could not evade the ubiquitous mud, which was after all the raw material of her husband's livelihood. She thought of it as a living organism, an alien and hostile force that kept her back door under permanent siege, forever waiting its chance to spread its sludgy empire and engulf her house. Mud, mud, detestable mud! It symbolised the dilemma that had ruled her entire married life: she loathed the farm and everything to do with farming, but she loved the farmer.

As she squelched and cursed in the yard, she was grateful nonetheless for this chance to leave the house and look for Tom. A greasy, troubled dawn was breaking over the village and lights were pricking the windows up and down the street. It was Christmas Day, but she had not seen her husband, far less greeted him or given him his present. Lately, they had often passed the morning, sometimes a whole twenty-four hours, without speaking, but today of all days she was determined to break the pattern. She had his present in her pocket, and she knew this because she herself had put it there last night. Every year she nursed the hope that he would write some extra message on the label she provided, and every year she was disappointed.

She stopped first at the farrowing house, wondering if he would be in his makeshift office among the pig medicines, a bolt hole he had almost made his home. She saw the light glowing at the far end of the aisle, but as she walked towards it a sow suddenly lurched forward, grunting aggressively and pushing her whiskery, blowing snout through the bars of her pen. Georgina started back in terror. She abhorred domesticated nature quite as much as its raw original. The bolt holding the pen door appeared to be shaking its socket loose. She ran back down the aisle and into the yard.

Catching her breath, she plodded to the fattening shed

which stood opposite, its long, windowless flint wall forming one side of the yard's quadrangle. To a student of
architecture this would have been a handsome example of
farm vernacular; to Georgina, it was an evil-smelling sty.
She pushed open its heavy corrugated-iron door and was
revolted as usual by the sight of the piglets scurrying to
hide in their litter of straw. Fifty or more weeners were
packed into a large pen with no more light falling on it than
was smuggled through the gaps in the roof left by a couple
of broken slates, and in this permanent twilight their pale,
shapeless bodies, writhing and climbing over each other,
always reminded her of maggots. There was no sign of Tom
here either. She shouted his name down the aisle between
the concrete dungeons reserved for the bigger baconers and
porkers, but was unwilling to walk any further. She could
hear the animals squealing and snorting in the darkness, for a
human presence generally signalled the arrival of food. Their
smell nauseated her, and she knew that if she looked into the
fattening units and saw the pigs slithering on their bare slats,
blackened with their own filth, she would indeed be sick.

Outside she breathed deeply, expelling every last trace of
the stench from her nostrils. She shouted into the barn and
tractor sheds without getting an answer. She crossed the yard
once more and in the middle of the quagmire realised she did
not know where to look next. Though the mud was clinging
to her skirt and soaking her stockings, she also realised she
did not want to return to the house.

Damp and immobilised, she felt the wind cut through to
her skin. It was a rowdy and mischievous wind. Careering
round the confined space of the yard like a manic child, it
seemed to blow from all points of the compass at once. As
she stood in the centre of this buffeted square of mire, the hub
of her husband's kingdom, she looked carefully at each of its
buildings in turn – the pig houses with their blood-coloured
tin roofs, the huge church-like barn, the open-mouthed
tractor sheds, the workshops and old stables where she had
once thought of opening a farm shop – and she was appalled
to discover how broken-down they all were. Wherever she

137

looked she saw broken tiles, heaps of rusting metal, sagging ridges, unhinged doors, loose and rotting weatherboard and empty windows with flapping plastic sacks nailed over them. Even the weather vane attached to the barn's gable-end had broken off its fixing and would soon smash its way through the slates. This had been a gift from the blacksmith to Tom's grandfather on his wedding and was wrought in the shape of a Suffolk punch cart-horse. It was one of the few bits of the farm site she liked. Now it was toppled over, pointing immoveably downwards, as if all Suffolk's gales finally blew themselves out in the inescapable mud.

The wind moaned and boomed, whipping little flurries of waves across the diesel blooms in the brown puddles. She was cold and she had nowhere to go.

She had failed as a housekeeper and could not return to her kitchen when a man she did not much like was cooking her Christmas lunch. She had failed as a wife and could not find her husband, who had stopped speaking to her and loved his sows. She had failed as a farmer because she hated mud and pigs and oil and tractors and broken-down buildings held together with binder twine and plastic sacks. Worst of all, she had failed as a mother because she had allowed her daughter to marry a fool and her son to be sent away, and she could not protect him from his father's coldness. She was stuck in the mud and did not know what to do.

'Stick-in-the-mud' had been her father's nickname for her as a little girl. The booming of the wind in the yard was the same, ceaseless booming that had shaken their house in Cromer as it blew off the sea and hit the cliffs. But there the wind had been friendly, exhilarating, a reminder of warmth and safety indoors. The sound of the sea had been in her ears throughout her childhood and she had missed it keenly when she married and moved to Slaughterhouse.

Her father used to stand at their drawing-room window and point to the horizon beyond the grey expanse of the North Sea, telling her that the waves had rolled all the way from the Arctic. If you were a bird instead of a Stick-in-the-mud, he would tell her, and you flew north, you wouldn't sight land until you'd gone over the top of the world and reached Siberia. That's where the wind comes from. Siberia. He was a solicitor, but he used to say he had a dash of pirate in his blood which was why he kept a boat at Blakeney. Any day he chose he could set sail for the South Seas in search of treasure. In point of fact, he had amassed a fair amount of treasure without voyaging any farther than his office in Cromer's high street, treasure which in due course had been invested in the Albion farm. This mud-bath was her inheritance.

The wind sighed through the ramshackle buildings, and at Cromer the waves would be crashing onto the stony beach. When Tom had decreed that Oliver be sent to a boarding school she had insisted on Bitterley Hall, because there he would at least have the noise of the sea in his ears. During the long weeks of his first term it had eased her pain to know that while he lay in his dormitory he was soothed by the same sea she had heard as a child.

Landlocked and imprisoned by mud, she had not seen the sea for ten years, not since her father had lain dying in Blakeney within earshot of his beloved boat. She had sat by his bed listening to the rigging as it tapped on the mast and ticked off the seconds of his life. She had watched his life ebb away like a tide while she listened to the wind moan across the salt marshes, the icy Siberian wind that had driven him home for the last time. She had heard the curlew's cry and the shrieking of the gulls and a croaking gasp in her father's throat. She had closed his eyes and now this same polar wind was whipping tears from her eyes.

Where could she go?

Four

Mary woke with the shreds of a dream clinging to her. Sweating, she remembered something about lying in a river, or maybe a bath, like a Victorian Ophelia, with flowers round her throat and another figure floating beyond her open legs, whether drowning or emerging she could not tell, whose hair was red like Liz's but whose face was a smiling child's. The damp sheet was knotted round her neck and her hand was between her legs.

It was Christmas Day. She had forgotten. Her mother, dead now twelve, no thirteen years, used to leave breakfast out for Tommy and her in the kitchen, tea leaves in the pot, loaf cut for toast, water in a pan for boiling eggs. They had opened their stockings there, in the warmth of the Aga, whispering and shrieking, their parents' bedroom just overhead, butter on the wrapping paper and orange peel squashed on the floor. Tiles then, not Georgie's awful lino. Sweet woman, her mother, but Mary's childhood had belonged to her father, just as Tommy's had belonged to his mother. She had 'worried' over him, and that had been the beginning and end of him. Her mother always bought her a new dress to wear at Christmas lunch, and that was fine and she was grateful and enjoyed looking nice, but her father's presents were magical – a puppy, a bike, a new saddle and bridle, a diamond brooch and then a car. Why they were *his* presents and not from both of them, she never understood. She had driven the same car to London that terrible day after Tommy's return and it had been worn out and sold for nothing by the time she had come home again. Home.

Christmas Day. She leaned out of bed and dragged open a curtain. Rain skittered across the glass and the sky was dish-rag grey. Liz had dreaded the winter solstice, light failing, darkness closing in, hope dwindling. Dead. Well, that was her choice, the silly cow, and see where it had got her. That morning the policeman had surprised her by saying they tend to do it at dawn. You'd think if they'd made it through the night, they'd decide to hang on for another day. Not *hang*; bad joke. You'd think they'd throw the dice again, have one more try in case something eased. No. To them it wasn't first light, but last dark, the end of the protecting night. A new day meant more of the same, more of what could not be faced. Too much suffering. Apparently.

Christmas. Day of birth, not death; she was going to put Liz behind her and celebrate. Outside, the wind was blowing, a clean, wet sea wind that would purify them. She would get up and see her father straightaway. Life had always grown from his hands: he had coaxed life out of the stony ground, out of the apple trees behind the summer house, out of his beloved pigs. He had shown her grain in the great dish of his palm and when he stirred and poked the seeds with his cracked forefinger she had seen them sprout.

She too would swell and sprout. It was time to persuade Michael. The noise of the telephone last night: had it been Michael, or Tom, or had she misheard? If Michael, who was he calling? It was probably Tom. Motheba had lost her only son, run down in the bush like a dog and no one to bury him. Now she had no periods; the torture had done something to her insides, making her barren. They had even taken that away from her. Where was she spending Christmas? Yet she had once said to Liz, 'I have a child; he happens to be dead, but I still have him in my heart. I will always be a mother.'

It was no good having children for its own sake, just because your parents had you and we're all animals under the skin. To understand tradition, you must know some history. Look at Oliver; better to be childless than to push an Oliver into the world, unloved and unenlightened. Producing neurotic sons, that was a good old Albion tradition, and one that she would break. That's what all parents believe, and so they should, that their child will restore us to Eden, no, forwards, usher in a new dawn, bring about the Millennium, every son of woman the Messiah, every baby the Christ. What must it be like to have a baby quickening inside you? Too old, she was terrified. Quickening. What a beautiful word, speed and life synonymous. Cut to the quick, that would be less painful, unzipping your stomach like a suitcase to get the baby out, no screaming, asleep, wake up to find the baby alive and kicking, sucking too, at your breasts. She always liked Michael doing that, but he would hate the baby for it. Bottle then. Bottle, yes; she would tell him.

Anyway, it would be a girl. She would have a girl who would be quicker than the wind, lovelier than the moon, deeper than the sea and twice as mighty as Jesus himself. Her name wasn't Mary for nothing. What was the point of having a baby with no ambitions for it? She would be the she-Messiah, a wonderful heroine, striding at the van of a great crowd, eyes blazing, the flag of Liberty and Truth wrapped round her naked torso, like that French woman in the picture. Red hair, as red as Liz's, but strong and brave, fighting on the side of Life.

Christmas Day. Time to resurrect herself. She threw back the blankets, not minding the sting of cold air, and sitting up in bed crossed her arms to lift her nightdress. Just as she was pulling it over her head, face muffled in its folds, she felt hands clasping her breasts. She screamed, struggling to free herself, but only tangling herself tighter. The hands caressed her. In her convulsions she ripped the dress. It was Michael. Still holding her, he leaned forward to kiss her shoulders.

'Happy Christmas, darling. Did I give you a shock? Were you expecting someone else?'

He grinned teasingly, and kissed her newly liberated neck. Was this the kiss of an adulterer, a maker of clandestine phone calls? Surely not.

'Michael! You terrified me. Don't do that again.'

He kissed her back, and she could smell cooking on his clothes, a homely, companionable smell, very different from his usual aroma of steely aftershave.

'Has Georgie put you to work in the kitchen?'

'I volunteered. Otherwise lunch would have been quite inedible.'

He continued to caress her and she wondered if they were going to make love. Christmas Day would be a propitious occasion to conceive, but she would have to tell him first. She couldn't deceive him.

'Here's a present,' he said suddenly. 'To be going on with.'

He reached under the bed and pulled out a parcel wrapped in gold paper and adorned with a single bow. There was no card or message. She tore off the paper and delivered from its nest of tissue paper a black mohair sweater. She held it up.

'The back's so low.'

'That's the point of it. Put it on.'

She dropped it over her head and sat upright to show him the effect. It suited her much better than it had Zara, whose back was stocky and waistless. Mary's back was lean and elegant, and the sweater's swooping lines looked exquisite on her.

'It smells of you. Where did you buy it?'

'Oh, a little boutique near the office. It's where all the secretaries go, I'm afraid. I think my aftershave must have leaked in my case. Everything reeks.'

He had dowsed it to expunge any trace of Zara's musky cupboard where it had lain, unworn, since he had bought it for her in the summer.

'I had such a strange dream just before I woke up,' said Mary, 'I can't get it out of my mind. I was lying in water somewhere and there was this child, with red hair, smiling at me, but I couldn't tell whether it was coming out or going under. And I didn't seem to care.'

Not really listening to her, he slid his hand beneath the silky wool and took her breast again, pinching her nipple with a subtly increased urgency which she knew was a preliminary to sex.

'I think it was a dream about giving birth, but I don't know why the child seemed to be drowning too. I suppose dreams are like that. Ambiguous.'

She was talking fast, almost gabbling; she had felt his hand stop and fall away from her breast at the word 'birth'. She turned her head and looked pleadingly into his eyes.

'We have to talk about it. I know I promised not to for a year, but I think about it all the time.'

'Let's not spoil Christmas,' he said, pulling out his hand and moving to the edge of the bed. She hugged herself to keep warm.

'Spoil Christmas! That's an odd thing to say when you think about it. I mean Christmas is a birthday, a day of birth, after all.'

Against her will, she had allowed her voice to acquire a sardonic edge. He stood up brusquely and walked to the dressing table where he looked at himself in the glass, smoothing his hair and adjusting his tie.

'What is this fetish for having children?' he suddenly demanded. 'Tell me, how many happy families do you know, truly happy families? Most people we know hate their fathers or their mothers, and now they're getting older their children are beginning to hate them. Do we want that? Do we want to put a child between us who'll grow up to hate us?'

'It doesn't have to be like that.'

'No? What about you and your father? And what about Oliver, for Christ's sake? Don't tell me he won't grow up to hate Tom.'

She frowned in frustration and pulled at her lip. She did not want an argument, only to tell him how she felt.

'What is the point of children? You tell me that.' He paced the room, plying an agitated course between the bed and the window. 'What are they for, exactly?'

'Oh Michael. You know what they're for. They don't have a point like a business plan or a military expedition.'

'I mean,' he said more softly, 'what do we need them for? We were happy before you started all this business. Just the two of us.'

Mary did not answer this, but said, 'Anyway, Georgie loves Ollie after her own bizarre fashion; you can't deny that. And it's not too late for Tom to come round. He's going through a rough patch – ' Michael snorted derisively – 'All right, he's always going through a rough patch, but it doesn't mean he won't come round. He loves Ollie, I'm sure of it, he just won't show it. And you're wrong about my father, I don't hate him.'

'I suppose you're going to tell me you love him now.'

'Of course I love him. That's what you can never understand. Relationships are messy and unpredictable, and they don't use just one emotion to drive them along. They're chaotic and full of stuff that neither person wants. They're not like your fucking furniture, all bright and sharp and stainless.'

She fell silent, regretting the insult. He stood at the window, his expression concealed from her. She decided to get dressed while he was facing the other way. She did not want to conduct this row from her bed; nor did she want to make herself vulnerable to him by letting him see her lower half naked. She slid quickly from the sheets, but saw his head turn slightly to watch her in the dressing table glass, his eye fixed on her groin and then her bottom as she bent to pick up her clothes.

'Don't spy on me,' she shouted. 'If you must stare at me, don't do it in that creepy way. I don't want a bloody Peeping Tom for a husband.'

She turned her back on him and pulled his sweater over her head. He strode over to her and span her round. She was completely naked now, and crossed her arms over her chest in an instinctive gesture of protection.

'I'm looking straight at you,' he said, hissing through clenched teeth. 'And what I see is a neurotic woman with a bloody stupid obsession planted in her head by another neurotic woman.'

'Liz did not plant the obsession, as you call it, in my head. It was my idea. It sprang up naturally, the way it does in the minds of millions of women every day. It's normal. Natural. Not that you'd know much about that, would you? If anyone's neurotic, it's you. You're the one

145

who can only get it up with women who look like skinny girls. That's what I call a fetish, when someone does more looking than fucking, and only wants to look at half-starved schoolgirls. And don't think I'm flattering myself: I know how old I am. What did you expect? A rubber doll. Did you think I was made of plastic? I'm thirty-five and like every other woman ever born, even the ones you've screwed, I'm perishable. I'm organic,' she said, plucking at her flesh. 'Dust to dust, you know. And before it's too late I want to put my body to one of the uses it's designed for. I won't let you make a fetish of me.'

He stared at her furious, frozen body, his eyes glittering. He made a small move towards her.

'You look very sexy like that,' he said hoarsely.

'Don't be disgusting.'

She grabbed her clothes in a heap and ran to the bathroom, slamming the door behind her.

Five

Down in the village, in Slaughterhouse Cottage, Rose woke
and felt a pang of joy at the memory of Gregory's return and
'confession'. Last night they had not woken until the fire had
burnt out, leaving them cold and aching on the hearth rug.
In bed, soon after, she had lain awake listening to him as he
moaned and sighed in his sleep. She leaned over to look at
him, but his head was turned away, his arm sprawled over
his face.

Suddenly she recalled it was Christmas Day. There would
be time enough later in the holiday to worry about his job.
She would tell her mother to mind her own business, and ask
her father for help, though without letting Gregory know.
Christmas Day! She hadn't yet seen Ollie back from school;
there was lunch to look forward to, and her vile uncle Basil
to dread; there were presents under the tree, and no office
to go to for five long days, and drinks in the pub tomorrow
when the hunt met outside in the yard, the very yard where
Gregory had first kissed her; there were sexy mornings in
bed, and Gregory's mother to amuse, and films on television
at night, and more sex. And there was Gregory himself. No
longer Something in the City, no longer safe and bankable,
no longer the Gregory she had married.

She left him asleep, creeping from their bed and going
downstairs to make the tea. She was still enough of a child
to get excited at the prospect of her presents. What would
her father's cheque be worth this year? £100? More? Less?
What was the price of bacon at the moment?

When she returned to the bedroom, a tray in her hand
bearing two mugs of tea and a neatly wrapped parcel, she
found that Gregory had thrown off the covers and was
lying naked – he had of course given away his pyjamas –

his arms outstretched, his head drooping on his shoulder, his legs straight and crossed at the ankles. Last night, in the glow of the fire and the passion of the moment she had not looked closely at his body, being too eager to hold it and feel his long limbs twined round her. But now, inspecting him in the bleak morning light, she was shocked by his emaciation and frailty. He lay like a corpse dragged out of the sea, a white body on a white sheet. His face was seamed with the lines of an old man. Never anything but thin, he now looked half-starved, as indeed he was, not having eaten a proper meal for more than a month. His ribs stood out like a wire cage and his legs and hips looked as if the flesh had been scraped off their bones.

She pulled the covers round his shoulders and kissed his poor rutted forehead. He woke at her touch, his eyes already anguished.

'Is it Christmas Day? There must be a shop open somewhere.'

She sat on the bed and held out his tea. He ignored it.

'I've nothing to give you. Nothing.'

'I don't mind,' she said soothingly. 'I only want you. I'm so glad it's over, whatever it was. You mustn't worry any more. You'll find a new job, and for the time being we'll survive on what I earn.'

He was not comforted by her words. His head fell back on the pillow and he stared hopelessly at the ceiling.

'Look. I've got something for you.'

He made no move to take her parcel, so she undid it for him, pulling out a long, multi-coloured woollen scarf. She bent to wind it round his neck, but he tore it off and threw it aside as if it were poisoned.

'I can't wear that,' he said to her with terrible intensity. 'You haven't been listening to me. There are people out there, children, who haven't got shirts to wear, never mind scarves. So many people, the streets are full of them, nothing to eat, nothing to wear, nowhere to go.' He snatched up the scarf again. 'This could save a life.'

'Gregory darling, you can't save the world on your own. It isn't your fault.'

'It is,' he shouted. 'It's everyone's fault.'

'Well, anyway, you haven't got any clothes left to give. Or money,' she added ruefully.

'I know,' he said. 'But I still have something to give. We all have.' He threw back the sheet again and pointed to his hollow abdomen. 'Organs. Blood. Marrow. I've plenty to spare.' He plucked at his skeleton to show her. 'I must get to the hospital now. They'll be dealing with emergencies. They always do at Christmas because of the drunken drivers. You'll come with me, won't you?'

'What are you talking about?'

'Transplants, of course. Corneas, lungs, that sort of thing. And blood, any amount of blood they need. Please say you'll come with me.'

Utterly bewildered, Rose was beginning to be frightened. Evidently Gregory had lost not only his job, but his sanity as well.

'I'll come with you,' she said in an effort to pacify him, 'but – '

'Wonderful!' he cried jubilantly. 'I knew you would have faith in me. And you can help too. We can do this together.' He kissed her fervently and then held her shoulders, looking at her body speculatively. 'Just a kidney or something at first. Nothing you'll miss.'

He sprang from the bed, hopping from one fleshless shank to the other as he searched his ransacked drawers for something to wear.

'Hurry, hurry, hurry,' he muttered. 'No time to waste.'

Rose stood beside him and put her arms round his spindly chest.

'You're ill,' she said gently. 'Go back to bed and I'll give you some breakfast. Look how thin you are.'

He brushed her aside.

'Better thin than dead,' he told her.

Suddenly grasping the logic of his ideas, she said, 'You'll be no use to them at the hospital if you're not healthy. No one will want your organs and things if you look like a famine victim.'

'You're right, you're right,' he said after a moment's thought, his face illuminated with joy. 'I love you Rose. You understand me. Yes, I must eat.' He skipped over to the bed and threw himself into it. 'I must fatten up and get myself in perfect condition. You too. We must both be as fit as fleas and then we'll be indispensable to them.'

He looked up at her, his eyes radiant with craziness and desire.

At this poignant moment they heard the sound of the back door opening.

'Yoo-hoo. It's me,' a voice called up the stairs. 'Yoo-hoo. Anyone at home?'

'Hello mother,' Gregory called back, sighing in disappointment. 'Happy Christmas.'

Six

Georgina was finally driven by the cold to uproot herself from the quagmire in the yard. There was one place where she might find some temporary solace, and that was the church, but first she had to tell someone where she was going in case Tom reappeared and asked for her. She trudged through the mud towards the house, her head butting into the wind.

Without bothering to take off her coat, she walked into the kitchen and was immediately smothered by a fierce, wet heat. Michael, a glass of brandy in his hand, a cigarette between his lips, stood by the Aga and stirred a pan from which thick clouds of richly odoriferous steam were rising, causing the windows to run with condensation. The Aga itself had been coaxed and stoked into a state of incandescence and was throbbing with power as if in readiness for some great feat of traction.

Georgina's store cupboards had been invaded and pillaged, their doors hanging open and their spoils littering the table. Mounted on a ring of onions and parsnips, the huge white breast of the turkey lay exposed like a sacrificial offering in its blackened roasting tray. Loops and swags of sausages festooned its legs and wings, long rashers of bacon were draped over the high arch of its breast bone, while little scrolls of rolled bacon filled every crevice.

'What do you think you're doing?' Georgina cried out, horrified by this orgy of wastefulness. 'That food's got to last us until the end of the week, so you can put all those sausages back where you found them. And the bacon.'

'Hello, Georgie,' said Michael, waving his spoon in her direction with an affable gesture. 'I thought I'd make a start with the turkey. By the way, how many mouths are we catering for?'

Georgina began to pluck the sausages off the turkey. What would Tom think if she squandered so much food in one meal?

'Contrary to whatever Mary may have told you,' she barked, 'we're not made of money.'

'My dear Georgie, I was only trying to lend a hand.'

Michael poured himself another brandy.

'If you must drink so early in the morning, kindly drink your own alcohol.'

'We all have to get through Christmas in our own way.'

Georgina took the bottle from him and screwed on the cap with a brutal twist. Then, not wanting to leave him access to it in her absence, she looked round the room for a suitably secure place but her whole kitchen was under his occupation. She shoved the bottle into the pocket of her coat.

'I have to go to the church to rearrange the flowers for this morning's service. Please tell Tom if he asks. And clear this mess up. I will be back shortly to do the cooking *myself*.'

'As you wish,' Michael said, sighing. 'Do you think I should peel a couple more potatoes.'

'Not unless you plan to pay for them. I have a budget to stick to, you know.'

She slammed shut the cupboard door above his head, and then slammed the kitchen door behind her.

'Merry Christmas to you too,' Michael said and went through to the office to see if Father Christmas had left his sherry bottle on the table.

Georgina took the path that led through the garden, across the meadow and over a stile, bringing her into the churchyard. The rain had eased off and when she looked up at the mock-battlements capping St. Anthony's tower, eighty feet above her, the whole flint edifice seemed to be swaying, drifting away from her, swinging like a ship on its moorings into the racing mainstream of cloud. The tower was a huge, ungainly construction, military in appearance and grossly disproportionate to the delicate nave and chancel below. It was also subsiding, cracking and possibly falling down. Or rather it had been until the parish council launched its Save The Tower fund. Ten years of jumble sales, fêtes, coffee mornings, bric-a-brac fairs, Sixties dances and sponsored swims, runs, walks, spellings and pancake marathons had been required to raise the money to have the tower's foundations secured and a great steel brace bolted round its hips. No one had been more assiduous than Georgina in her efforts to keep aloft this mighty, flawed erection.

She hurried into the porch protecting the south door and turned the iron handle to lift the latch inside. Despite its weight and sagging hinges, the door was no match for her hearty shove. Inside, a faint glow of unfamiliar warmth wafted towards her, emanating from a pair of gas heaters left alight by the vicar following early communion. She tutted automatically at this extravagance and turned them both down to their lowest point.

Because there were so few flowers at this time of year, and buying them was out of the question, Georgina had contributed to the decoration of the church by filling a large vase with sprigs of holly and mistletoe, of which there was a great abundance on an old apple tree in her kitchen garden. She had set her vase in one of the deep window sills on the south side of the nave and had been very pleased with the effect her arrangement had made against the coloured glass. But, as she now discovered, most of the berries had dropped off her holly, bombarding the nativity tableau below which had been constructed by the village primary school.

The madonna, a plastic doll with blonde nylon hair, movable limbs and a Jane Fonda figure, lay on her face in the straw, perhaps the victim of a falling holly berry. Joseph, a battle-scarred Action Man, stood over her, indifferent in his combat fatigues. In toppling over, Mary appeared to have struck down an elephant, one of the menagerie of improbable creatures, including some monsters and a robot, gathered to pay homage to the infant Jesus. He lay snug in his matchbox crib, peering at the Adoration through a tin foil halo.

Feeling the weight of the brandy bottle in her pocket,

Georgina put it down on the nearest pew and began to clean the stable. She reorganised the figures so they stood in a precise circle round Mary, whom she placed immediately behind the manger where she belonged.

When the job was done she sat in the pew and read, as she had done a thousand times before, the epitaph carved in a monumental plaque attached to the wall beside the window.

> Here lyeth the mortal remains
> Of Rachel Baylham
> Beloved Daughter
> Seemly Wife
> Patient Mother
> Just Mistress
> And Steady Friend
> Gone to Her Wardrobe of Dusty Clothes
> 1654

Georgina wanted to pray, but could not. Her mind would give vent to nothing but thoughts of Tom, Oliver, Rose . . . These were not prayers, they were dreary, everyday anxieties. She wanted to beg and confide and weep; she wanted to be comforted and refreshed; above all, she wanted to be listened to – not merely heard, but attended to with care and respect. She would have knelt down and put her hands together if she had not been afraid that the vicar might catch her in that compromising position. She did not want him poking his fleshy nose into her business.

Immediately after the death of her father she had found consolation in this church, and had become the first member of the Albion family in three generations to be a devout church-goer. 'Our Father which art in heaven . . .' she had pronounced with fervour every Sunday, thinking of her own father, and hoping that he was indeed in some kind of heaven. The image of God the father was in fact the only concept of God she could accept and understand. She had found it easy to humble herself in front of this God, readily acknowledging her manifold sins and wickedness. Making her confession she gave voice to her faults with a booming ardency that horrified her less conscience-stricken neighbours. Oh yes, she had erred and strayed. Yes, she had left undone those things she ought to have done. Every Sunday she could think of a dozen, a hundred things she had left undone. There was no health in her. She was a most miserable offender; and she did indeed crave a godly, righteous and sober life.

These were familiar sentiments and she enjoyed the rare luxury of putting them into words. Daddy had always made her feel guilty, but she had never worked out a way of showing her penitence. And then he had died, and though she had sobbed sorry, sorry, sorry into his ear as he lay on his death bed, he had only stared back at her in mute bewilderment. No absolution for Georgy-porgy.

While she mourned her father she made herself indispensable to the old vicar, whose wife had died many years since. She sat beside him on innumerable committees and played a zealous part in all the church's many fund-raising projects. She collected old clothes from the village and bought them at jumble sales, selling them back to herself over and over again until they stank so badly they had to be burnt. She cleaned the church every third Wednesday and did the flowers once a month. She even washed the vicar's smalls, which he left out for her in the vestry, discreetly wrapped in brown paper. She became a pillar of the church, revelling in the business of husbanding its pitiful budget and worrying over its crumbling fabric.

But for all her loyalty to the church she never learnt to pray. During those parts of the service when Mr Simpkins invited the congregation to pray and he himself creaked onto his bony knees and bowed his silvery head, Georgina was invaded by a great emptiness which, unless she prevented it, would slowly fill with grief and longing for her father. To pray to him, instead of God, seemed impious, so she trained herself to concentrate her thoughts on church business. Deprived of her father's rubicund cheeks and bloodhound eyes, God never shaped into a living personality in her imagination; he remained a word, a code, a liturgical device. Nor did the God of Mr Simpkins' visions ever unveil Himself to her. To Mr Simpkins God was a notion which could only be dimly glimpsed after scaling the Himalayan heights of eloquence, but whenever he set off on these verbal expeditions, seeming almost to levitate from the pulpit, Georgina always found herself left behind at base camp guarding the baked beans. Without a God to receive her supplications prayer was meaningless, no more than whimpering in the void, but in spite of throwing open the doors of her mind God did not visit her, at least not in a form which she could understand. Miserable sinner though she was, God, as far as she could tell, had not taken mercy on her.

Her religious, or rather ecclesiastical life suffered an abrupt change with Mr Simpkins' retirement. His successor, the Reverend Michael Brickhill ('Call me Mike; everyone does') had a wife and therefore no need of Georgina's humble skills. Mistaking her for one of those power-hungry parish matrons who are the bane of every rural cleric's life, Mr Brickhill treated her with a fruity condescension and this had completed her sense of redundancy. With no Mr Simpkins to care for, she turned her attention to the church itself and virtually took over the cleaning roster, bringing the place to a state of polished immaculacy she had never achieved in her own house. She took to haunting the church, passing whole afternoons in its chilly sanctuary. She never allowed herself to be still, far less contemplative, and if she was ever on her knees it was to buff the flagstones, not to pray. But nor did she drive herself at the same frenzied pace as she did at home; in the church she worked slowly, relishing laboriousness as if fulfilling the steps of some ritual. She hoped that perhaps she would reach God through housework.

It was fortunate that she had not taken to her knees because at that moment the vicar himself entered the church, banging the south door behind him and hopping ponderously on each of his enormous feet in turn to remove his cycle clips. Once he had liberated his flapping grey turn-ups, he strode down the nave, iron-tipped heels ringing on the flagstones.

'Ah, Georgina, m'dear, it's you. Merry Christmas. And will we be seeing you and your family for morning service? I think we can promise you something rather special.'

We! Who was this we? He spoke for himself and God, no doubt; and probably for the entire Trinity.

'I'm afraid not, vicar,' she said shortly. 'My sister-in-law is not a church-goer, and Tom, as you know, is a confirmed heathen.'

Mr Brickhill laughed merrily. He would have laughed with no less merriment if she had told him that Tom was a head-hunter and a cannibal. He held out his large red hands to the gas heater's feeble glow and made as if to turn up its heat, but a look from Georgina stopped him and instead he took to rubbing his palms together.

To her great annoyance he began to rearrange the figures in the tableau, breaking up her regimental lines.

'These children are such martinets,' he said, distributing the animals in an 'artistic' pattern and leaning his head back to squint at his efforts. 'After all, the beasts have come to worship the Christ, not to queue for a bus.'

He said this with a mischievous twinkle to show that he was being humorous. Georgina did not smile in return.

She noticed that he positioned Joseph much nearer Mary than she had done; indeed, she was shocked to realise she had put Joseph as far away as possible from Mary and her child and had stood the crib between them like a barricade.

'What sort of marriage do you think they had?' she asked, pointing to the Holy couple and asking the question before she had really considered it or the insight that might be inferred from it concerning her own state of mind.

Mr Brickhill, however, was not a man to discern subtleties. He laughed uproariously as if she had said something daringly satirical, for he prided himself on his ability to be amused by blasphemous teasing.

Subsiding at last, he said, 'I suppose they had their little tiffs and differences like all married folk, but I don't imagine they had any more need of the Nazareth agony aunt than you or I have, Georgina.'

She smiled at him this time, but so bleakly he was forced to turn away and cough. For the first time he noticed the brandy bottle on the pew where she had been sitting. She saw the direction of his glance and his change of expression. Without a word, she thrust the bottle back in her pocket.

He fiddled with the tableau for a moment, his handsome forehead knotted in thought. Then, flushing brick-red, he suddenly said to her, 'Would you like to pray with me, Georgina? Just a short Christmas prayer and a blessing.'

Scarlet now, but unstoppable, he went on. 'You are, I believe, a good woman who does not get her due. But God sees everything and knows your true worth. Your goodness will not go unrecognised, or unblessed.'

Georgina was no less astonished by the impertinence of his remarks than by the fumbling attempt at kindness which lay behind them. Mr Simpkins had never made so intimate a proposal; in fact, he had never appeared to take any interest in her spiritual comfort. She stared at Mr Brickhill, dumbfounded and embarrassed, her face as red as his.

'No. Well, I shall pray for you all the same,' he muttered. He put his hand on her shoulder and squeezed it roughly for a moment.

'Happy Christmas, Georgina.'

He strode away, unable to look her in the eye. She heard his footsteps clanging down the nave and the south door bang as he left the church.

The man was a fool. A good woman indeed! How dare he patronise her. And yet, in his blundering way, he was trying to reach out to her, offer her some relief. She rubbed her shoulder where he had clasped it. Tom had not shown her even that much affection in the last twelve months – longer probably; she had forgotten when they had last lain in the same bed.

If she felt uncomfortable making ordinary conversation

with the vicar, she could hardly kneel down and pray with him. In any case, she would have felt a hypocrite: if God did exist, which she very much doubted, He had long since vacated these premises. Like Tom, He had withdrawn, folding himself within a fog of reticence which no communication of hers could pierce.

One of Mr Brickhill's first sermons had been on the theme of God's ordinariness, for according to him God was to be sought and found in the most mundane place and, by the same token, in the most ordinary hearts. 'God,' he explained in his inimitable fashion, 'is not a snob. He is just as much at home among the cobwebs in some humble cottage as He is among the portraits and porcelain of a big country house.' This proposition had given great offence to the majority of his congregation, ladies who themselves lived in humble cottages and resented this slur on their standards of housework. But Georgina was outraged for different reasons. Mr Brickhill's God, his Ordinary Bloke who knocked on cottage doors like a tradesman, no doubt accompanied by Jesus, His Lad, was her idea of anathema. Ordinariness was a prison she had come to hate. She hungered for a God who would release her from ordinariness and transport her to His house of many mansions where presumably cobwebs were unknown among the jasper and gold.

She sat down and put her head in her hands, staring down at the tattered hassock by her feet. Grey stuffing extruded from its perished seams and its tapestry design was worn colourless and threadbare. She knew this place too well and it possessed no mystery for her. She knew that behind its black curtain the sacristy was cluttered with floor mops, brushes, candle stumps, tins of dried-up polish, cloths torn from the frayed remains of Mr Simpkins' underwear, oil for the lawnmower, old parish newsletters and spare hymn books which the mice were eating. She knew that the church's vacuum cleaner, which belched more dust than it consumed, lay like a discredited relic in the iron-bound treasure box behind the font. She knew that the old oak benches, so admired in all the guide books, were impossible to clean properly because polish gathered and hardened in the clefts and gaps of their carving. She knew that beneath its white damask cloth the altar table was riddled with woodworm. And now she knew that she hated being God's housewife.

The arm of the bench she sat on had been carved in the shape of a bird perched on the rim of a crudely shaped nest, its neck bent in a hoop, its long pointed beak stabbing its own breast. According to Mr Simpkins, this was the medieval idea of a pelican, and it was a symbol of Christ's Passion. The story was that the bird killed its fledglings in a fit of irritation with their constant demands, but then relented after three days and brought them back to life by tearing open its own breast so the blood flowed onto them. It was the story of Man's Fall and Redemption and Mr Simpkins never tired of showing the bird to visitors and telling them its gruesome legend.

But to Georgina the pelican was a symbol of motherhood, a symbol in fact of her own lot. There were three chicks in the nest, their necks stretched up, their beaks gaping to receive the blood dripping from their mother's chest. The blood was represented by two large knobs of wood which seemed to ooze from a long, open gash cut across the feathers. Georgina had polished this treasure many times, bringing a mellow shine to the lips of the wound and making the globules of blood glow like black pearls. She laid her finger inside the wound now, feeling its ragged centre between the smooth edges. The wound of Christ. The open, unhealable wound all mothers bore. Those three chicks were hers, and the biggest and greediest was Tom himself; he had sucked her heart's blood, bleeding her white, and yet his beak still yawned, insatiable, unthankful and sharp-toothed. She had given milk gladly to her children, to Rose and Oliver, but Tom had drunk her very blood. No Fall, no Redemption, only his spear of a beak forever pecking at her breast. But now he too had fled the nest, leaving her to sponge away the blood herself.

She unscrewed the brandy bottle and put it to her lips. The

unfamilaiar spirit burnt her mouth and tore her throat. She took another, smaller gulp and felt its warmth penetrating her innards.

Like Martha in the bible, she had been too harassed by chores to listen to God, and now He had departed. She could never have thrown duty to the winds, as Martha's sister had done, and simply sat at Jesus's feet, indifferent to the efforts of others, careless of the food that had to be cooked and the tables that had to be laid. Instead she had scrubbed and polished and brushed this church so thoroughly she had cleaned out God Himself. And at home she had driven away that other god, her husband.

She stood up and looked around her angrily. She hated these lumbering, blackened benches. She hated the musty, dank smell that never left the place no matter how many flowers were put out. She hated the flowers too, pathetic blobs of colour that only made the stone feel colder, the light seem gloomier. She hated the stupid saints in their windows, staring down on her so complacently from their resurrection.

Georgina took a sip from her bottle.

And there was Mary in the south aisle window opposite, grinning like an idiot at her baby, as fresh and radiant as an ad for washing powder. How many hours did her labour last? Was that night of stars and angels and shepherds split with her screaming, or did she bite out the side of her cheek trying not to scream, as Georgina did with Rose. Or perhaps she cried out to God – who, after all, was responsible in more ways than one – begging Him to take away the pain. And who delivered the Babe? Did Joseph call out the Bethlehem midwife, and did she demand water and rags from the Inn? Who cut the cord? Joseph? With his carpenter's knife? Did her milk come at once, or did the baby gnaw and scream and twist in hunger like Ollie because her raw nipples were dry for the first day? These things were never mentioned in the Christmas story. Did Mary wash His nappies and wipe the holy Bottom? They never showed that in pictures, far less stained glass windows. And Joseph – surely he was jealous, the kid wasn't even his. Did he ever smack his step-son, or did he just ignore Him, as Tom ignored Ollie?

Mary had been chosen to be the mother of God. *Lucky her*! She had been given a divine mission and all she had to do was fulfil it, passively, gracefully, with dignity. Once, Georgina had thought she knew her mission, which was to rescue Tom from his father's extravagance and be the thriftiest – the 'seemliest' wife in Suffolk. For Tom's sake, she had turned herself into a miser. She had done it willingly – not gracefully, but willingly – for she was confident that every penny saved would be another penny's worth of love for her. What a joke! She had only been robbing herself. Far from loving her, Tom was repelled by her tightfistedness. She knew that now.

Mary was the wife of a carpenter, but she was always shown in lovely, luminous robes. Georgina was the wife of a large land-owner, and yet she wore clothes that were old, stained, patched and shapeless. Mary was beautiful, Georgina was ugly, but God had presumably made them both. Mary never had to nurse her demented father-in-law; nor was she less loved than pigs. No, Mary was adored and venerated, while Georgina was mocked and despised. Mary, for all her anguish beneath the cross, was never alone; but Georgina had been pushed aside by her husband and deprived of her son. Now she had been abandoned by God.

Raising her hand above her head in a fist, she smashed it down on the nativity, destroying the stable and scattering the Holy Family. She pulled her vase off the window sill and hurled it onto the tableau where it broke, sluicing water and leaves and berries over the cardboard and straw. The Infant Jesus fell to the floor and cracked its head open on the flagstone. She left it there.

With her bottle under her arm she marched down the nave and switched the gas fires onto full power.

Seven

Mary took her time getting dressed, lingering behind the locked door of the bathroom in order to compose herself. Christmas Day was not the occasion to fight a marital duel, and anyway she had too much pride to expose her private conflicts to the scrutiny of the family. The thought of giving Georgina the chance to gloat was unendurable.

On the other hand, her anger with Michael forced her to confront the question of last night's overheard telephone call. Georgina had been out of the house at the time, Oliver had been asleep in bed, and it seemed that Tom, who anyway had a notorious aversion to the phone, had ceased to communicate with the outside world by any medium. Which left Michael. But if Michael had been making a clandestine call there was only one conclusion to draw. Who does one telephone surreptitiously at midnight, out of the wife's hearing, at the first opportunity of privacy, except another woman?

Michael had always been an inveterate flirt but not, as far as she knew, a philanderer. He was one of those men who automatically radiated an extra wattage of charm in the presence of women. Let a woman enter the room, any woman, no matter how old, ugly or unavailable, and he immediately glowed and twinkled for her benefit. It was a way of fingering the cloth with no intention to buy, of licking the spoon when he wasn't hungry. But lately, it was true, she had noticed that his casual, social encounters with women seemed to be electrified by a new urgency, a questing impatience. But an affair? No. Surely he was not capable of being so deceptive; nor was she so naive.

Yet that's what last night's furtive telephoning seemed to imply. An affair. Had a little mushroom of infidelity been

growing, unseen by her, in some lightless corner in the cellar of their marriage? And was the little fungus now beginning to seek out the light and invade the upper floors? No. She could not believe it. If in fact he was betraying her, it meant he was guilty of a monstrous dishonesty. It meant he could lie to her face, smiling at her and caressing her as he did so. She didn't think he could do that. It meant he had been turning their marriage into a farce, twisting yes into no, love into a mask, sex into a trick to avoid discovery. No. He couldn't be such a shit to her. It meant that she was only living with his shadow, while the real man sang and danced in another house, kissing another mouth. No.

She brushed her hair with vigorous, angry strokes. Well, there was only one way to find out the truth, and that was to ask him, and watch and listen for the slightest flicker of pretence.

As it happened, the object of these unhappy suspicions was at that very moment tiptoeing down the passage from the kitchen to the office, where the only telephone in the house was located. His attempt to phone Zara last night had proved abortive because the perverse girl had not been at home. He had to move quickly now to seize his second opportunity, which would probably be the last of the day, for he knew Zara well enough to know that if he did not do as she demanded the consequences would be dire.

He closed the office door, squeezing the latch slowly into place and challenging it with a terrible grimace to make a sound. The phone stood on the desk, next to the window. Muffling it with a corner of the curtain and standing well out of sight of the yard, he dialled the number Zara had given him for Christmas Day. Her mother's number she had told him, though these days he believed very little she said. She was an atrocious little liar.

The number connected and began to ring. He crouched in an agony of impatience, muttering, 'Come on, come on.' Mary might be down any moment. He would have to pretend he was ringing his aunt, or a colleague who was ill. The twofold pulse warbled in his ear half a dozen times. Finally, a voice drawled, 'Hello.'

'Hello,' he whispered.

'Hello!' the voice boomed. 'Who's that?'

'May I speak to Zara, please.'

'Who? Speak up. This is a very bad line.'

'Zara,' he hissed a fraction louder.

The phone rattled at the other end and he heard footsteps retreating. A longish silence ensued while he rocked to and fro, pressing the receiver painfully to his ear. Then nimbler footsteps clicked closer and closer.

'Hello?'

'It's me. Michael.'

'Michael. My hero. Is there something wrong with your voice? Have you caught a cold?'

'Of course not. I'm whispering.'

'Why? Aren't you alone?'

'Yes, but it isn't easy to phone in this house. I told you. Where were you last night? It doesn't matter. I'm just ringing to say Happy Christmas, as you asked. Now I've got to go.'

'Oh Michael,' she sighed, 'I miss you passionately.'

'I miss you too,' he said hastily. This was dreadful; he must rid himself of her as soon as possible. 'We'll see each other right after Christmas. I really have to go.'

'We were thinking of dropping in, perhaps on Boxing Day.'

'What?'

'My mother says she knows your part of Suffolk awfully well. She might even have met your father-in-law. Is his name John? She certainly remembers the village. Slaughterhouse isn't a name you forget easily, is it? Anyway, we vaguely thought we'd drive up tomorrow and pop in for tea.'

'Are you mad? You mustn't come here. Do you understand?'

'Don't you want to see me, Michael?'

'Yes – very much – but not here.'

'You could always say I was a colleague, or a client, or a long-lost cousin. You'll think of something. You always do because you're so clever, Michael.'

'Zara, you are not to come anywhere near here. You are not to set foot in Suffolk. Is that clear?'

He spoke in a suppressed bellow, through gritted teeth.

'You're not being very Christmassy. But never mind. We may not be able to come after all. My mother's got a bit of a cold, like you.'

'I haven't got a bloody cold,' he roared hoarsely.

'If I'm not allowed to see you, say something sexy to make me feel better. Say something dirty in your sexy whisper.'

'Don't be fucking stupid.'

'That's a start, I suppose. Look I'll help you. I'll tell you what I'm doing and you try to imagine you're here with me.' She adopted a husky whisper of her own. 'I'm sliding my hand . . .'

'For God's sake, Zara! Stop it. I can hear someone coming.'

'Well, it certainly isn't me.'

'I'm putting the phone down. Happy Christmas.'

'In that case, I will pay you a visit. I knew you were getting bored with me. See you tomorrow, darling.' A kissing noise squeaked down the line, which then went dead.

Like an actor in a bad film, he repeatedly banged the phone's switch hooks, shouting, 'Zara! Zara! Damn you!' in his loudest whisper, even though he knew full well she had long since cut their connection.

Now on his knees, he moaned into the indifferent mouthpiece, 'Oh, please, Zara, please.'

As he grovelled on Georgina's threadbare carpet he knew he was learning a lesson: where sex is concerned, intelligence, sophistication, good looks and a smooth tongue were no guarantees against folly. And when a proud man stoops to folly he must expect to look a fool. Michael felt exceedingly foolish, and he feared that his persecution at Zara's hands had only just begun.

His lamentations were suddenly interrupted by the sound

of creaking floorboards overhead. Mary was coming downstairs at last. He scuttled to the kitchen and seized a sprout.

Shortly afterwards Mary came in and he knew from her expression that the next few minutes were going to be uncomfortable. She had drawn her hair off her face and secured it at the back of her head in a perfectly moulded bun. She was wearing her glasses and a pair of heavy brogues. These were bad signs.

'Michael,' she said in her severest tones, 'there is something I must ask you.'

'Fire away.'

He looked her squarely in the face, his own features sculpted, not without considerable difficulty, in an expression of candid helpfulness.

'Did you speak to anyone on the phone last night, around midnight?'

'No.'

He was able to say this in perfect honesty, having failed to get through to Zara, and he pushed his luck a little further by adopting a look of mild puzzlement. Within, however, he was bracing himself to field the question that would inevitably follow. And, indeed, Mary's lips were in the act of shaping the first unassured syllable of her enquiry into Michael's feelings for her when Georgina lurched into the kitchen.

She unbuttoned her coat with a violent ripping movement and threw it in the direction of a chair. It fell on the floor with a dull clunk and the brandy bottle rolled out of its pocket.

'Have you put the turkey in the oven?' she demanded of Michael.

'Yes. Ten minutes ago. Was that too early? I wasn't sure when you wanted us to eat.'

'Show me.'

He went to the Aga, pulled out the blackened roasting tray and presented the still white bird for her inspection.

'What do you think this is? A workhouse?' she shouted at him. 'We're not paupers, you know. Nor misers. Today is Christmas Day, in case you hadn't noticed. Where are the sausages? There are no sausages on that bird.'

Michael pointed an uncomprehending finger at the fridge. 'You told me not to use them.'

'This is not a workhouse, Michael,' she barked at him, punitively. 'We country people know how to enjoy ourselves, even if you don't. We know how to lay on a good spread. We have a tradition of hospitality here in Suffolk.'

She strode to the fridge and pulled out the bag of sausages and bacon, throwing them in handfuls of sticky pink meat onto the turkey. Small pieces of paper bag clung to the bacon rashers.

'What are you two staring at? Haven't you ever seen a proper Christmas lunch being prepared before?'

'Are you all right, Georgie? Has anything happened?' Mary asked in an astonished voice.

'Don't patronise me. Of course, I'm all right. Never better. Now, out of my kitchen; I've got work to do.'

Like dismissed children, Mary and Michael slunk from the room, involuntarily finding themselves in the scullery. Wordlessly, they put on their coats and boots and walked into the yard.

'What has come over her?' Mary said, laughing. 'Suffolk hospitality indeed! That's a contradiction in terms if ever I heard one, and she's always been the most tightfisted of the lot.'

'She's drunk,' Michael told her. 'It's as simple as that.'

Here was his opportunity, and he did not waste it. Taking her arm and putting it through his own, he guided her across the quagmire, and as they picked their way between the potholes and mud ruts left by tractor tyres he narrated in his most animated, amusing manner the story of Georgina, the brandy bottle, the sausages and potatoes. He kept her engaged while they circled behind the pig houses – still no sign of Tom – and walked down the path that led to the spinney a mile away. Many Christmases ago, Mary's father and grandfather used to shoot in the early mornings, bagging a few pigeons and maybe a wild partridge to bring back to the house for cold suppers on Boxing Day. The path ran beside a paddock at the back of the farrowing house, and they stopped at the far end, leaning on the fence and looking back over the farm.

Standing immediately in front of them, surrounded by a wet porridge of mud and dung, was a ramshackle shed made of breeze blocks with a couple of sheets of rusting corrugated iron for a roof. This was a temporary home for sows which had just been separated from their litters and were gathering strength for their next farrowing. Mary and Michael's appearance at the fence attracted the interest of a large, mud-encrusted matron who squelched her way to the fence, grunting and blowing with curiosity. As she moved, her twin banks of teats swung below her sagging belly in majestic syncopation. Her reddened udders were still a little swollen with unwanted milk, while her teats were rubbery and stretched. She pushed her snout under the lowest bar of the fence, snuffing at their boots with her wet, sawn-off trunk, which had been pierced with a trio of punkish metal rings. Michael picked up a stick and scratched her scaly, bristled back. Her skin had the consistency of tree bark, but she seemed to derive pleasure from his raking strokes. Then, snorting and flapping her ears, she ambled to the shed and propped her considerable bulk onto one of its corners. With a limber roll of her hips, she shimmied her flank against the crumbling breeze block, scraping and rubbing her horny skin. Mary and Michael were presented with her oscillating buttocks and a close view of her battered, protruding vagina.

'That's what you think I'm going to look like if I have a baby, don't you?'

'Don't be absurd,' said Michael, appalled.

'Yes you do,' she insisted.

Michael was now in a jam. He did not want to return to the dreaded baby debate, but nor did he want Mary to press him any further on the subject of last night's telephone call. If Zara really was going to descend on him tomorrow, he had less than twenty-four hours to repair relations with Mary and build up sufficient trust to withstand Zara's poisoned barbs. He put his arm round Mary's shoulders, hugging her affectionately, and led her away from the sow, which was now relieving itself in a seemingly ceaseless gush of frothing urine.

'I just don't think I would make a very good father,' he said, inspiration suddenly striking him. 'I never hit it off with my own father, as you know. He was abroad all the time, then they sent me away to school and, well, frankly I don't think he liked me much.'

'But that's the point,' said Mary, turning to him and speaking with vehement intensity. 'We must break these sterile old patterns and make new opportunities of our own. Look at this farm.' She swept the horizon with her arm. 'This is my father's landscape. He built the place up and turned it into his idea of a modern farm. It made him rich and gave him satisfaction, but it's killing Tom because he can't create his own landscape.'

'Don't get cross, but I still think Liz is behind all this. If she hadn't died, you wouldn't want to have a child so badly. You'll get over her, but it would be crazy meanwhile to bring a new life into the world as a way of replacing hers. After all, that would hardly be fair on the baby.'

'No, it wouldn't. But in the end, new life's the only weapon we've got. Liz did a dreadful thing and it should die with her. For me, having a baby would be a way of defying the things that defeated her.'

'I don't really see how.'

'I still don't understand why Liz did it, or why she did it that way. Of course she was neurotic. You're right. But I've been trying to credit her with a rational motive as well as a neurotic one. I believe she was making a symbolic gesture. She was saying there's too much suffering in the world for books to make any difference. That's how I interpret her note.'

Mary sighed and stared up into the sky's grey blanket, struggling to control her tears.

'But that's not an argument for having a child. If anything, it's an argument for not having one.'

'Only if you accept her vision of the world. But I don't. Books and politics and ideas aren't the only ways of being creative. I mean, you've got to stand up for justice and all the things Liz felt so deeply about, but there are other other principles. Love and so on. You've got to have . . .'

She shrugged as her voice trailed off. She was crying. She shrugged again, wordlessly, and made a miserable gesture with her hands.

Michael looked at her helplessly. He had no means of consoling her.

They walked on in silence. The track took them along the perimeter of one of the farm's largest fields, an expanse of land which in her childhood Mary remembered being a mosaic of meadows, patches of woodland and small fields. Now it was a featureless tract of more than thirty acres, demarcated by rectilinear ditches with bald banks. Spring barley, planted in faultlessly regular lines, was beginning to put a green blush on the earth's brown corduroy.

'What on earth are those?' Michael said, stopping abruptly.

He pointed to the centre of the field where they could make out hundreds, perhaps thousands of some species of bird covering the ground like a pestilence. Each bird seemed to stand alone in the crowd, motionlessly studying the soil at its feet and shunning its myriad neighbours.

'They're peewits,' Mary told him. 'Can you see, they have little curved crests on the top of their heads that look like surgeons' needles?'

Suddenly, she clapped her hands violently and shouted, 'Bugger off' at the top of her voice.

Every creature took to the air at once, and the whole field seemed to rise as a solid crust. The flock wheeled and climbed in a huge revolving cloud, its rim fraying while it rolled, the skirr of feathers audible above the wind. With their round black wings and white underparts, the birds resembled a flight of living flints. The cloud gradually scattered in the grey sky, then gathered itself up again, and swirled in a cautious, sweeping circle until, bird by bird, the entire flock had returned to the soil and its teeming solitude.

'Look,' Mary said, 'it hasn't made any difference. After all that upheaval they settle back as if nothing had happened.'

She clapped and shouted again, but this time she only disturbed a few birds at the outer edge, which lifted in a curling eddy and dropped back.

They followed the track to the corner of the field and then broke away, taking a footpath back to the farmyard.

'This place is falling apart,' Mary said as they approached the back of the weaner shed, whose weather boarding was patched with tattered plastic sacks. 'Maybe we should sell up and be rid of it.'

'You couldn't! This is your home!'

'No. It's Dad's home. Poor Tom; he never stood a chance.'

She drew him into a corner of the building out of the wind and gripped the lapels of his overcoat.

'Michael,' she said, 'I love you. Please try to listen to me. Ever since Liz died – killed herself – I've been trying to extract something positive from it. You can't get more negative than committing suicide, but if the people left behind don't work for the opposite then every suicide claims more than one victim, if you see what I mean.'

He was pulling away from her, but she tightened her hold on his coat.

'You say you wouldn't make a good father. But that's like killing off a part of you before it's had a chance to grow. It's like a small suicide.'

She stroked his face. 'Don't look so scared.'

Michael lit a cigarette with a hand that was being made to shake by more than the cold wind.

'I must know that you love me, Michael.'

'I do,' he confirmed, glad to be able to say something simple that would not invite interrogation. 'I really do.'

She smiled and to his relief did not press him on the subject of fatherhood.

'I don't want to go back to the house yet. Let's go in

there,' she said, pointing to the farrowing house. 'It should be warmer than out here.'

They skirted the yard and pushed back the heavy sliding door. Inside, the building smelt of meal and straw dust. From one of the pens near the door came the noise of scampering and squealing as a litter romped round its prone dam.

'I'm sorry to confront you with so many icons of maternalism,' she said, waving at the rows of sows and laughing.

It was his turn to smile. Still feeling himself to be under an obligation to respond to her speech, but not knowing how to do so, he resorted to a less compromising expedient. He kissed her. She surprised him by reciprocating instantly, as if she had been waiting for him, pressing her body passionately against his through the double thickness of their coats.

'I thought I'd lost you,' she said.

'Never.'

'Let's go in here.' She opened the door to one of the empty pens. It was knee-deep in freshly forked bedding. Hitching the heater lamp a couple of feet above the straw, she turned it on and the outsize bulb immediately began to radiate warmth. She lay beneath it and unzipped her coat.

'It's getting hot.' She patted the straw beside her, invitingly.

'Someone will come.'

'You and me, with any luck,' she said, using a joke that seemed to have become the leitmotif of his morning.

She pulled off her sweater and reassured him. 'Now they've finished feeding, no one'll be in here till this afternoon. You're quite safe.'

She was all but naked now, glowing pink under the lamp.

'I love you, Michael.' She opened her arms for him.

He was sure she would not trick him into conceiving a child; he could trust her to take her pill as usual. Yet he also knew that if he joined her in the straw, made love with her, he would be saying yes to everything she had offered outside. She was asking him to endorse the principle of their having a child together. If he lay down with her, their Christmas child,

174

though no more than an idea, would be born today, here in this stable among the beasts. If he refused her, he would be killing their Christ-child, for Christmas would never come again for them. He knew that too.

He stared at her splayed body, and saw a stranger, the nameless woman he had always had sex with, a creature, a thing of parts – breasts, lips, patches of hair, legs, bones, red skin. Blood throbbed in his head. But then Mary reached up and pulled him into the straw beside her, and, perhaps for the first time, he stopped looking and closed his eyes, simply feeling her warmth.

Eight

As soon as Gregory heard his mother's tinkling halloo, he sprang out of bed, decency restored in a trice, and pulled on his sweater and trousers as he tumbled down the stairs to greet her.

Gregory had not inherited his great height from either parent. His late father's stature had been as modest as his achievements, while his mother, Irene, in her youth had been admired, not to say yearned after, for the sake of her rounded petiteness. From this union of miniatures had sprung the beanstalk Gregory, and because she and her husband were both so small his mother attributed her son's unfurling loftiness to genius rather than genes. Gregory, in her eyes, was a self-made phenomenon: he had willed himself to his astonishing altitude and every time she scanned his summit, craning her neck at an ever-steeper angle, she tingled with pride. Viewing him on Christmas morning she marvelled again at the sheer length of him, and on looking closer at his haggard attenuation she wondered if he had not improved himself lately by yet another half inch.

Jack-knifing at the hips, Gregory swooped down to kiss her upturned face.

'Merry Christmas, darling. You're looking as elegant as usual.' She removed her hat and gloves, and arranged herself daintily on a sofa, announcing she had something most important to confide. But before she could do so, Gregory himself began to talk, vociferating with his usual intensity and complete lack of coherence. His height notwithstanding, Gregory had inherited this quality from his father and Irene knew from long experience that she had no choice but to sit out the monsoon of his oratory. She lit a cigarette, fiddled with a ring beneath her glove and tried idly to pick out the odd intelligible phrase.

By the time Gregory's outpouring finally slackened she had formed the impression that her magnate-son was now so rich he could afford to dedicate himself exclusively to charitable works for the benefit of people with one eye. Or was it one lung? In any case, it was noble; it was splendid. Naturally, she was thrilled for him, and she said as much. She was effusive with her congratulations and though they did not seem to strike quite the right note, he looked pleased all the same.

Relieved that the crisis was behind them, they fell to chattering of other things with the same perfect absence of communication. Rose, now dressed, joined them and all three spoke gaily in repetitive unison as if performing an operatic trio. Gregory reminded Rose that he could eat a horse, whereupon Irene, forgetting her own news, took command of the kitchen and soon had the cottage reeking with the smell of frying bacon and burnt toast.

When a suitable moment occurred, Rose absented herself, quietly closing the front door as Irene and Gregory waxed indignant about the vulgarisation of Christmas. 'I don't know what the world's coming to,' Irene was saying, and Gregory, who did, was about to tell her.

Glad to have the noise of her mother-in-law's voice out of her ears, Rose walked up the empty village street and cut through the churchyard into the garden. Once in the Manor's steaming kitchen she was no less astonished than Mary to see the truly epic quantities of food her mother was preparing. The turkey could be heard sizzling and spitting in the oven, but Georgina had decided to augment it with a cooked ham she had been keeping back for Boxing Day. Her eyes gleamed with recklessness as she plastered the pink meat with a thick, dribbling layer of yellow honey and stabbed a hedgehog's coat of clove nails into the goo.

'What are you gawping at?' she barked at Rose, forgetting to wish her daughter a happy Christmas, or any kind of

Christmas. 'If you're going to stay, make yourself useful. Otherwise, I suggest you keep away until lunchtime.'

'All this food, Mum. What's come over you? I thought it was only the usual gang for lunch.'

'It is. But for once I'm going to go the whole hog and your father can like it or lump it.'

She scraped the last of the honey out of its pot and dolloped it onto the ham.

'What do you think about apricots?' she said, consulting her cookbook with a gummy finger. 'Well, why not?' She sluiced an entire can of apricots, juice and all, over the ham and honey.

'That should do the trick,' she said, and wrapped the whole sticky chunk into a tinfoil parcel.

'How's Grandpa?' Rose asked, continuing to watch her mother in amazement. 'Can I see him?'

'Don't disturb him. He's asleep and he needs all his strength for this afternoon. He's determined to come down to eat.'

'Where's Dad?'

'Your guess is as good as mine. Better probably. He can be in Timbuctoo for all I care. Only he'd better be back for lunch.'

Rose was still more amazed by what she was hearing than what she was seeing. In all the years of her childhood and adolescence she had never heard her mother speak so mutinously, so slightingly of her father. She had heard her argue with him, even abuse him, but this was the first time she had heard her speak contemptuously of him behind his back. Whatever Georgina's complaints of him, whatever injustices she groaned under because of him, she had always deferred to him as the boss, the king of their little state.

'What's happened? Have you two had a row or something?'

'Nothing of the sort,' replied Georgina haughtily. 'I have simply resigned my job as the family miser. In fact, I have appointed myself family spendthrift.'

She reopened her foil parcel to hurl in a few shots of brandy.

'I don't suppose you've noticed, but your father is letting this place go to rack and ruin. Well, if he won't keep his side of the bargain, I'm not going to keep mine.'

Rose sighed with irritation. 'Come off it, Mum. You sound like Grandpa.'

Georgina threw open her cupboard door and surveyed its shelves.

'Still,' she said, absently putting the bottle to her lips, 'at least we can have one last almighty beanfeast before they cart us off to debtors' prison. And if you think I'm exaggerating,' she added, turning fiercely on Rose, 'ask that father of yours – when you find him – how he thinks he's going to pay for those buildings out there to be repaired. Have you seen the state of them? I'm amazed this wind hasn't brought the whole lot down.'

With a terrible clang of metal she thrust the ham into the Aga's second oven.

'I'll come back later and help you lay the table,' Rose said, at the door. 'And Mum, please don't make me sit next to Uncle Basil.'

'He will sit where he always sits, between you and Mary. This silly joke about Basil is most distasteful.'

Rose growled in frustration and left.

Walking as briskly as she could against the wind, she crossed the garden again and took the track leading up to the meadow which overlooked the house. This was known as Queen's Piece and it stood in the lee of a dense wood called the Spanish Thicks. According to her grandfather, who was however far more fanciful than reliable in such matters, the Thicks was a piece of ancient woodland which in medieval times had been managed by monks and later had furnished oaks to repel the Spanish Armada – hence its name. Rose had always relished this little legend, and she thought with affection and concern about her grandfather as she tramped up the meadow's slight incline.

Rose was a simple girl – not a simpleton by any means, but a girl of simple insights, simple ambitions and simple loyalties, to which she clung with a simple obstinacy she had inherited from her mother. One of those insights concerned Georgina. At a certain moment in her late adolescence, a year or two ago, she had looked up from the breakfast table and realised that her mother, who was chasing round the dining room as if pursued by an invisible cattle prod, was not behaving naturally. On thinking about it, she came to understand that Georgina's rules and obsessions, her budgets and systems, were not inborn features of her character, they were the consequences of a life passed in disappointment and thwarted love. She saw that her mother had adopted these habits as a strategem to secure her father's love, and that it had failed. She began to see the woman behind, or rather within, the parent, and it is not every child who makes this elementary distinction.

Up in her room, while studying for her A-level English, she had tried to illustrate the geometry of love within her family by means of triangles and quadrilaterals, an idea she took from a short story. However, she could not devise diagrams complex enough to do the job, so she settled for verbal formulae instead, copying them with sacramental formality into her diary.

The first two read as follows:

Georgina loves Tom more than he loves her; G. loves Tom more than she loves either Rose or Oliver, though she loves O. more than R.

Tom loves Rose more than he loves G. or O.

Thus, she taught herself one of life's most problematic truths: love is not evenly or fairly distributed; love is not always returned as warmly as it is given; nor is it necessarily bestowed where it is most deserved. But this was a lesson she already knew, and had always known, otherwise she would not have spelt it out so explicitly. As her father's favourite, she could afford to view this asymmetry of love with a certain complacency. On the other hand, her sense of justice, a tender organ, was distressed by her father's partiality. She, Rose, had done nothing and was adored without reservation, yet Georgina, who had done everything, was spurned. Once she had recognised that Georgina's cheese-paring was not intended for her persecution, she began to pity her mother, a condescension which was enhanced by the knowledge that while she was ripening into a pretty, desirable woman, Georgina, her lumbering, frantic, unhappy mother, was corroding into an ever uglier one. Rose rejoiced in being her father's favourite – he was the rock on which her simple life was built – but in her new-found sympathy for Georgina she tried to encourage her in little acts of defiance and rebellion against Tom. She even entertained the fantasy that her queenly benevolence would at last unite her parents in conjugal devotion. This did not happen. On the contrary, Georgina was infuriated by what she took to be Rose's bolshiness and lack of respect. Family relations deteriorated all round: mother and daughter strove to avoid each other, while husband and wife were still further divided. And Oliver was the universal loser.

Then along came Gregory, good old Gregory, and provided Rose with the perfect means of escape. By marrying him and staying in Slaughterhouse she could leave the Manor but continue to see her father on the farm. Contrary to popular belief, it is quite possible, as Rose proved, to live in a small community and still have nothing to do with your neighbour.

During its first few months her marriage had been blessed with many of the gifts that make for happiness, and it was only as autumn was giving way to winter that Rose noticed her father had declined into a blacker melancholy than was usual with him. Being his daughter, she automatically blamed herself for this development.

Never a vociferous man, Tom had sunk into a monosyllabic gloom, from which even Rose could not rescue him. His terse utterances had acquired a new note of spleen, and all his movements had become violent. His handsome face, of which Rose's was a small and lovely replica, was permanently cast in an expression of baleful hostility. He seemed to hold everyone in contempt, and one of the few words he used with obvious relish was 'fool'. There were fools everywhere and their favourite occupation was to visit him and persecute him with their foolishness. Drivers, reps, milkmen, postmen, vets, tradesmen were all fools, to a man. As for politicians, they were not merely fools but bloody fools, and so were news-readers, sports reporters, weathermen and indeed everybody in public life. Fools, the lot of them. The only exceptions were his family, on whom he passed no comment whatsoever. Even Gregory, a champion fool in any father-in-law's eyes, was never censured. But it was Rose alone who could soften him, coax him into talking a little, and she was horrified to find that on the few occasions when he dropped his misanthropic mask the face beneath was harrowed with a look of desperate sadness.

At weekends or sometimes in the evenings before Gregory came home, she would join Tom in his hide-out at the back of the weening house where the medicines were kept, and try to comfort him and uncover an explanation for his depression. Her efforts invariably met with surly resistance. She resorted instead to gossiping about her own small pleasures and anxieties, and it seemed to soothe him. Then Gregory had begun what she feared was his gradual desertion, emptying their cottage of his possessions. This could not be confided in her father, whose vengeance would have been sudden and bloody. And so, as the December nights grew colder and longer, the two of them had fallen into the habit of sitting silently for an hour or more, each sunk in an incommunicable misery, he sipping whisky, she smoking innumerable cigarettes.

But today was Christmas. A day of joy and celebration. She had not lost Gregory, after all, and he had lost no more than his job, a problem which to her simple way of thinking had the eminent virtue of pointing to its own solution – the getting of another job. In that matter her father would surely be helpful. She had decided not to tell him about Gregory's state of mind; she would merely indicate that he was unwell, not himself, that the strain of the last few weeks was making him act a little strangely. Privately, she reassured herself with the hope that rest, plenty of food and the prospect of a new job would cure him and restore the old Gregory to her. She would ask her father to use his influence and find him work closer to home, in Colchester perhaps, or better still in Ipswich, in a nice, safe office. If he worked in Ipswich, they could have lunch together.

She stood for a moment and looked down towards the village, picking out her own roof with its black and brick-coloured pantiles. She traced the line of the Crow flowing from west to east and cutting through the village like the life line on the palm of a hand. And, indeed, the river did trace the line of Rose's life, for it too sprang into existence just outside the village, oozing from the spongy pores of Strangeways Fen and swelling into a rill that took its first tinkling steps in a ditch at the edge of her father's largest meadow – Crow meadow. Not far away, in the next-door parish, it merged with the Gipping, which in turn flowed into the Orwell, and together these parochial waters made their way across the county towards the coast, their course followed by the A45, the very road Rose travelled every day as she drove to work. From her office above the Ipswich docks she could watch the brown, turbid river pouring the last of its fresh life into the grey salt of the estuary. The sea was as foreign as the grave to her: she had never crossed it and had no desire to do so.

She walked along the track which took her round the edge of the Spanish Thicks and put the village and then the Manor out of sight. Stepping over a stile, she came into a second meadow, prosaically named Upper Meadow, whose scant grass was dotted with the rotund figures of her father's pregnant ewes, all Suffolks with white bodies and black heads. A trailer, piled high with rolls of wire, stakes and wooden hurdles, stood beside a stack of straw bales. In a week or so her father would use these to construct a small village of his own, a maternity village, comprising a delivery yard where the ewes would await the term of their pregnancy, and a street of back-to-back pens, roofed with straw, where the new mothers could feed and bond with their lambs. Like any other well-organised community, it would be equipped with running water and power, the electricity giving light to the strings of bulbs running up and down its single street and round its compound. For three weeks her father would take up monastic residence in the shepherd's hut on wheels that had been dragged for shelter against the edge of the wood. A thin coil of smoke threading from its tin chimney confirmed her guess that her father had already retreated to this, the most remote of his hide-outs.

Unusually, the door of the hut, which consisted of two halves, like a stable door, was closed top and bottom. Before putting her foot on the lowest of the four little wooden steps that led to its threshold, Rose hesitated, suddenly overtaken by an apprehension of tragedy, a sense of something terrible hanging over the hut.

Terrified, she listened at the door but the wind, thrashing in the ash trees and cracking their long branches like whips, stopped her hearing anything within. Why were the doors shut? Where was her father and what was he doing? Where were his dogs? She looked round the field hoping in vain to see him among the white shapes of the sheep.

Pulling back from the steps, she walked in dread round the side of the hut. She stood on tiptoe to look into the window. Through the half-light she saw her father's head in profile, tipped back a little as he held the gleaming barrels of a shotgun to his forehead.

'Daddy! No! Daddy!' she screamed.

She ran to the door and tore it open.

'Merry Christmas, Rosy.'

His voice was sardonic, but hardly suicidal.

He peered once more down the barrels and snapped the breach shut.

'Don't worry, I'm not shooting myself. Not yet.'

He wiped the gun with a rag and hung it from a pair of hooks over the window lintel. A box of orange cartridges was scattered over the table.

'God, you gave me a shock.' She kissed him. 'Put those horrible things away.'

He scooped the cartridges into his coat pocket and offered

her the whisky bottle. She refused, asking for coffee. As he boiled the kettle on the stove, she lurched without preamble into her request for help on Gregory's behalf. He had been made redundant, not his fault at all, and he had tried, ever so hard for a whole month, to find another job, but jobs didn't grow on trees, not in the City, and now he was well and truly broke, with no prospect of finding one, and he looked so thin and ill, it worried her that he was going to have a breakdown or something, he was so *gaunt*; and so she wondered if he, Daddy, could use his influence, pull a few strings, and get him a place in the accounts department of a firm in Ipswich, where they could have lunch together, and she could see he was eating properly (and make sure he wasn't going off his head), something in a fertiliser company, or an agricultural machinery place, or a seed merchants maybe, and could he be very kind, dear Daddy, and stump up a bit of money, just to tide them over this difficult patch?

At the end of this breathless oratory, she looked at him pleadingly, but also with confidence, for never in her life had he refused her.

He gave her a mug of coffee and invited her to sit on the bunk while he stood by the window staring out at his flock, a glass of whisky in his hand. During the lambing period he slept in his clothes, using an old army greatcoat as a blanket, and over the years the bunk had acquired a pungent odour, which only ripened with each season. To Rose, however, its cocktail of smells was not altogether offensive: coke dust from the iron stove in the corner, whisky, disinfectant, sheep muck, lanolin, and other, bloodier sheep smells, and above all the smell of memory – the memory of as many lambings as she could recall.

'You must burn this coat, Dad. It really reeks.'

'What would your mother say? There's plenty of wear left in it.'

It was a ritualised joke between them, repeated every year, but this time Tom spoke his line in a resigned, empty tone as if there was no more humour to be wrung from it.

'I can't help you, Rosy. There's no money left, for you or anyone else. I'm finished.'

'What do you mean? That's what Mum said.'

'She doesn't know the half of it.'

'The half of what? Tell me.'

He looked at her, seeming to assess her strength.

'There's a new manager at the bank and he's given me three months to bring down the overdraft. The bloody fool!'

'What are you going to do?'

'Nothing. There's nothing I can do. It's too late.'

She joined him at the window.

'The ewes look well. If you get plenty of big lambs, won't that make a difference? You're always nervous the week before lambing, but things will look better when you've got all your pens up and the lambs start coming. You won't have time to worry then.'

'Listen,' he said angrily, 'if every one of those ewes produced triplets, and every sow produced twenty bloody piglets, and the harvest was the best since the war, we still wouldn't even meet the interest charges, never mind the capital. And anyway, the three months are up. He gave me until Christmas.'

'Grandpa says we should expand the pigs. He says it would make us rich.'

'Expand the pigs!' Tom shook his head wearily. 'That's what he's done all his life, and see where it's got us. Whenever he was in trouble he would dream up some new scheme and sweet-talk the bank into lending him more money. Not that they needed much persuading, those smooth bastards, because they had him sewn up. They knew that if the worse came to the worst they could sell the place and cover themselves. And now it's happened. They've given us the chop.'

'I can't believe it.' She lit a cigarette. He could tell she was frightened.

'I'm telling you, they've given us the chop. No cheques, no more overdraft, nothing. After all these years we're getting the chop. They give you all the rope you want so you can make a good job of hanging yourself. For the last three years we've been borrowing just to pay the interest. Now they've decided they can't bleed us any more so they're sending us to the knackers.'

'I can't believe it.' She pointed to the sheep again. 'All those lambs waiting to be born. They must be worth something. You're so good with the sheep.'

'You don't understand.'

He opened the door, took her by the arm and led her into the field. The nearest ewes lifted their heads to watch them without breaking the rhythm of their cud. Their bellies were as round as barrels and looked as solid.

'That's one of the best flocks we've ever had. In fact, it's one of the best in the county. Most of those ewes will have twins, and yet it'll be a bloody disaster because I won't be able to feed them. The more lambs they have, the more food they'll need, but I owe so much money to the feed suppliers they've shut my account.'

He kicked at the scrappy grass.

'This won't feed them. They need hay, but I can't afford that either.'

'Oh Dad.' She put her arm round his shoulders. 'What's going to happen?'

'I can't even afford to feed my fucking dogs. They'll have to be sold along with everything else.'

'But surely you're not going to sell the sheep. Or the pigs. What would you do?'

'Everything.'

'You mean the whole herd? Boars and all.'

'Rosy, I mean everything. Tractors, combine, machinery, pigs, sheep, dogs, shovels – the lot.'

'And the crops?'

'Certainly the crops. And the buildings. Down to the last shit house. The entire property will have to be sold, lock stock and barrel, if we're going to avoid bankruptcy.'

'But not the Manor. You won't have to sell the Manor?'

'I have to sell every piece of property I own. Every one. We'll have to take Ollie out of his school. At least that will please your mother.'

'But you can't sell her home over her head. I thought she'd put money into the farm. Doesn't that give her some rights?'

He shrugged. 'All the farm houses must be sold.'

'Have you told her?'

'Not yet. I thought I'd leave it until after Christmas. I didn't want to spoil her Christmas. Or yours.'

She shivered. 'It's cold. Let's go inside.'

Climbing the steps of the hut, she tried a little joke. 'You'll have to bring Mum to live here.' He didn't smile. 'It can't be as bad as you say, Dad. It can't be.'

'It's worse.'

'What do you mean?'

'Your cottage.'

He looked at her again, this time with shame in his eyes.

'The bank can't touch the cottage. It's ours. Or at any rate, it's mine. You gave it to me.'

He sat on the bunk and put his head in his hands.

'The bank wouldn't release the deeds when you got married. I didn't tell you. I was still hoping thing would improve. The bank want to put it on the market before the farm. They think it will fetch nearly as much as the Manor would.'

'It's only a little cottage. It's my home.' Despite her bravest efforts, she was crying now.

'I know, but the Manor needs a fortune spending on it, while your cottage is in perfect nick. It's a valuable property, Rosy. The bank want us to sell your cottage now to bring down the overdraft.'

'The bank! The bank! They can't treat us like this.'

'They can. We've no choice. They've got it all planned out. They're going to sell the farm with its crops in the spring and put some of the money into the Manor.' He sighed. 'It's going to be converted into maisonettes. Mum and I will live in one of them. With Grandpa, I suppose.'

He winced at the prospect.

'But where will we go? Gregory and me. Do we get a maisonette?'

'No. I thought you could live with Gregory's mother in Stowmarket. For a while. Until things pick up. See how Gregory feels.'

She sat beside him on the bunk. 'Oh Dad.' She wept.

For the first time in her life the clear flow of her mind was muddied and clogged with so many bad emotions she did not know what she felt. She felt betrayed by her father, her beloved father, the rock of her life, yet she pitied him as well: not only was he trapped in this wretched humiliation, but he had made himself keep the secret week after week. And of course she pitied her mother too. All that scrimping, mending, making-do, meter-watching, coupon-hoarding, all that self-denial and sacrifice, all that jumble-sale drabness had gone for nothing. Eviction and bankruptcy were her only rewards. But perhaps she would be happier in her maisonette.

As for herself, Rose was terrified. It seemed as if every anxiety of childhood had been gathered in a great cistern and someone was holding her head under the water. No house, no money, no husband – none that is to protect and keep her. And now no father.

'Don't cry,' he said. 'I can't take it.'

She wiped her eyes, blew her nose and lit a cigarette.

'I'm sorry. It's the shock. You know. I've had a lot of shocks lately. Gregory's been behaving very strangely – because of losing his job. I think he's ill.'

She took a sip of whisky from his glass, shaking her head at its sharpness.

He stood up, looking at his watch. 'We must go home. Don't say anything until this afternoon. I don't want to spoil Mum's lunch.'

He opened the door and whistled to his dogs. They sprinted from the bales and lay shivering on their bellies beside the wheels of the hut, their eyes fixed on him. Walking down the steps, he slipped drunkenly. Rose took his arm.

Nine

Ever since the death of her father Georgina had arranged for the Albion family to spend alternate Christmas Days in Norwich with her sister and brother-in-law, and every other year they were invited back to the Manor at Slaughterhouse. No one could have said just when or how this exchange had hardened into custom, but over the years a tradition had become consecrated and it was now as rigid as the date of Christmas itself.

From the start, however, the Norwich team had brought a far more inventive spirit to these celebrations than the Albions, who were of course restrained by Georgina's frugality. Her sister Helen added all sorts of small and inexpensive touches to the Manor's plain routine, most of them reproduced from their Cromer childhood and therefore irresistible to Georgina, but it was Uncle Basil Fanshawe, Helen's husband, who proved the most fertile source of festive innovation. Drawing on the memory of his own childhood, a seemingly mythical epoch set in some fabled corner of Norfolk, he appointed himself high priest of Christmas and slowly transformed the Albion Christmas lunch from a big meal into a baroque ceremonial whose every moment was prescribed by rituals that grew more elaborate with each year.

Basil it was who decreed that the family's presents should be distributed at precisely twelve o'clock, that lunch should commence no less precisely at one o'clock, and that the table should be cleared by three o'clock in order that the Queen's speech should receive the attention and reverence it merited. The presents, he directed, should be piled in an orderly but decorative heap round the tree in the drawing room and should be opened to the strains of King's College

190

choir singing carols (on record, naturally; even Basil did not demand the live choir). Finally he insisted on champagne being drunk throughout and would permit no exemptions; children, teetotallers and invalids alike were all required to swell the hilarity. With Basil the rule was, enjoy yourself – or else. And Georgina was powerless to defy him: every year, despite her sternest resolutions, she did indeed enjoy herself.

And so it was that as the hall clock gathered itself in a whirring of springs and levers to strike half past eleven the Fanshawes' sleek BMW pulled onto the gravel in front of the terrace. Basil's merry tattoo on the front door coincided precisely with the last note of the chime.

Mary, making sure that no straws still clung to her clothes, shouted to Michael, who shouted to Oliver, who ran to the kitchen to summon Georgina, and she hurried through to the hall. Bundling her apron into the umbrella stand, she readied herself and took up a formal pose of reception.

'Let them in,' she boomed at Michael. 'Open up the doors.'

With a fine ceremonious gesture he did as he was ordered, ushering in a howling gust of wind which whirled leaves and dust round the hall; and there in the eye of the maelstrom stood the beaming, rubicund Basil, hat aloft, short arms outflung.

'The merriest of Christmases to you, dear Georgie!'

He sprang forward, hugged her, kissed her, and hugged her again.

'I can see you are in the pink, the absolute pink. Wonderful to see you.'

Georgina was not merely pink, but carmine. Brandy and embarrassment, but mostly pleasure were making her blush, for nobody kissed and embraced her as Basil did, with the same palpable affection.

Behind him stepped her elegant, shy, self-effacing sister, whom Georgina, taking the initiative this time, kissed with happy delight. And behind them both, but tripping daintily with no hint of subordinacy, came their eight-year-old daughter, Alice. She had had the good fortune to inherit her mother's prettiness with her father's curling titian hair, and on her neat head it burned with a radiant glow, which a large emerald ribbon did nothing to damp down. Mary was painfully stuck by its resemblance to the burning bush that had crowned Liz's head. She wanted to put her hand on the child and warm her fingers in those innocent flames, exorcising the flames that had raged inside Liz's head.

'Mary!' said Basil, turning to her and opening his arms again. 'Merry Christmas, you stranger.'

He bore down on her, making the first move in a curious game of chess whereby Mary, without giving way to impoliteness, attempted to position herself so she could direct his impending kiss to the safety zone of her cheek, and whereby Basil, under cover of seasonal bonhomie, contrived to plant his lips squarely and juicily on her shrinking mouth. As usual he outmanoeuvred her with ease, mating her within a couple of moves and taking possession of her whole face with a deft, rapacious assault. Revolted, she scrubbed her lips with the back of her hand, and yet she did it covertly, not wanting anyone to witness her shame. Meanwhile Basil himself had turned to hail Michael.

'Mike!' he called out, 'Happy Christmas to you, old chap.'

He clapped him heartily on the shoulder, a man-to-man greeting from which Michael shrank in repulsion.

'Give me a hand with the fizz, there's a good fellow.'

He trotted back to the car followed by a smouldering Michael and threw open the boot to reveal a wooden box stamped with the name Dom Perignon.

'Nothing but the best for Georgie, the pauper of Slaughterhouse.'

He winked confidentially to Michael and handed him the box.

'Straight to the fridge, if you please. There's nothing worse, I always say, than luke-warm fizz. And stand them upright.'

From a plastic cool-box he extracted a separate bottle, which he held to his cheek for a moment.

'Perfect! As cold as a witch's tit. Isn't that the expression?'

The man was immune to embarrassment. Within a minute he was standing in the middle of the drawing room and lecturing Gregory on the correct method to open champagne in a stentorian voice that brooked no competition.

'A clean white cloth is of course indispensable,' he declared. 'The trick is to twist the bottle and hold the cork still. Don't ever force it out with your thumbs; that's how yobbos and racing drivers do it.'

Gripping the coy bottle between the vice of his knees, he inflicted a lethal wrench on its neck. The cork expelled itself with a modest pop and the wine gushed its frothing spasm tidily down the side of the glass held out by Gregory, his acolyte.

'And champagne must always be drunk from tall glasses like this. Flutes, as they are charmingly called.' He took the expiring glass from Gregory, holding it fastidiously by its foot. 'On no account must it be drunk from those nasty little flat dishes. I'm right, aren't I Mary?'

'Quite right, Basil,' she said archly. 'As always.'

'Ah Tom, there you are.'

And indeed, there he was, sidling into the room, unnoticed by everyone except the ever-vigilant Basil.

'Pour the drinks, Gregory. Let the revels begin. Happy Christmas to us all.' He held up his own glass, gallantly waiting for the others to be served before broaching his own bubbles with a complicated sniffing and slurping procedure.

'I don't know why I bring you this stuff,' he continued. 'It's coals to Newcastle. I'm not fooled, Georgie, by this down-and-out act of yours.' He put his flipper of an arm round her waist. 'I bet you and Tom guzzle champers every night when no one can see what you're up to. You farmers are all the same. You never stop whingeing about the weather and bad harvests, you go about dressed like scarecrows, but there's always a Range Rover tucked away in the garage. And all transactions are strictly cash only, aren't they Tom?'

'You don't know what you're talking about,' Tom muttered.

Rose stared at her father, wondering how he kept his temper, how he concealed his secret under this provocation. Yet his face was blank – the mask not of a man controlling his responses, but one which hooded emptiness. His face, she thought, was like the lid on an empty pot.

Basil had other fish to fry. Bumptious he may have been, obnoxious even, yet he did inject into the proceedings a much-needed brand of adrenalin. He was the life and soul of their hectic party, at once its host, ringmaster and chief entertainer, its sommelier, jester and most boisterous guest. Catching sight of Gregory, who had become immobilised beside Rose and was apparently hesitating to refuel her outstretched glass, he seized the bottle, filled Rose to the brim, and toured the rest of the room.

'Your attention please, ladies and gentlemen, lads and lassies,' he called out, and with his pen, an obese Mont Blanc, Mary observed, tapped the side of his glass. As its fluting notes died away they were answered by the mellow melody of the hall clock chiming midday.

'Now, does everyone have plenty of shampoo? Good, then I propose we reward the patience of certain small people by dispensing the presents. Shall I be Father Christmas?'

He settled himself in the chair placed for that purpose near the tree and propped a pair of half-moon glasses on his little rubber bung of a nose.

'Rose, my dear, will you make yourself responsible for the carols? No sticky fingers on the playing surface I beg of you. Our record is brand-new for the occasion. And you children, will you be my Mercury and Hermes?'

With a trembling hand Rose stabbed the stylus, which was original to the ancient Albion gramophone, into the surface of Basil's virgin vinyl and, after two gouging attempts, secured the second verse of 'Hark! The Herald Angels Sing'. Fortunately, these excruciations were buried beneath the cries of the children as they ran about the room, calling names out and delivering parcels – 'Aunty Helen from Uncle Michael!'

'Uncle Tom from Aunty Georgie!' 'Gregory with *love*, ugh, from Rose!' and so forth.

This frenzy of giving and receiving reduced Gregory to a state of glassy-eyed bliss and he hardly noticed that though he had not bought a single present he was being continually thanked. Rose had, of course, done his present-buying for him, but the prophet of Charity had transcended these dingy practicalities and was bathing in the pure, bright element of universal philanthropy.

The loudest shrieks of gratitude came from the children. Oliver's were more polite than sincere when he responded to Aunty Mary's leather-bound copy of *Ivanhoe*, but he needed no champagne to intoxicate him once he had opened his grandfather's 'special' present, which realised all his wildest hopes and broadest hints by proving to be an air rifle.

'O brill!' he gasped. 'Where's Grandpa? I've got to thank him.'

'I'll bring him down in a minute; he's going to eat with us. Don't use that language, Ollie dear. I suppose you've picked it up at school.'

Gregory was instructed to circulate once more with the bottle, Basil doled out the last few presents and Georgina left the room, signalling to Michael that he should join her in the kitchen. Ten minutes later he returned and announced that they were to take their seats in the dining room. As soon as they were ready, the turkey would be processed with full honours to the table.

The family straggled across the hall, only to gather in a bunch at the threshold of the dining room, craning over each other's shoulders to peer inside. As if rubbernecking in a stately home, they seemed to be restrained by an invisible silk rope slung across the doorway.

Georgina had ransacked the Manor's cupboards and chests, many of which had remained sealed since the death of Tom's mother a decade ago, and unearthed every piece of silver, glass and linen that could conceivably be used to decorate a banquet. The entire length of the table was crammed with candelabra, finger bowls, ash trays, cigar cutters, match holders, cruets, pepper mills, water jugs, sauce boats and salvers. Each place setting was stocked with an armoury of bone-handled cutlery and garrisoned with a platoon of glasses. Georgina had seen to it that there was nothing from snails to lobster, raw steak to knickerbocker glory, that her guests were not equipped to eat, nothing they could not crack, grind, wrench, tear, slice, winkle, chop, spread or scoop, and nothing they could not drink, from beer to Benedictine.

At one end of the table a pack of silver hounds snarled and strained to sink their teeth into a silver stag which stood, nobly defiant, among the bonbon dishes at the other end. Surmounting the whole crazy *mélange* was a huge Victorian fruit bowl, a ruby tazza, its swelling bowl cut with deep, slashing incisions, which appeared to bleed in a long red shadow.

'How many courses is she going to serve?' Helen asked in an awed tone.

'What's come over her,' demanded Basil, who was still hovering on the threshold, for even he was nonplussed by the extravaganza within. 'Have you come into money, Tom?'

Rose looked at her father, but he did not respond to the question, or show any sign of hearing it. He simply stared at the table, seemingly bewildered by the great heap of his possessions on display. She longed to say to him, surely all this stuff can be sold to pay off some of your debts? That grotesque stag, which she had never seen before in her life, appeared to be solid silver and must be worth a fortune on its own. She wanted him to smile, gasp with relief, begin to make amateur valuations; she wanted him to flash her a secret signal to indicate that their bacon was saved (what a phrase!) and they could still call their homes their own. But he said nothing and did not look her way.

Pushing through the crowd, Oliver was first into the room. He picked up a vicious-looking table instrument, gleaming with ratchets and springs. 'What's this for?' he asked.

'It's for tearing fingernails off inquisitive little boys,' said Basil humorously, his confidence restored. He shooed the others inside, and when they clustered nervously behind the door, not knowing where to sit, he despatched them to their places with the authority of a general disposing his troops. As Rose had feared, he reserved the seat between her and Mary for himself. 'A thorn twixt two roses,' he murmured in her ear, slyly laying his hot palm on her thigh as he took his chair.

'Quiet everyone, please,' he called out, studying his watch.

In the silence they heard the servile hall clock prepare to chime the hour, and all eyes turned expectantly on the door. At the precise stroke of one o'clock it swung open, but instead of making way for Georgina and her steaming trolley, it revealed old Mr Albion, who tottered across the threshold, his throat red and wet with blood.

Mary sprang from her chair. 'Oh Dad, no! You silly old fool,' she cried out, suddenly understanding the meaning of the 'arrangements' he had talked about yesterday.

'Michael, ring the doctor quickly. Give me your napkin.'

She pulled her father to a sofa by the wall, forcing him to lie down.

'I don't want to go to bed,' the old man protested. 'I've only just got up. I want my lunch. Where's Georgie?'

'It's all right, Mary,' Tom told her. 'He's only cut himself shaving. He can't see his face properly so he slashes it to ribbons. The nurse usually does the job for him.'

Mary cleaned his neck and cheek with a napkin dipped in water and found that beneath the smear of blood there were indeed only a few harmless nicks which were already beginning to clot. She kissed his other cheek. 'You frightened me, you daft old sod,' she told him.

'You frightened *me*,' he said with feeling, 'rushing about and screaming like that.'

At that moment Georgina appeared in the door, bending low as she put her weight behind the trolley. Loaded onto its top shelf was the turkey, its skin crisp and blistered, stuffing oozing juicily from its rear, and beside it was the ham, now cased in a carapace of blackened honey. Surrounding them were a dozen opened tins of sardines, tuna, pilchards, corned beef, luncheon meat and frankfurters, their jagged lids standing up in a row like a crest of scales along the tail of some primitive reptile. The shelf below was packed with vegetables: potatoes, roast, boiled, mashed and chipped; cauliflower with and without cheese sauce; carrots, diced, sliced and whole; peas, garden and mushy; beans, broad and runner; as well as parsnips, cabbage and courgettes. There was gravy, clear and thick; bread sauce; jelly, redcurrant and cranberry; mustard, English, French and German; there was tomato sauce, brown sauce, Worcestershire sauce, tabasco, pickle, piccalilli and chutney in three varieties. In addition, there was butter, marmalade and a rack of toast.

A stunned silence greeted the sight of this mobile cornucopia, but then the whole party rose to its feet and cheered Georgina's entrance. Tom clashed his carving knife against the steel, Michael assisted Georgina in parking her cumbersome vehicle, Mary began to pour the wine and Irene chirruped, 'Alleluia! Alleluia!'

'Grace, we must have grace,' shouted Basil, interrupting them. Everyone bowed his head, though more out of embarrassment than piety.

'Oh Lord,' intoned Basil unctuously, as if the Lord were in literal earshot, 'we thank Thee humbly for these Thy blessings' – he looked up for a moment at Georgina's mountain of blessings – 'for these Thy most bountiful blessings bestowed on us, Thy unworthy children, by your beneficent hand. And let us not forget as we consume our viands, so handsomely prepared by Thy handmaiden, Georgina,' (who made an indignant grunt) 'those whom in Thy wisdom Thou hast seen fit to favour on this day of days less abundantly than ourselves.'

A mumbled Amen sounded from the bowed heads round the table.

'Perhaps we should give our meal to someone else, said

Gregory, running to the window, apparently hoping to spy a hungry unfortunate in the park.

'Certainly not,' said Basil briskly. 'That would be a most patronising gesture. And anyway the food would be ruined by the time we found anyone truly deserving. It may be Christmas, but we are not living in Dickens's England, you know.'

Tom took up his knife once more and made a hacking gash in the turkey's breast.

'No, no, no,' cried Basil. 'You are not digging ditches now, Tom. Carving is an art and not to be confused with chopping logs.'

He took the knife from Tom and put an extra edge on its blade with a flurry of whipping passes against the steel.

'You farmers are used to serving yourselves half a bird each, but we ordinary folk' – he winked archly at Mary – 'have had to learn to economise.'

Assuming a professional stance, he deftly slit the brittle skin away from its breast and shaved off a slice of white meat that was as thin and perfectly formed as a leaf. His next slice was the very match of the first, as were the next three, and he laid them across the plate in the shape of a succulent fan.

'Now, whom am I serving first. You, Irene, have right of precedence, I think.' He bowed gallantly in her direction, and then took her through the entire catechism of choice relating to skin, wing, leg, onion, bacon, sausage and so on. Every single person round the table, children included, was treated to the same methodical interrogation, a procedure which allowed Basil to hog the centre of the stage throughout. Plate by plate, he handed Georgina a small masterpiece of proportion and colour. She, however, overrode these delicate preferences by smothering his artistry with heaps of vegetables and topping them off with dollops of corned beef or pilchard.

'Eat up, eat up,' she kept shouting. 'I don't want a scrap of this lot left over.'

As soon as Basil had served the whole table, she snatched

the knife from him and inflicted second helpings on every plate, ignoring all refusals and appeals for mercy. Empty glasses were an abomination to her, and she continually bellowed at Michael to fill them; then, as people felt the effects of claret on top of champagne and began to drink more slowly, full glasses became an abomination and she bellowed at everyone to drink up.

Despite her bullying, conversation round the table flourished. Swilling his claret with a carefree hand, Oliver described the male pig's anatomy to an incredulous Alice, using a silver corkscrew for graphic demonstration. 'And Carter says they squirt out pints of sperm,' he told her. Helen confided in Mary how difficult it was to buy a decent pair of shoes in Norwich. Michael, when not circling the table with a new bottle, was obliged to listen as Irene rehearsed, in a penetrating whisper 'so as not to swell his head', the many dazzling talents possessed by her son. The phenomenon himself confined his exchanges to grunts and nods, keeping his mouth constantly plugged with gross forkloads of food. Only Tom and Rose kept silent; she occasionally looked up the table, hoping to catch his eye, but he never lifted his head from his plate.

When everyone had suffered at least two helpings, Georgina had the table cleared and instructed Basil to pour the dessert wine while she wheeled away the bones of the turkey. On her return she rammed open the dining room door as if she were attacking a castle gate with a siege weapon, for her trolley was ablaze with flames rising from three cannon balls of puddings which she had doused with brandy. This time the lower shelf was loaded with brandy butter, ice cream in half a dozen flavours, custard, cream, thin, thick and whipped, jams, chocolate sauce, syrup, treacle, honey and, for good measure, a pint of brandy in a milk bottle. To avoid any impression of niggardliness she had also heaved on board a monumental slab of cheddar.

Though the thought had been uppermost in every mind throughout the meal, no one had dared to ask Georgina what had brought about this astonishing change in her catering policy. Michael, glancing with distaste at Gregory, who appeared to be fattening himself for the oven, did manage to say, in a teasing voice, 'This is a Lucullan feast, Georgie.'

'Lucullan, indeed,' echoed Basil.

Not knowing what the word meant, but instinctively sensing an insult, Georgina was furious. 'It is a perfectly ordinary Christmas lunch,' she said hotly. 'Christmas was always a big occasion in our house, wasn't it Helen? And lunch was always a big meal. A blow-out in fact. I'm just continuing a good old family tradition.'

She stared pugnaciously at Tom.

'All this food is a bit disgusting,' said Mary, laughing. 'Not that I'm complaining,' she added hurriedly, smiling at Georgina. 'I just think that over-eating is a very primitive way to celebrate. It's not as if we starve during the rest of the year.'

'Nonsense,' said Basil. 'Eating large meals is the English way. It always has been. Look at the Victorians. Georgie is quite right. Even if we don't all go to church, Christmas is one of the few family traditions we've got left and we should preserve it at all costs.'

'It's outrageous,' declared Irene, who had not quite followed his train of thought. 'No church, no lunch is what I say. No church, no presents.' She pushed her paper crown off her forehead and suddenly rounded on Oliver. 'Can you recite your Lord's Prayer without a single mistake?'

'Of course he can't,' said Basil. 'Nor can my heathen daughter. But people don't need religion any more, they've no use for it. And you know why? Because they've never had it so good, that's why. Oh yes, Mac was right. Look around you: people have never been as well off. They've got everything – car, television, holiday in Spain, washing machine, the lot. Even the poorest man can buy his own house. We are living in a paradise on earth, only we don't recognise it. As the lady once said, we should rejoice, rejoice.'

To emphasise his point, he held up his glass, then drank its contents in a single gulp.

'Come off it, Basil,' Mary protested. 'If this is paradise, it's a pretty wretched affair. I mean . . .'

Before she could continue, Gregory rose from his chair, staring at Basil with bulging eyes. He shook his fork at him and his face writhed in an agony of dissent, yet he was unable to speak for the great wad of food he had just rammed into his mouth. He strode up and down the room, struggling to chew and swallow, still brandishing his fork. Rose stood up and led him back to his seat.

'Not true, not true,' he managed at last. 'The streets of London are full of hungry people. I've seen them. Thousands of them.'

'Have a drink, my dear chap. You'll choke if you're not careful. Perhaps I should have said we are as close to paradise as we are likely to get. All right, we have our poor and homeless,' – he bowed in deference to Gregory – 'but we have far fewer of them than any other society you care to name.' No one contradicted him. 'Look at *us*. We are only ordinary folk; not princes, dukes, or millionaires, just ordinary, respectable folk, and yet we live like gods. Look out of the window: can you imagine a more beautiful landscape? An English Eden. And this house. It may be a little ramshackle, it may need a lick of paint, but it's a palace in its way: comfortable, well-proportioned and solid. As for ourselves, we surely represent a pinnacle of civilisation. Our women are beautiful, intelligent,' – he laid his soft, glabrous hands on the shoulders of Rose and Mary – 'and fertile. Our children are healthy and well-educated. And the rest of us have teeth that do not hurt. Never underestimate the misery rotting teeth have inflicted on mankind throughout history. We have interesting work to do, elegant clothes to wear and exquisite food to eat.' He raised his glass in a courtly gesture to Georgina. 'We are not oppressed and we do not oppress others – well, not too much anyway. We live in peace and we stand a reasonable chance of dying in old age with our dignity intact and our loved ones to lay us to rest. What more has any generation of humans ever asked for?'

'Dignity, my arse,' said Mr Albion. 'You wait till you've had a stroke and can't pull up your own trousers.'

He put his glass to his lips, spilling more than he drank. Georgina steadied his arm.

'Look. I can't even get drunk without a nursemaid to help me.'

Basil shrugged and smiled, yielding to the crankiness of age rather than Mr Albion's point.

'Do you know what those bloody socialists have done?' the old man continued, wine dribbling down his shaving cuts. 'They've made it a law that all gravestones have to be the same miserable size. Oh yes. I've looked into it. The rich aren't allowed to have bigger gravestones than the poor. Bloody poppycock! You watch out, they'll ban burials altogether. That'll be the next thing, you mark my words. We'll all end up in little regulation-size pots. That's paradise for you. Bloody jam jars!'

'Calm down, Dad,' Mary said. 'You're not dead yet.'

'No, but I want to get it right. I don't believe in this cremation crap. I want to be buried down there,' – he waved his good arm in the direction of the churchyard – 'six feet under with a good, big monument on top of me.'

'Oh, I don't,' said Irene with drunken vehemence. 'I can't bear the thought of rotting away on my own in the dark. I want to be cremated, Gregory dear, and you can spread my ashes in the City somewhere.'

Georgina intervened. 'This is Christmas Day and we don't want any more morbid talk.'

'Quite right, Georgie,' said Basil. 'We must celebrate life – our life. We've earned all this,' – he made a sweeping gesture up and down the table – 'and we shouldn't be ashamed to enjoy it. With any luck, we'll go on earning it for many Christmasses to come. Let's face it, we can't lose. I'm a lawyer, you Albions are honest yeomen farmers and Gregory's in the City. Oh yes, and Mary's a publisher.' He threw her an ingratiating smile. 'Law, land, money and books, those are the four pillars of civilisation and they're all sitting round this table. God keep *us* merry, ladies and gentlemen.'

He stood for a moment, but his short legs failed him and he fell back into his chair.

'A toast.' He flourished his glass. 'I give you Prosperity! Prosperity and Youth!'

In the general hubbub of responses, some of which were less hearty than others, Basil leaned over to clink Rose's glass. With his free hand he hugged her round the waist and then slid his ardent fingers down her back to her bottom, giving it a vigorous, delving squeeze.

'Fuck off, you disgusting little man!'

She sprang to her feet and sluiced wine into his lap.

Basil jumped up too, but when everyone stared at the wet stain on his grey flannel groin he sat down.

'What do you think you're doing, young lady?' he blustered.

She ignored him.

'Tell them, Dad,' she cried out, beseechingly. 'Tell them.'

A terrible silence followed while all eyes turned on Tom.

Wearily he put down his spoon and sighed, his head drooping. At last he said, 'We're bankrupt. We've gone bust. The farm's got to be sold. Everything's got to be sold. Everything.'

Another brief silence was blown apart by an uproar as everyone reacted at once.

'Balls! Balls, you fool!' shouted Mr Albion.

'Oh Tom, how could you?' Mary reproached him. 'It can't be true.'

Helen put her head in her hands and sobbed, 'Georgie, you poor thing.'

'Gregory will sort it out,' said Irene complacently, pouring herself another drink.

Basil stumbled round the table, a napkin clutched to his shameful loins, and gripped Tom by the shoulders. 'Chin up, my dear fellow. We'll get you out of this somehow. I'll ring my accountant. He's a top man in the field. Don't worry. I'll pay.'

Only the children remained silent, solemnly thrilled by the drama and, in Oliver's case, frightened by his father's words.

Suddenly, one voice soared above the pandemonium, quietening the rest.

'Rejoice! Rejoice!' roared Georgina, her glass aloft, a manic look on her face. 'I've hated this farm since the day I first set foot in it, and now we're free of the ruddy place. Happy Christmas everyone!'

.As she swigged her wine, the hall clock was heard to chime three sonorous tones.

'Basil,' she said. 'The Queen. We must not let standards slip.'

Ten

Running across the yard, Mary was suddenly conscious of the wind, which was raw and damp, cutting through her clothes. She stopped, thinking of going back for her coat. The sky was as grey as slate and in the failing light the house looked lifeless and defeated, sinking into its own mire. Impatient to speak to Tom, she pressed on.

When Liz had died she had been tormented by the sense that somewhere within her was a frozen core which was impervious to the sufferings of others, a watchful, calculating centre which remained impassive while her outer self wept and raged. She felt that her heart was like a cave, a cold, vacant hole whose dead air was never stirred by the storms that blustered at its mouth. She feared she lacked that deep well of humanity from which an empathy for Liz's despair should have sprung; she was hollow, and the sound of her grief was no more than wind blowing across the top of an empty bottle.

But now, as she struggled to understand Tom's announcement, which she instinctively knew to be true, every fibre of her being was invaded by feeling; no part of her was aloof or invulnerable. She was riven with an emotion she could not name, but one that seemed to have attacked the daughter in her, the sister, the woman and even the mother-to-be. Without Slaughterhouse, they would all be orphaned, and so it was not only for herself, but for her father, her brother, and all the others, especially Georgina, that she was determined to fight and rescue what she could from Tom's catastrophe.

She found him at the door of a shed next to the fattening house. He was loading sacks of meal onto the back of a trailer. As she approached he turned his back on her, throwing the plastic bags with hostile vigour. She stood in front of him, but he said nothing. The cold was intense and she was shivering violently.

'Tom. Please.'

He swung a sack and would have knocked her over if she had not dodged back.

'Tommy!'

He grabbed her elbow and pulled her inside the shed. Years ago her father had used it as a dispensary, keeping the pigs' drugs and medicines in a locked cupboard. Now the cupboard door yawned open, a jumble of old syringes and dirty bottles falling off its shelves. In her father's day the walls of the shed had been covered with charts showing the farrowing dates and litters of all his sows, but they were bare now except for a girlie calendar advertising paper sacks.

'Has Dad been in here recently?' she asked. 'It's a pig-sty.'

'What do you expect? It is a pigsty, you bloody fool.'

'Just tell me what's been going on.'

He pointed to a table which was heaped with ledgers, invoices and envelopes. He picked up a fistful of paper and let it drop.

'It's all there. Look for yourself. Paper and more bloody paper, that's all that grows here nowadays.'

'What's happened? You can't really be bankrupt.'

He shrugged.

'I want to know. I have a right to know. My money's tied up in the farm too.'

'Kiss it goodbye.'

He went outside again. She ran after him.

'For God's sake, Tommy, talk to me.'

'Ask Rosy. I've told her all about it.'

Before she could say anything else, he climbed into the tractor and switched on the engine. Immediately, a terrible screaming filled the yard making conversation impossible. The noise came from a quadrangle of pens near the house where the sows in seasons were kept in close proximity to the farm's two boars. These giants were so attuned to the routine of the place they could distinguish between the noise of one machine and another. As soon as they heard the first cough of the tractor that brought their food they began to roar in anticipation, setting off the sows which added their shrieks to the chorus of hunger.

Mary ran after the trailer and sheltered in a corner of the small yard while Tom piped water to the troughs and shook feed from the sacks into each pen. The yard was pandemonium now. The smell of food and the throbbing tractor had excited the waiting pigs to a frenzy of screaming and agitation. The heaviest sows slashed with their teeth at the shoulders next to them and stood with their fore-quarters in the troughs, their snouts and ears powdered white by the meal spilling from Tom's sacks. The younger sows, slithering on the slimy concrete, lost their footing and were trampled squealing into the dung beneath the scrum of trotters.

Hugging herself to fight off the cold, Mary stood next to the pen housing the older of the boars, a massive creature with a gnarled, bristling head. Grunting furiously, it ground the iron bars above its trough between its long curved jaws, producing a yellow froth of saliva which the wind whipped away in lumps. Its wrinkled balls protruded from behind its thighs like two large, elongated gourds, and with its arched back and quivering legs it seemed permanently poised for sex.

In the half-light these white monsters, these solid ghosts, howling in their cells and chewing the bricks in their prison, appeared to Mary to be true denizens of hell, and she shrank into her corner of their inferno, her fingers in her ears. They were the pigs of nightmare, ravening stomachs and giant crocodile jaws crying out for food, food, food, but getting nothing save pap to bite on, nothing but slop to crack between their axe-head teeth. They were the pigs of abuse, pigs of greed and filth, machines for shitting, wallowers in the bogs of their own dung, idling in beds of their own making, guzzling to make themselves fit to eat, fat enough to have their fat throats slit, their fatty flesh skinned, boiled, butchered and rendered, their dainty trotters melted into glue, their lazy bones pounded and powdered to buy more food for their slobber-chops to gobble. These were the pigs of passion and disgusting appetites: they snuffed the boar's stink on the air and clamoured for his corkscrew love, offering him their gaping vulvas through the bars and begging for the great gallonage of life he would hose into their barrel bellies, where litters the size of hamlets would spring up and leap from their wombs, screaching for the teat. These were the pigs of ignorant motherhood, who would kill their own piglets out of carelessness, eat their suckling corpses and screw with their corkscrew sons to fill their pork bellies with the litter of more flesh, more fat, more greed and filth.

And what of Tom? Was he the slave of these gross beasts, a gaoler more gaoled than his prisoners, the hungry guardian of these gorged hogs, the eunuch door-keeper of their bog-brothel? Or was he the king of this crazy kingdom of boars?

Mary cowered in her corner until he had finished his round and the yard had fallen quiet. With a curt gesture, he signalled for her to climb up beside him in the tractor cab. He drove them round the corner to the shed.

'What can you see in there?' he asked, pointing inside.

'Bits of paper? I don't know what you mean.'

'What else?'

'Nothing.'

'Exactly. Nothing. That was the last of our feed. There's none left, not a sack, and no money to buy any more. This is their last supper.' He laughed abruptly.

'It can't be as bad as you're saying.'

'I'm telling you the truth,' he said savagely. 'Tomorrow they'll starve. In the morning there'll be five hundred pigs shouting for food, and two hundred sheep out there, just giving up the ghost.'

'How can this have happened? What have you done?'

By way of answer he slammed the shed door and drove away on his tractor, leaving her to shake in the darkening silence.

Eleven

Still wearing her paper crown, Georgina held court in her kitchen. However, her throne room now resembled the bunker of a doomed monarch whose reign was at an end and whose kingdom has fallen into the hands of her greedy financiers. The ruins of her late magnificence lay all about her – plates piled high with the bones of her final banquet, empty champagne bottles rolling round the floor like skittles. As a valedictory gesture to her *ancien régime*, she had commanded that the Christmas cake be lit and cut, and it stood, blazing smokily beside the turkey skeleton, on a monumental silver plinth. She had dismissed the royal children, but the last of her loyal courtiers were gathered round her person, prostrated in various states of despair and lamentation.

And yet, as is often the case with the victims of historic crisis, the queen herself was displaying unforseen qualities. The little woman, suddenly bereaved, expands into a. formidable widow; the doormat wife, deserted at last by her philandering husband, blossoms into a femme fatale; and Georgina, rudely dispossessed of the home for which she had sacrificed so much and worked so dutifully, was behaving more like a liberated slave than a deposed sovereign.

Ensconced in the chair usually occupied by Elsie, who lay snoring at her feet, Georgina comforted her distressed comforters.

'Do stop crying Helen,' she said. 'Put the kettle on and make us all a cup of tea. You'll feel better if you're busy.'

She pushed the brandy bottle in Michael's direction.

'Georgie. What can I say?' He sighed and poured himself a consolingly large measure.

'I should just enjoy your drink. It's the last free one you'll get in this house.'

Moving like a zombie, Helen filled the kettle and placed it on the Aga's hot plate.

'Poor old G.,' she said. 'Poor old thing.'

'Do stop saying that,' Georgina snapped in something like her old style. 'I am poor but I don't need reminding of it every five minutes. And I certainly don't want to be pitied.'

'Good for you, Georgie,' said Michael, saluting her with a slow-motion gesture. 'I think I'll just make sure the sitting room fire hasn't gone out.'

He stumbled towards the door, the brandy bottle discreetly concealed inside his jacket, but before he could depart Basil burst into the kitchen, waving aloft a bundle of documents.

'All may not be lost,' he announced in ringing tones. 'There are spars to cling to, my dear Georgie, planks from the wreckage which may yet carry you safely to land and new life. You have gone under once and you may go under again before your ordeal is over, but you won't necessarily drown. There is still life!' He shook the papers. 'Life, I tell you!'

'What are you babbling about, Basil?'

'I've been through this correspondence, and there's no question, I regret to say, that Tom has been culpable of the most irresponsible negligence. I cannot understand what the man has been doing all these months. But fortunately the situation may not be as bad as he believes. From a cursory look at these letters, it appears to me the bank has been precipitate, not to say foolish. They may yet be persuaded to reconsider, especially if a little pressure from above is brought to bear. It so happens that I am on very cordial terms with the manager of the Norwich branch, who is of course many ranks senior to this Stowmarket wallah. I think I can safely say that a word from me in the right ear may well win us a little time. Only a stay of execution, you understand, but if we work damned hard we may be able to turn it into a reprieve.'

Georgina did not respond to the straw he had put within

her grasp, instead she reminded Helen that they were still waiting for their tea.

'The kettle won't boil, G. There's no heat in the Aga.'

'What I suggest, Georgie,' said Basil, her tenacious rescuer, 'is that first thing Monday morning I get my chum at head office to prod his man at Stowmarket and then you see him in the afternoon. Perhaps it would be best if Tom didn't attend. I recommend a diplomatic illness.'

Georgina stood up and removed the kettle to look inside the Aga's stoke hole.

'It's empty. Tom must have forgotten to fill it this morning.'

'Unfortunately, the bank will have to know about every penny and pearl you possess in your own right, Georgie. My advice is to prepare a comprehensive inventory of your private assets so you can take it along on Monday. I'm afraid all your little secrets will have to be revealed.'

Georgina pushed past him, threw open the door and despatched Michael to the coal shed with the empty coke hod in his hand and a befuddled expression on his face.

'We must be patient,' Georgina told Helen. 'The water will boil in its own good time.'

'Time is something you don't have,' shouted Basil, suddenly angry with her. 'You've run out of time.'

He could not understand her indifference to his proposals, which were surely as wise as they were charitable.

'G., darling, you must come and stay with us. Let Tom sort out this horrible mess. He got you into it, he must get you out.' Helen looked round the room, shivering a little. The metaphor of Tom's mess was translated for her into an Augean reality among the filthy plates, the cold grease and gravy, the half-chewed bones. 'It's getting chilly in here.'

Basil had cleared a small space for himself in the debris on the table and was laying out his papers in orderly heaps.

'The bank . . .' he began, but Georgina put up her hand to silence him.

'You must think about poor Ollie then,' said Helen. 'I'm

sorry, I mean little Ollie. What about his school fees and everything? I am sure we can help, can't we Basil?'

'The boy's education is the most important investment of all. We cannot allow his future to be ruined.'

'Ollie is never going back to Bitterley,' said Georgina flatly.

'My dear Georgie, don't be hasty. Give yourself time to gather your wits.'

'My wits are perfectly well assembled, thank you Basil. I never wanted him to go in the first place.'

'The decision is of course yours to make, but my offer still stands,' Basil said stuffily. Her churlish spurning of his generosity was less offensive to him than her obstinacy.

'Look,' he said in his kindliest tone, 'you don't seem to realise what I'm trying to do here.' He pointed to his little office on the pine table. 'If we're going to persuade the bank to relent, we must convince them that from now onwards this place will be run with prudence and efficiency. And that means you're going to have to apply your undoubted gifts. There's more to farming than mucking out and driving tractors; farms must be properly managed like any other business. Unless you take charge, you will lose everything.' He waved his arms round in an all-inclusive gesture. 'Everything!'

'And you don't seem to realise what I'm doing,' Georgina shouted back at him. 'I'm getting out of here. I meant what I said at lunch. I hate this place. I don't want a maisonette. I don't want to keep so much as a room. If there's any money left over we'll buy a cottage somewhere. If not, we'll rent one or live in a council house. I don't care so long as we never see this muck-heap again.'

'A council house,' cried Helen in horror.

'People lead perfectly normal lives in council houses.'

'This is madness,' Basil said in anguish. 'I meant what I said at lunch too. You have a piece of paradise here – a corner of beautiful English land. Don't throw it away. You have so much to lose: your family heritage, your son's future, your respectability.'

'Respectability!' Georgina snorted.

'Don't despise it.' Basil was on his feet now, his face flushed, his hands trembling. 'Respectability gives you freedom. No one respects a bankrupt, I can tell you that.'

This remark silenced Georgina. She slumped back into her chair and the light thrown by the naked bulb hanging from the ceiling reduced her sallow face to a mass of waxy planes and black hollows.

They heard the back door bang and then someone stumbling in the scullery. Finally, the kitchen door opened.

'I can't find the coke, Georgie. Sorry.' Michael showed her his empty hod, making a shamefaced grimace. His face was smudged.

'You seem to have found the coal house, but not the coke,' Georgina said sarcastically.

'The coal house was empty.'

'Tom must have forgotten to order it in time for Christmas.'

'He didn't forget,' Basil told her grimly. 'He didn't pay. The coal merchant is one of your many creditors.' He waved a clutch of bills in her face. 'He refuses to deliver.'

'Oh G., what will you do?' cried Helen. 'What will you cook on? Poor you, poor you. Come home with us. Bring Ollie. Let Tom stew in his own juice.'

'I'm not leaving my husband for a cup of tea. We can boil the kettle on the hob next door. We still have plenty of wood, if nothing else.'

But she did not move from her chair.

'Tom has behaved inexcusably,' Basil said, punching his chubby fist into the palm of his hand. 'Inexcusably. A man in his position has responsibilities. This farm was once the pride of the county and now look at it. A disgrace. He's let you all down. Where is he now? Skulking. Skulking. What sort of man is he?'

'Shut up, Basil. For God's sake shut up!'

Georgina thrust her face in her hands, her shoulders heaving. Helen put her arm round her, but Georgina shrugged it off.

Basil and Helen exchanged despairing glances. Basil returned to fiddling with his papers. Michael put the hod back in its place beside the cooling Aga.

Wiping away her tears, Georgina left the armchair and walked irresolutely across the room. Somewhere between the table and the door she hesitated and stopped.

Elsie looked up, thumped her tail and dragged herself back to the familiar comfort of her chair.

Georgina sat at the table opposite Basil, staring at the piles of paper in which Basil had arranged her life, but seeing nothing.

'He was so handsome,' she said, crying again. 'I had never seen such a handsome man.'

Twelve

The friendship between the cousins, Oliver and Alice, was intimate, harmonious and characterised by high seriousness. Had anyone been watching them as they walked away from the house he would have been struck by the gravity of their manner and the earnestness with which they conversed. With his new gun broken correctly over his arm, Oliver led her towards a pair of tumble-down barns that stood beyond the church and beside the road. Their heads bent down, her red curls almost mingling with his black locks, they made slow progress against the wind.

'What's your school like?' she asked.

'I hate it.'

'I hate mine too.'

But Oliver's emotions were never pure, they were always muddled with conflicting loyalties and ambiguous affections. And so he corrected himself. 'Some bits are all right though. Carter – he's my friend – I'm looking forward to seeing him next term.'

'I've got friends too,' said Alice, 'but I never see them in the holidays.'

After a few more steps Oliver said, 'Maybe I won't have to go back next term.'

He spoke the words with painful hesitation. This very thought had occurred to him as soon as his father had announced he was going bust. Thanks to his summer eavesdropping Oliver knew all too well that his school fees had placed a great strain on the family purse, and therefore it seemed more than likely his father's downfall would mean he would be taken away from Bitterley Hall. What a Christmas present! Yet the idea filled him with guilt, for his happiness would be a sort of celebration of his father's misery, like dancing on his grave. On the other hand, part of him wanted to see his father suffer, for his father wanted to get rid of him, his father was nice to him one minute and horrible the next, his father threatened to hit him, his father never smiled at him.

'What'll your dad do with no money?'

'Dunno.'

The phrase had a terrifying, yet thrilling ring to it. No money. Everything would have to be sold, he had said. Where would they live? In a caravan like gypsies, or maybe the shepherd's hut? Would they send him out to work? Get rid of him that way?

The barns were set at right-angles to each other and were used to store old machinery, rolls of wire netting, chicken coops, empty fuel drums. The roof of the nearside barn had caved in, its ridge forming a low-slung curve, like the roach back of an old horse. Oliver found a piece of chalk and drew a crude circle with a bull's-eye on the gatepost. He took Alice across to the other barn and put her in a place of safety, protected by a rusting harrow. 'Got to be careful of ricochets,' he said. He loaded a pellet in his rifle, raised it to his shoulder, took careful aim and pulled the trigger. The pellet made a beautiful ripping noise as it left the barrel, and the polished stock felt like silk against his cheek. He ran over to the gatepost. 'On target,' he shouted back to her, 'four o'clock, two inches from the bull.'

'Give me a go.'

He loaded a fresh pellet, loving the strength of the spring and the oiled smoothness of the breech as he snapped it shut. He loved the dull rattle of the lead pellets in their tin, he loved the cool smooth steel of the barrel and the snug curve of the trigger waiting to embrace his finger. He could probably keep his family by hunting; he could poach pheasants and rabbits off the new owner of the Manor. That would be a fine revenge for his father. Pigeons were his favourite; he would bring them home by the dozen for his mother to cook in their caravan. He'd soon be skilful enough to kill deer, and in the holidays Alice and Carter could help him and they'd carry the deer back on a pole and he'd wear the skin when his clothes wore out.

He showed Alice how to stand, one foot in front of the other, the stock tucked well into her shoulder, her cheek pressed against it; how to line up the sights and hold her breath while she squeezed the trigger. All this she did dutifully and was rewarded by hitting the post just outside the chalk circle.

'He's dangerous now,' shouted Oliver, 'because he's wounded and angry.' He gave her the gun again. 'Finish him off.'

She fired and hit the target.

'Got him. Right in the heart.'

As he pushed home another pellet their attention was caught by movement in the grass at the side of the barn. Stealthily, they crept to the corner of the building, keeping out of sight. Perhaps it was a rabbit. His first catch. He would show them what he could do.

At the edge of the field, where the spring barley was pricking through the flints in its orderly green ranks, a hare was capering in a circle. Lolloping clumsily on its oversized back legs, it pursued its circuit in a manic frenzy. Occasionally, it tripped over its buckling forelegs and sprawled in the mud, eyes bulging, only to rise with a struggle and set off on another pointless round. Its brown and grey fur was matted and seemed worn through by this continuous circling.

The children peered round the corner of the barn; the creature failed to see them, and they were able to advance to the very margin of its orbit. Suddenly, it sensed their presence and bolted, fleeing with crippled terror for the open territory of the field, but it was drawn inexorably back to them as if confined to a circular rail track. Writhing and hobbling, it careened past the toes of their boots. It lay still for a minute, crouched and flattening itself into the grass, but another convulsion seized it and drove its legs into motion.

'It's ill,' said Alice. 'We must take the poor thing home and make it better. Your dad will know what to do.'

She tried to intercept the animal, but it only ran faster, in more frenzied loops.

'It's mad,' said Oliver. 'It must have caught that disease rabbits get.'

'We've got to do something. Look at it.'

'I'll have to shoot it,' said Oliver.

'No. Please no.'

Oliver put his rifle to his shoulder and aimed, but his arm shook and he could not control the barrel. Finally, he pulled the trigger. The shot made a different noise out in the open, just a quick hiss. The hare's movements were so agitated it was impossible to tell if he had hit it or not. Certainly, he had not killed it. He fired again and this time the hare stumbled. It rose immediately and started its crazy circle, but on three legs now, its left forepaw drooping. He fired a third time, but without effect.

Alice was crying, begging him to stop.

The hare had lost control of its circles and was darting to and fro in a crippled fit. Oliver took his rifle by the barrel and held it above his head like a club. As the hare staggered past he struck at it, landing the butt on the brittle ridge of its spine. The animal lay in the mud, as helpless as a fur hat. Oliver hit it again, bursting its skull. He hit it once more – a blow that broke Rogers' head and avenged Carter's fish; a blow that broke his father's head and showed him he too was a man; a blow to repay all Mr Peach's blows; a blow to end the hare's suffering and make it suffer as he had done; a blow to vent his violence and a blow to plead that this should be the last of his life. A victim's blow.

They stood over the battered corpse, Alice weeping, Oliver panting.

'We must bury it,' said Alice, looking round for fear someone should be watching. She dropped to the ground and began scooping out the earth with her hands.

'You'll get dirty. I'll do it.'

'I want to help.'

Together they scratched out a shallow trench. Neither wanted to touch the corpse. Oliver found a stick and prodded the hare into their hole. They kicked soil over its bloody fur and jelly eye.

'You had to do it,' she said, carrying his gun home for him.

But he knew he was not a hunter, nor his family's saviour. He knew he was a murderer.

Thirteen

'Oh by the way,' said Irene from her taxi, as Rose and Gregory stood outside their cottage to wave her off, 'I forgot to tell you, Gregory dear, I'm taking a little cruise next week. Just ten days to the Canaries and back, but who knows, I might meet a millionaire.'

'May we look after your house for you?' Rose asked. 'We should have found somewhere of our own by the time you get back.'

Irene looked at her very doubtfully. 'I don't understand these things. I never have. I thought you Albions were frightfully rich, but it's all above my head. I'm sure you and that nice Mr Fanshawe will sort it out for them, won't you, Gregory dear. I really don't think you should have been so rude to him, Rose. But then I understand nothing, not a thing.'

'We'd just camp there while we looked for somewhere to rent,' Rose persisted. 'And we could feed the cat.'

'Ah well, I suppose so, Rose. But only on condition that you promise me you won't pay more than an ordinary rent. I don't want any privileges. Gregory will know what's fair; we'll leave it to him. And talking of lolly, I don't suppose you've got a ten-pound note handy. I must pay this darling man' – she patted the taxi driver – 'and it's so long before the banks open again. I don't know how the nation is meant to survive without cash for weeks on end, but, as I say, I understand nothing. Not a thing.'

Having neither a ten-pound note, nor a ten-pence piece for that matter, Gregory did not move. Fuming, Rose strode back to the cottage.

'They're rather a dotty lot, these Albions, aren't they? Be careful, Gregory. Don't give them any money; don't give them anything except advice. And make sure you charge them the proper professional fee. They won't thank you for charity. Their kind never does.'

Rose thrust the note through the taxi window.

'Too kind, my dear. Treat it as a deposit. I must love you and leave you. A merry Christmas to all, and thank you, Gregory, for my perfume. So thoughtful. How you find the time, I shall never know.'

Winding down the window, she protruded her cheek. After a nudge from Rose, Gregory swooped down and like a blundering bird of prey pecked at it, missed, and soared back to his airy perch in the sky.

'Toodle-pip.'

She waved to them with a giddy kiss of her hand and sped away, chattering to the driver without a backward look.

Gregory raised an arm in a lofty salute and stood immobile until her car was out of sight. Indeed, he might well have remained thus if Rose had not taken his elbow and led him down the street.

'Where are we going? I'm cold.'

'You should have worn your scarf,' she said bluntly.

He shook his head in bewilderment.

If it was possible to be drunk on food, then Gregory was intoxicated almost to the point of helplessness. His face, though still wretchedly gaunt, was reddened and puffy, while his movements were stiff and precarious, as if he was in extreme danger of exploding.

'That's the first good thing that's happened today,' Rose said.

'What?'

'Your mother's house, of course. You haven't grasped it, have you? Our cottage, or rather the bank's cottage, is going to be on the market next week. I'd move out now if we could. I love the place, but now I never want to see it again. We'll move to your mother's as soon as we can and find a flat or something.'

They walked in silence along the narrow pavement, Gregory dropping behind her. She stopped abruptly.

'We can live anywhere we like now,' she told him. 'Anywhere on earth.'

He looked at her, puzzled. Like his mother, though in a very different sense, he seemed to understand nothing.

They turned onto the wooden footbridge connecting the two streets of the village and stood at its centre. Rose looked around her, contemplating the little world which for nineteen years had been as familiar and unconsidered as the temperate air. With a jolt she realised her childhood was at an end, for the village suddenly seemed a strange place, or rather, a place from which she felt estranged. She was surprised to find that she was filled with a sense of liberation.

She and Slaughterhouse had evolved together, trickling down their gutter of history with no more urgency or drama than the Crow in its placid bed. During their mutual existence no catastrophes had befallen them and no enemies had laid siege to them; nor, by the same token, had they exulted over victories, or celebrated anything more historic than royal weddings and harvest festivals. Change had come to both of them in gradual, intelligible portions; there had been no mysteries, persecutions or secret dissent; no miracles or shameful vices; everything had been even-tempered, even-flowing, even-handed. But that was gone. That was the era of her childhood. Yesterday. Now everything was flux and opportunity.

She looked up at the Manor, whose roof and teetering chimneys were still visible as black shapes against the black sky, and did not believe what she saw. That lumpy silhouette was only a building now, a mocked-up front to keep the clouds from rolling over the village like breakers, a sign to reassure the natives that their landscape had not folded up its tents and disappeared. But the Manor that had been her home was gone, and now her parents were refugees, exiles in their own house with bundles strapped, carts loaded, their past buried in the cellar like tinpot treasure. She was the only one to have escaped with anything of value: she had got away with her childhood, but now she must wrap it up, put it away in some secret drawer of her heart, and sharpen her knife for the war to come.

And her husband, which epoch did he belong to, her lost, irrecoverable, unmourned childhood, or the new combat? She stared into the shallow hurrying of the Crow's inky current, which ran like a black ribbon round the graveyard of her old life, and the more she studied the action of this self-appointed little moat the more anxious she was to break free of its protection. She wanted to change the course of her existence and flow in an utterly fresh direction, away from Suffolk, away from England even, out across some sea quite beyond the dreams of the Crow's tiny pulse.

'Where shall we go?' she demanded of Gregory. 'We can go wherever we like. We can do anything we want.'

'I have so much to give,' said Gregory, rubbing his stomach.

He was sobering up after his lunch-time orgy, but instead of being punished by a hangover he was suffused with the most delightful feelings of wellbeing. The painful distension of half an hour ago had been replaced by a gratifying sense of amplitude. All his organs were humming and pumping with the sweet efficiency of tiptop health. He thought of himself as a sow with a belly full of piglets which were fattening nicely and would soon be ready for consumption. He was swollen with a sense of fulfilment, of purpose realised.

'I am rich,' he told her, stretching and breathing deeply. 'I am rich and getting richer all the time.'

'What are you talking about?'

'Organs. You know. Our plan.'

He reached out, meaning to pat her abdomen, that treasure trove of vitals.

'Oh grow up, Gregory,' she said, slapping his hand aside. 'You must get a job, and I must put in for a rise. We have people to look after now.'

'You're right, you're absolutely right. So many people.' He looked up and down the empty street.

'All that nonsense must stop now. We have responsibilities.'

For a moment she sounded exactly like her mother, and Gregory was horrified to see her neck, her beautiful, graceful, sexy neck, shrink into her shoulders giving her that look of burdened roundness so characteristic of Georgina. But Rose was discovering her own way of playing out the drama of her life: unlike her father, she would not allow the struggle to waste her in bitterness and anger; nor would she falsify herself as her mother had done, bending until she could no longer straighten. No, she would be the heroine of her own story, and, like it or not, Gregory would be the hero. She squared her shoulders, threw back her head and shook her hair into the wind.

'I must hold myself in readiness,' said Gregory, 'and keep myself fit and well fed. The call may come any day now.' Seeing Rose's glare of disapproval, he hastily added, 'Perhaps for the time being I might help at a hostel or something, giving out soup to the homeless, that sort of thing.'

'You idiot, Gregory. My parents are homeless. And so are we, for that matter. Everything has turned round, don't you understand? We are the breadwinners now. You must ask Basil what to do about getting a job.'

'A job?' Gregory turned to her in bewilderment. 'But what will happen to my mission?'

'You have a new mission,' she said fiercely. 'To help those you love, the people who've helped us in the past. It doesn't matter where we do it, or how, but we must make money to keep my parents. We've been set free. Can't you see that? We're not the children any more.'

Gregory could see nothing. His face paled. He would have put his hand out to her if it had not already been repulsed.

Suddenly he lurched forward, hung his head over the bridge and vomited his lunch into the Crow. Since he had eaten like a dog, gulping down his food in huge unchewed lumps, his digestive system had hardly touched it, and Georgina's feast was returned in much the form it had been despatched. The polychromatic fragments vanished beneath the bridge and reappeared on the downstream side, bobbing in line towards the pub, towards Ipswich, the estuary and the sea, where perhaps they would at last be consumed by albatross, porpoise, shark or even the fabled dugong. Or perhaps the Crow itself, unable to resist such rich carrion, would dispose of it inside the parish boundary. But, whatever its destiny, Gregory's final act of charity would not be wasted. He had given his all.

Rose held her baby's head as he retched drily into the stream. She knew now what sort of husband she had, and she knew this was not the marriage she wanted with him. Yet she took Gregory's clammy hand and led him home.

Fourteen

When Basil's car finally pulled away from Slaughterhouse, the white horns of its headlamps seemed to have stolen the last of the Manor's light. Lifting her hand in a futile, invisible wave, Helen looked back at the black space above the village roofs but could see nothing of the farm or the house.

As the ruby glow of tail-lights vanished, Tom crept out of the darkness and slipped into the kitchen without a word. Mary who had been trying in vain to clean up the kitchen, a task made impossible by the lack of hot water, decided her best course was to leave man and wife alone. Though the temperature in the kitchen had been no more than tepid, the passage and hall felt bitingly cold and she hugged herself as she hurried towards the drawing room where the only fire in the house was to be found. This running from the piercing cold outside to the ambiguous warmth of rooms heated by smoking grates and the combustible moods of her family evoked the winters of her childhood, the dark days and nights when her mother had shivered beside the hottest fires and her father had chopped down half a wood in his efforts to warm her.

Her parents had tried to keep time at bay by means of rituals, anniversaries, birthdays, repetitions of all sorts. If this year is the same as last, so the unspoken argument ran, then we can't have got any older or iller, and therefore we can't be any closer to the last ritual of all. And as her mother had indeed become iller, they invented more events to celebrate, more habits to ceremonialise. Her final Christmas had been prolonged well into February, and perhaps she had only died then because that time of year is so lean of feast days.

During the shortening days of her invalidism they did everything in their power to confound the idea of linear time; they tried instead to twist time into a corkscrew, a spiral that would put an endless length into the same distance, allowing them to come round and round to the same place without advancing, without declining. Life, they fought to persuade themselves, was not a sparrow's flight from the dark into the brief light and back into darkness; life was more than a rat's dash across the road, more than an ignominious sprint to dodge the careless scythe of death. No, as her mother grew weaker, they deluded themselves that life was a grand gyre down which she would slowly roll gathering grace and elegance.

Of course, nothing was delayed or postponed; there was no grace or elegance. Her mother died a young woman in years, an old one in pain and decay. But in their efforts to hobble time and win her a few more seasons they only managed to put a glass case over her. Unwittingly, they closed her inside an airless cage where her disease thrived all the same and the nursery prevailed: here her daughter was forever a tomboy, her son forever an ailing little boy and her husband a blundering intruder. Her feathers lost their gloss, the sawdust leaked out of her and her nest of dried flowers crumbled to dust. She became lonely. Mary and her father suffocated in her stale atmosphere and only Tom – always Tommy to her – was able to draw breath under her glass dome. Indeed, when she died he seemed to have lost the gills to breathe in ordinary air.

Mary had never mourned her properly, for the job was done for all of them by Tom whose pain was pitiable to witness.

In the drawing room, which had been her mother's bell jar, Mary found Michael and her father sitting on either side of the fire surrounded by crumpled wrapping paper and champagne glasses.

'Good God, not another long face,' her father said. 'We've had enough doom and gloom for one day. I've just been telling Michael here that there's no such thing as disaster in business, only new opportunities. We're going to have to start again. Fine. Fine. We don't belong here anyway.

We've had a good run for our money, but now it's some other bugger's turn. Good luck to them. Let's clear off and set up shop somewhere else. They tell me vines are the new thing. A couple of acres in the right place and you can make a killing.'

'Dad,' she said wearily, 'Tom isn't up to it.'

'To hell with him. I'll do it myself. That ass Gregory can help me; he's looking for a job isn't he? The fresh air will bring him to life, and I bet he's got a few bob tucked away.'

He rubbed his hand gleefully and stared into the fire, seeming to see Gregory's gold shining among the flames.

'We're a family of pirates. That's what your mother could never understand. She wanted us to behave like gentry and make people think we'd been here since Domesday. Well, she had her reasons,' he said hastily with a glance in Mary's direction. 'My father, the old bastard, bought this whole estate for a song,' he told Michael. 'In those days, just after the first war, anyone with a couple of quid in his pocket could buy land and a bloody great house and call himself a squire. My old man loved all that. He loved being called sir and the village grovelling to him whenever he rode through, but he never let me forget where we'd come from. You're the son of a market gardener, he'd say to me, so don't give yourself any fancy airs and graces. When I was sixteen he set me to work and put me in a cottage, and do you know, the tight-fisted bugger used to charge me rent, taking it straight out of my wage packet. I hated him then, but I'm grateful now because he taught me I wasn't Lord Tom Noddy and people are only as good as their money.'

'Come on, Dad, we've heard all this before.'

'Take a chance, Moll.' He leaned forward and gripped her wrist with his good hand. 'What do you say? Stump up some cash and let's have a go at something new. Pack in this publishing lark. What do you say? It'll be fun.' He turned back to Michael. 'You've got plenty of money. Come in with us. Bang some sense into her head. Show her she can have a new life – it's there for the taking.'

Mary was surprised to see Michael nodding earnestly at the old man. Before he could commit himself to verbal encouragement, she intervened.

'I don't want a new life, thank you. I am more than content with my old one.'

Now she was still more surprised to find Michael nodding at her, and beaming. He was, she assumed, drunk to the point of imbecility.

'Don't be so bloody spineless,' her father roared at her. 'This is your chance to get even with Tommy. He once chucked you off the farm, remember? Now it's your turn to put him in his place. We'll make a fortune, you and I. You've got a head on your shoulders and you're not frightened of hard work. We'll look after him, don't worry. He can play with his pigs somewhere and we'll give him his pocket money. But we must build a new business for Ollie to inherit. I have to start before it's too late. I may drop dead tomorrow, you know. Or turn into a cabbage.'

Rubbing his head violently, he looked behind him in his half-blind way, as if expecting to see the angel of death lurking in a corner.

Mary could hardly believe what she was hearing. He had never before acknowledged that she had been 'chucked off' the farm and for him to do so now, while in the same breath trying to incriminate Tommy, was an act of such unscrupulous hypocrisy she was tempted to laugh. But this was the opportunism of a desperate man, a mad old man on his last hunt who did not care whom he trampled or hurt. She despised his last efforts to manipulate her, yet had to admire the tenacity with which he pursued life and its dwindling possibilities. He was not greedy for money or things, and power over people in itself had never given him pleasure; he was simply one of those men for whom existence was action. Do or die was a literal motto in his case.

And here was her dilemma. Offering him the slightest encouragement would involve her in some crazy venture which would cost her money and probably cost Tom his health and sanity. And yet to deny her father this last chance and lock him up in his dressing gown and slippers, was to condemn him to death. Whose life to sacrifice then, the son's or the father's?

'It's not my problem,' she said feebly. 'You must talk to Tom. And what about Georgie? You can't accuse her of social pretensions, but this is her home, you know. She has rights too.'

'Ah yes, Georgie,' he said thoughtfully. 'She took us all by surprise today. Maybe she's not as poor as she pretends. That father of hers was pretty rich, wasn't he?'

'Don't even consider it, Dad. She's suffered enough without you stealing her money – if she's got any, which I doubt.'

She loved her father, but looking at him now, as he rubbed his frowsy hair and shifted his false teeth away from his tender gums, she was repelled by his senile energy. What was the meaning of this tireless, fevered urge to be up and doing if nothing was created as a result, no enduring home, no family bond, no private traditions; if it achieved nothing but its own solipsistic relief?

Suddenly her father was on his feet.

'That bugger. Where is he? This is all his fault.'

He lurched with crabwise clumsiness towards the door.

'Tom, you bloody failure, come here,' he shouted into the empty darkness of the hall. 'Come here and face us like a man.'

Reeling slightly, he gripped the door jamb and leaned into the hall. He peered in the direction of the green baize door, mumbling and blinking.

'Come here, you useless bugger . . .'

Mary had moved towards him, but it was Michael who took his arm and pulled him back into the room.

'You mustn't say those things,' he told him. 'What if Ollie were to hear? We must all think of him.'

Michael guided the old man back to his chair where he sat rubbing his scalp with diminishing vigour. Finally his hand dropped into his lap and his head slumped. His energy appeared to be spent.

'Where's Georgie with my tea?' he demanded petulantly.

'I'll go and see,' Mary said.

As she was about to leave the room, he turned his head sideways to look at her, his face suddenly alive and cunning.

'I'm not giving up, you know,' he told her. 'I'll be hanged if I'll lie down and die.'

Fifteen

Half an hour later, having delivered her father into Georgina's abrasive care, Mary returned to the drawing room and found Michael as she had left him, slumped beside the fire in an attitude of befuddled meditation. The log basket was empty and the cooling hearth contained nothing but ash and grey embers. She drew the curtains but they did little to block the draughts that played round the room and sighed in the windows.

'He will go roaring into his grave,' she said. 'He's quite incorrigible. The minute he saw Georgie he asked her how much money she'd got and offered her a partnership in his new business. He said he'd make her a millionaire and name his first vintage after her. Apparently, she's going to be a household word, like Bollinger.'

'You've got to admire him.'

'I suppose so. But there's something monstrous about him too. As he says, he's like a pirate. A new ship, new crew, new voyage, new treasure to capture, that's all he thinks about. He doesn't care what he leaves behind. He seems to have no attachments, no roots. He doesn't belong here, like Tom does. He never did. This was never a home to him, just his headquarters. It was always my mother's home. She chose all the furniture and pictures and stuff, but to him it was simply a place to use. He hasn't aged. He has no history. He's the same as he always was, only now he's struggling with broken-down equipment and won't admit it.'

'But do *we* have a home, Mary?'

'What do you mean? Of course we have.'

She looked at him closely, but was unable to fathom his elated expression. Once again, she put it down to drunkenness.

She shivered. 'This room used to be unbearable in my mother's day. She kept it so hot I couldn't help falling asleep, which is probably why our relationship wasn't much good. She wanted me to be witty, and I just yawned.'

Michael took off his jacket and put it round her shoulders.

'No, but is our flat really a home, or is it a place we just use? I mean, is that where you want to bring up your child . . . our child?'

She laughed at him, but in nervous confusion.

'I'm serious. Do you want to bring up a child in London, never mind our flat? When your father was talking about coming down here and starting a new life, it suddenly sounded like a good idea. Maybe he has a point.'

'You're drunk, Michael.'

'Well, naturally I'm drunk. How else is one supposed to get through an Albion family Christmas? But I'm not so drunk I don't know what I'm saying. I've had a very remarkable day.'

'Haven't we all?'

'Listen to me.' He leaned forward and spoke to her intently. 'I certainly drank my fair share at lunch, though I may say I was well and truly stupefied long before we sat down, and for that I blame you and your farmyard debauchery. Anyway, what with one thing and another, I was in urgent need of fresh air by the time the Queen had finished uplifting us, so I went outside and walked down the drive to the summer house. And who should I find there, weeping his eyes out, but young Ollie.'

'Poor kid. He's had an awful Christmas.'

'He didn't mention the bankruptcy or his father or anything. He kept going on about a hare he and Alice had killed because it was sick. It all had something to do with a goldfish at school. I couldn't understand the connection, but he was very upset about it.'

'What did you do?'

'I offered him a cigarette.'

'Oh Michael, you didn't.'

'It did the trick, I can tell you. He cheered up immediately. And I'm damned sure it wasn't his first. He has a very fancy way of lighting up and blowing the smoke through his nose. He smokes like a prisoner with his hand cupped in case someone sees him, which is how he learnt, I imagine.'

'You were lucky Tom didn't see you.'

'Don't worry, he didn't smoke it all. He said he usually shared them and wasn't used to smoking whole ones. So I helped him out; in fact I smoked most of it.'

'Since he hardly ever sees you, I suppose he won't suffer too much from your wicked influence.'

'He's hopelessly corrupted already, but then that's what private education does for you. The point is, though, I wanted to give him something from the adult world, my world, that was friendly. I can't explain properly. I wanted to make some gesture that would tell him I thought he was a nice kid. I don't know. Maybe the cigarette wasn't such a good idea. But then he did the most extraordinary thing. Extraordinary to me, at least.'

'What?'

'It was getting dark so we began to walk home. The cheeky little sod asked me if I'd got a mint to kill the smell of fags on his breath. I said I hadn't and we went up the drive. Then he put his hand in mine. Just like that! He held my hand! I hadn't asked him, or made any move. He just did it.'

He put out his hand to show her, looking at his open palm in wonderment.

'I don't think he knew he was doing it. How old is he? I don't know about these things. But that's the point. He was doing something simple and natural. Quite unimportant to him, no doubt. Yet to me, it was a completely new experience, a revelation. I suddenly realised I had never held a child's hand before in my life. Never. The only people I have held hands with are women, and I've never wasted much time on their hands, if you know what I mean. This was a new kind of touching. Did your mother touch you often? Mine never did. I paid the first woman who touched me.'

236

He was on his feet now, not looking at her but apparently reliving his experience with Oliver.

'He called me Uncle Michael.'

'You were kind to him,' she said gently.

'He made me reconsider my conviction that all children are vile brats, that's for sure.'

He lit a cigarette of his own and sat down again, throwing a covert glance at her through the smoke to see how she was receiving his confession. It was important to strike the right tone; yet, try as he might, he could not control the shaking of his lip.

Michael's customary poise had deserted him, and alcohol was the least of the forces undermining him. During the course of his long, eventful day, his mind – that finely tuned instrument of duplicity – had arrived at certain strategic decisions, only to have them endorsed, overwhelmed and utterly transmuted by feelings for which there was no precedent in his emotional experience.

For example, his policy of ingratiating himself to Mary as an insurance against Zara had simply been nullified by events in the pig house. Lying in the straw, panting after his exertions, he had suddenly been convulsed by a pure, authentic love for her, a tenderness so exquisite he had been driven to helpless tears. He did not pause to consider the origins of this onslaught of feeling, he only knew that sexual passion had somehow generated a deeply heartfelt love that was new, new to him and their marriage.

He had cried all the more desperately because he also knew that his game of sexual infidelities still had to be played out. With the noise of last night's telephone attempt still fresh in her memory, Mary was bound to be suspicious if he expressed his devotion to her with unwonted passion. Accustomed to giving voice to sentiments he did not genuinely feel, he was now in the paradoxical position of having to dissemble what he did feel. Of course, the option was always open to him to tell the truth and confess to Mary about his liaison with Zara. He did not doubt that he would be forgiven, but he had been on ambiguous terms with the truth for so many years he no longer trusted himself with it.

Confounded by these riddles, he resorted to the only honourable course left open to him; he became drunk. Not boisterously or even festively drunk, but quietly, celestially drunk. Oblivious and dreamy, he went into a drunken retreat.

Throughout lunch, it occurred to him that an acceptable way of showing Mary his new feelings, which would at the same time bind her to him with hoops of steel, was to hint to her that a conversion of his views on the baby business was beginning to occur. But here again the truth and his guilefulness converged in the most alarming fashion. No sooner had this crafty plan wormed its way into his brain than he did indeed feel some weakening of his prejudice against motherhood for Mary. While pregnancy and parturition in the abstract remained unthinkably repellent to him, the idea of Mary the mother nonetheless grew more alluring with each drink; for did it not carry in its womb the idea of Michael the father?

True egotist that he was, Michael immediately saw paternity as a means of aggrandizing himself and raising a mighty bulwark against mortality. But there was more to it than that. All his life he had been obsessed with possessing new things, stainless, uncorrupted, perfect things from which he sought an absolution from his own stains and corruption; and what, after all, was a baby, if not the very quintessence of newness? A brand-new baby would surely confer on him, as its brand-new father, the grace of its freshness and innocence? And how eagerly he craved a new life, a life wiped clean of Zara and the fiction he had invented to conceal his visits to her sordid flat, a life cleansed of his old, foolish, deceptive, unloving self. His beautiful daughter (for his child was bound to be a silky-skinned, golden-haired girl) would redeem him, and Mary would love him all the more when he was a father. He had been so short-sighted not to see how loveable a father he would make in Mary's eyes.

This picture of his transfigured self entranced him throughout lunch and he barely noticed the drama that broke over the rest of the family. He wandered through the day's timetable, doing as he was told and consuming whatever was put in front of him, but attending to nothing except the vision of his miraculous fatherhood.

Then Oliver held his hand, and for a moment the egocentric spiral was broken.

The boy asked, and Michael, hardly knowing what he was doing, gave. And that was the end of the matter. When they reached the house, the boy took his hand back and ran off, shouting, 'See you later, Uncle Michael.'

Perhaps in reality this was how redemption offered itself. It was not a mystical experience; there was no parting of the clouds, no divine hand reaching down to sponge away sins and cloak the white body in a clean mantle. Redemption was just the gift of a brief, fleeting opportunity to make a small change in oneself. No more – yet no less. A forty-year-old adulterer, used only to taking and lying, could not reasonably hope to win salvation except by means of small, hard-won changes. Moreover, he was helpless without the intercession of others: a woman who was willing to put her trust in him despite his betrayals, a child who offered him the charity of affection. In a word, love. Love could save.

To Michael this was a novel and revolutionary concept, which he glimpsed only obscurely, though with enough clarity to realise that it had turned his Christmas Day into a momentous event.

Under the circumstances, it was therefore galling to find that Mary was not receiving his glad tidings with the joyfulness he had anticipated. Indeed, she appeared not to have heard him.

'Don't you understand, Mary? I think you're right. We should have a child.'

For the first time in their marriage he held out his arms to her in a gesture of physical tenderness that was quite innocent of any sexual intention.

She did not respond. He crossed the hearth-rug and knelt beside her.

'I love you Mary.'

'I love you too Michael. We'll talk about children when we get home. But for the moment we must think about helping Tom and Georgina.'

She hurried to the door, leaving Michael on his knees in a state of agonised confusion. His conversion to parenthood could not have been more sincere, yet it had brought him no protection from Zara. He was no less exposed to her wiles than he had been before Oliver had taken his hand.

Lighting another cigarette, he stared sadly into the now dead fire. For some reason he fell to comparing himself with the rich young man in the Bible who was not able to face the eye of the needle because he had too many possessions. It occurred to Michael that he had got himself in a moral fix for which there was no relevant parable. He had shed enough selfish baggage to enter the gate, but not enough to get through. He was stuck, incapable of movement either way, the butt and victim of any passing joker who cared to pillory him. Zara.

He was in sore need of help.

Sixteen

No light issued from the house, but the clouds had lifted to expose a half moon whose pock-marked ghost-twin was obscurely visible. A soft lunar glow fell on the yard concealing its disrepairs and purifying its mud. Though the wind had slackened, the cold had sharpened and rime glittered on the roofs of the pig houses and along the crests of the tractor ruts.

Darkness and cold pervaded the house too. Downstairs, coiled tightly on her armchair, Elsie slept in the now unheated kitchen, while upstairs Oliver was likewise curled beneath his thin blankets. Lying beside him, repacked in its box with its stock polished and its barrel oiled, was his air rifle.

Michael, for all his new-found fatherliness, had been wrong in imagining that his rakish cigarette had restored the boy's spirits. Oliver had told his murderous story of the hare to Basil, and then to Helen, and then again to Georgina in whom he also confided many incoherent details concerning Carter, his beautiful fish, Rogers, Mr Peach and the vicissitudes of life at Bitterley Hall. He had wanted to tell his story to his father as well, but Tom had disappeared, putting himself beyond the reach of all those who were eager to speak to him.

Despite his best efforts, Oliver wept as he recounted his experiences at school, and Georgina in her turn wept too. Nothing was said by either of them about his returning to Bitterley next term, though Oliver did ask her where they were going to live and what they were going to do without any money. Georgina told him not to worry, an answer they both knew was inadequate. When at last she put him to bed and helped him clean his rifle, he was still red-eyed and she was sure he would not close his eyes before giving way to tears once more. She was right: for the second night running, the second night of his homecoming, he cried into his pillow until he fell asleep.

In his attic bedroom Mr Albion was sleeping noisily, his toothless mouth working continuously at some argumentative strife. Georgina pulled the blankets over his agitated shoulder and closed his door, leaving the light at the top of the attic stairs to shine onto his ceiling. If he needed her in the night he could ring his bell, for she had decided to sleep in her own bedroom with Tom, if he returned. Where was he?

Taking off her clothes she defied the piercing cold for a moment and glanced at her naked torso in the hand-mirror balanced on her chest of drawers. A rectangle of white flesh against the white-washed wall. Plain Jane her father had called her, one of his special names for her. Plain Janes had no need of mirrors except to see their faces were clean and hair tidy. She possessed inner beauty, he used to say, one of his special jokes. But Tom, in the days when he used to crack jokes, private jokes between the two of them which did make her laugh, had once said he'd only married her for her tits. One summer's afternoon, when Rose was at school, he'd taken her upstairs to this very bed and undressed her, telling her they were beautiful. He'd been drunk and she hadn't believed him, but she'd never forgotten. Big white things they looked now, with red knobs that looked sore and shrivelled in the cold. Plain Jane.

Was she a bride or a corpse in her white nightdress? Had she undressed for bed or the grave? She turned out the lamp beside her bed, but went to the window and searched the black pit of the yard below for a trace of Tom. The moonlight was blocked out by the barn opposite which cast a long, fathomless shadow, more liquid than lightless, as far as the back door. Which way was the moon turning – towards its other face or away? Was that the old face that had been, or the new one to come? She never knew.

The sheets were painfully cold and her side of the bed, unoccupied for three weeks, felt clammy with damp. Her new house would be small and clean, with fitted carpets and a boiler pumping heat into every room. How much? The habits of a marriage were not going to be broken in a day. She had made herself a miser to be loved, but no one loved a miser. What could she be instead? Or was she too good at being mean to change? Rose didn't love her and never would, miser or not. Ollie did love her. Ollie! Oh God. He must never go back to that place. Helen loved her, and Basil. He had given her two hundred pounds before they left, and made her keep it. And Tom? Everything came back to Tom, who was out there in the dark and cold on his own, leaving her alone here, in the dark and cold. Didn't he realise she was frightened? Terrified. She could not help him if he hid from her. Come to bed, Tom, please.

Lying in the blackness, shivering in her icy sheets, her mind turned for warmth to the remembrance of her famous feast. She smiled. Lucullan; that was a word to treasure. A fortnight's food blown in a single meal. And the table had looked so beautiful with its shining silver and all their faces gawping round it in amazement. Even Basil had shut up for a couple of seconds, too shocked to speak, just his little chin wobbling. She had been peeping at them through the green baize door to see their reaction.

But the laugh was on her now: no food in the larder and no money in the bank. No husband in her bed. She was tempted to carry Ollie through and put him next to her, but Tom would be furious. In any case, this was no place for Ollie. Too cold. His bed had been cold at Bitterley, so he'd said. He couldn't get his feet warm even when he'd kept his socks on. She'd put a hot water bottle in his bed, but it would have cooled by now. He'd hated the noise of the sea. Poor Ollie.

Exhausted, she lay with her arms straight beside her, as if in a boat, becalmed and lost; as if in the ground, cold and alone. She looked up at the two-faced moon, sleep overtaking her. Today she had deserted God and smashed his crib, but she had cooked a Christmas feast that would always be remembered. Always.

Seventeen

Standing at the top of the bale stack at the back of the old barn and feeling his way in the half-dark, he slung his rope over the beam and pulled the noose down so it hung level with his neck. Behind him, the straw was slimy and rotten beneath a hole in the tiles. Moonlight filtered between the broken rafters and he could see the line of the rope dangling in front of him. He adjusted the noose downwards to give a good drop of a foot. This distance was critical: any less and the job would not be done properly, any more and he would pull his head off.

Doing it up he could be sure that Freddy would be the first to find him in the morning when he drove the tractor in to collect more bales for the pigs' bedding. It had to be somone and Freddy was the man; he had seen plenty of dead animals in his day and one more was not going to addle his brains. The old fool was only nineteen shillings to the pound as it was.

The noose had been round his neck for months, tightening all the time, and now it was only a matter of stepping off into the dark, into peace, into silence.

He held the noose in place and wound the rope end round the beam twice, securing it with a knot. He pulled on it with all his weight, forcing the rope to creak and stretch, but the knot held. They could put his body into the wool sack he had left below. Freddy would see it and understand. There was string for the neck in a bag hanging on the wall.

He sat on the edge of the stack and pulled his hip flask out of his pocket. His hand was trembling so badly he could hardly unscrew the cap or get the whisky into his mouth. He put the flask back in his coat, shaking it to see how much was left. What did it matter? Rain fell on his face and neck

through the hole in the roof. He craned to see the moon. Like him, it was half-alive, half-dead.

Grasping the rope, he hauled himself upright and stood leaning over the brink, looking down towards the floor of the barn which was invisible in the darkness. His body would stay here, but he would go down there, into the pit, dropping, dropping, until he was free. All he had to do was let go and be rid of himself forever.

But not tonight. He could not do it tonight. The others had already suffered enough because of him. Georgie. Rose. And Ollie, poor little sod.

He stepped back and slid his hand up the rope as far as the knot.

There had been too much suffering for one day.

He tugged at the knot to loosen it.

For their sake, he would have to wait.

The knot had jammed and he broke his nail unpicking it. He would never untangle the other knots; they were snares that could only tighten, choking him like a dog in a trap.

He coiled the rope neatly, tying it to prevent it from unravelling, and hid it in its place under the roof.

One night he would drop into the darkness; one night soon he would be gone.

Eighteen

She woke.

He was beside her, his chin pushing into the hollow of her neck, his arms reaching round her, his hands seeking her breasts, his stiffness prodding into the folds of her nightdress. He was shivering and she could feel a wetness of tears in the scrub of his bristles. Or rain. He yanked up her nightdress and entered her violently, as if trying to bury his whole being in her.

Tom, she whispered. Tom. He was silent.

She wanted to take off her nightdress to feel him against her, but his grip on her was too urgent. And yet he was holding her and moving inside her the way she liked, her special way which always brought her to a flood. He seemed to be waiting for her, his body poised like a fish riding the current. Until she surged beneath him.

He turned over, but not away from her. She put her arms round him and her cheek against his shoulder. He was as silent as it was dark.

She woke.

Ollie was shrieking. The lights were on, Tom's side of the bed was thrown back. The screaming gave way to sobbing and Tom, naked, carried Ollie into their room. His eyes were still staring at some nightmare horror, but his body in Tom's arms was drooping back into sleep. Tom put him in the middle of their bed where he hugged his knees and closed his eyes again without a word. The light went out. She felt Tom's weight pressing the bed as he got back in.

I love you, Tom. He said nothing, but she sensed his hand reaching over Ollie towards her. He laid his palm on her head for a moment, just a light, gentle touch, like a blessing.

As she sank to sleep once more, she heard the church clock chiming midnight. She did not hear the twelfth stroke.

Christmas Day was done.

A Selected List of Fiction Available from Mandarin

While every effort is made to keep prices low, it is sometimes necessary to increase prices at short notice. Mandarin Paperbacks reserves the right to show new retail prices on covers which may differ from those previously advertised in the text or elsewhere.

The prices shown below were correct at the time of going to press.

☐	0 7493 0780 3	**The Hanging Tree**	Allan Massie	£5.99
☐	0 7493 1224 6	**How I Met My Wife**	Nicholas Coleridge	£5.99
☐	0 7493 1064 2	**Of Love and Asthma**	Ferdinand Mount	£5.99
☐	0 7493 1368 4	**Persistent Rumours**	Lee Langley	£4.99
☐	0 7493 1068 5	**Goodness**	Tim Parks	£4.99
☐	0 7493 1492 3	**Making the Angels Weep**	Helen Flint	£5.99
☐	0 7493 1364 1	**High on the Hog**	Fraser Harrison	£4.99
☐	0 7493 1394 3	**What's Eating Gilbert Grape**	Peter Hedges	£5.99
☐	0 7493 1216 5	**The Fringe Orphan**	Rachel Morris	£4.99
☐	0 7493 1510 5	**Evenings at Mongini's**	Russell Lucas	£5.99
☐	0 7493 1509 1	**Fair Sex**	Sarah Foot	£5.99

All these books are available at your bookshop or newsagent, or can be ordered direct from the publisher. Just tick the titles you want and fill in the form below.

Mandarin Paperbacks, Cash Sales Department, PO Box 11, Falmouth, Cornwall TR10 9EN.

Please send cheque or postal order, no currency, for purchase price quoted and allow the following for postage and packing:

UK including BFPO   £1.00 for the first book, 50p for the second and 30p for each additional book ordered to a maximum charge of £3.00.

Overseas including Eire   £2 for the first book, £1.00 for the second and 50p for each additional book thereafter.

NAME (Block letters) ....

ADDRESS ....

....

☐ I enclose my remittance for ....

☐ I wish to pay by Access/Visa Card Number

Expiry Date